T0165856

Cocaine

Pitigrilli

RONIN

Berkeley, CA

The dazzling classic of Paris in the Twenties

PITIGRILLI

Translated by Eric Mosbacher

Hamlyn 1982 UK Translation

Cocaine

Pitigrilli

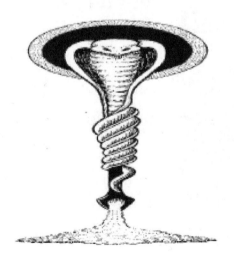

Cocaine by Pitigrilli
Isbn: 9781579512187
Copyright 2016 Ronin Publishing
Copyright 1974 And/Or Press
Copyright 1933 Greenberg Publishers

Published and Distributed by
RONIN Publishing, Inc
PO Box 3436
Oakland Ca 94609

All Rights Reserved. No part of this work may be re-produced or transmitted in any form by any means electronic or mechanical, including photocopying recording or translating into another language, or by any information storage or retrieval system, without written permission from the author or the publisher, except for inclusion of brief quotations in a review.

And/Or Press
1974 cover

Production:

Editor: Beverly A. Potter

Cover Design: And/Or Press

Library of Congress Card No:

2016930255

Distributed to the book trade by

Publishers Group West

Table of Contents

PITIGRILLI
cocaina
romance
ARTURO VECCHI & FREITAS BASTOS &
EDITORES

INTRODUCTION

Dino Segre, who wrote under the name of "Pitigrilli", was bom in Turin, May 9, 1893, under a conjunction of the sun and Venus in Taurus, the classic indication of a sensual nature. little is known of his personal history, but it is possible he spent some time in Turkey in his youth, and that in the 1930's he moved to Argentina, He returned to Italy in 1945 and soon after converted to Catholicism, publicly renouncing his earlier novels as "immoral."

Like Tito (the hero of *Cocaine*), Pitigrilli worked as a journalist throughout the "twenties and 'thirties in Italy, during which time he published at least 10 light novels in which sensual love is the predominant theme. Apparently he became fashionable for most of his books were translated into Spanish and French, a few into German and Russian, and three, including the present, into English, The other two titles in English, *The Man Who Searched for Love* (New York; R. McBride, 1932) and *Mr, Pott* (London: John Lane, 1933) were both translated by Warre B. Wells, and while *Cocaine* lists no translator on the title page it is possible that Wells had a hand in it also. Other memorable titles by Pitigrilli include La Vergine a 18 Carati (1924) and I Vegetariani deii' Amore (1932).

Cocaine first appeared in Milan in 1921 and was reprinted in 1923, The Spanish translation, *Cocaina*, appeared around 1925; the German edition, Kokain, in Berlin, 1927; and the earliest French edition recorded came out in 1939, by Michel in Paris, translated by Robert Lattes. The English translation reprinted

here was published originally in New York by Greenberg in
1933.

Although the cynical tone and the light-headed sryle are characteristic of many between-wars authors, Pitigrilli surely ranks at
the top. The reader is reminded of Nathanael West, but in a more
abstract, less personal mood, the mood engendered by cocaine
herself. Perhaps it is no wonder that Pitigrilli's Cocaine has had
to wait for rediscovery by the drug-energized consciousness of the
70's, while the novels of his alcohol-influenced contemporaries,
Fitzgerald and Hemingway among them, found immediate success,

Pitigrilli's journalistic background is evident in his bony
prose and the speed of his dialogue; the rapid transitions are ex-
hilarating. After the burial of the beautiful Kalantan's husband,
Pitigrilli does not elaborate: "How Tito ever became the lover of
the Armenian Siren, the reader will find amply described in any
other novel, but not in this,"

A fruitful comparison might be to Aleister Crowley, whose
Diary of a Drug Fiend appeared in 1923, just one year after
Cocaine. Both Crowley and Pitigrilli are occult authors in the
sense that they are probing the astral zones. Pitigrilli fixes his
attention on the sexual impulse that moves his characters through
the Parisian demimonde. For Tito, desire becomes so related to
L'Universelle Idola (his favorite brand of cocaine) that he begins
to call Maud, the object of his obsession, Cocaine. Compared to
Tito's aphoristic journey, Crowley's hero moves along a linear
course of unfoldment which appeals to the Will in us, but leaves
the reader with an abstract, Utopian conclusion, Pitigrilli prefers to
elucidate his goal by circumnavigating it, and the end is profound
as well as amusing. Pitigriili's art, however, cannot approach
Crowley's dense evocation of drug-induced states, which identi-
fies Crowley as an experienced adept.

In exploring Tito's boredom with mundane reality, Pitigrilli almost incidentally criticizes sexual suppression. Though an important factor in Pitigrilli's modern conscience, it is not freedom from the morality of the day that is his theme. Instead his interest is in auto-suggestion and self-suppression, the accumulation of desire that results in jealousy.

Tito and Maud follow in the tradition of the decadent heroes who have spent their life-forces in sexual and narcotic excesses before the age of thirty. Tito Is consumed by jealousy which he prods with generous doses of cocaine, and though he realizes its glandular source, he remains ruled by desire. If only he could see the meaning of the cryptic senrence both women repeat to him: "The past is no longer ours."

Instead Tito flits from the worldly Maud to the aloof Kalan-tan, trying to assuage his misery. He is held by jealousy for Kalantan's past and for Maud's present. At length, tired of reveling in fictiousness with Kalantan, he leaves her, but not without taking the coffer in which her rich husband had deposited a gold coin each time he made love to her in order to experience the pleasure of having a courtesan.

But with Cocaine-Maud, the venom-woman, his exaltation and ruin are more intricately woven. Departing for Argentina with her, Tito thought that age and the loss of her beaury would at last bring him Maud's loyalty, but the untiring Maud announces that when she is no longer able to sell her pleasures, she will buy them back! True to the nature of desire, Pitigrilli gives no relief: the end brings us back to the beginning, and one imagines a faint cocaine-crazed smile crossing the author's face.

Tito at length comes to welcome death, as he had welcomed cocaine, as the only escape from his suffering. Back in Italy he meets his old friend Pietro from their Paris newspaper *The Fleeting Moment.* Always the wiser of the two, Pietro says:

Sure, we all kill ourselves. All of us, men of our times,
And the spreading cocaine venom is but a symbol of the
death to which we all succumb. Cocaine is not merely the
hydrochlorate of cocaine; it is also the fierce and subtle
and sweet death—truly, a thing of black shadows, like
some nameless cataclysm, which we inflict upon ourselves
voluntarily, with different voices and different words, while
waiting for the consummation of our fate.

William Dailey
Director, Fitz Hugh Ludlow Memorial library
Los Angeles Branch, October 1974.

PITIGRILLI
& JIM OSBORNE

There are marriages made in heaven, and others consummated in places far less savory. The pleasures attendant upon the latter type may be guilty ones, but they are so captivating that one returns to them again and again—ashamed, perhaps, of oneself for continuing to be attracted, but unable to break away.

This is an apt description of the plot of *Cocaine*, and an equally suitable way to look at the relationship between Pitigrilli's writing and the illustrations in this edition, by Jim Osborne.

Osborne (1943-2001) was an early member of the coterie of underground cartoonists, a group best known for the work of Robert Crumb and Gilbert Shelton—and for giving a start to cartoonists who later moved into more-mainstream work, including Art Spiegelman ("*Maus*") and Bill Griffith ("*Zippy the Pinhead*"). Osborne worked in underground comics for only about five years, starting in San Francisco—ground zero for underground cartoonists—in 1968. He then dropped out of the field and did little artistically for the remainder of his life.

His influence, though, was substantial. It was violence that Osborne explored in intricate, often excruciating detail, again and again; his portrayals of horror-soaked scenes were admired by, and had an effect on, the work of other artists of the grotesque, including S. Clay Wilson and Kim Deitch. Osborne's work appeared in many of the same venues as theirs: Yellow Dog, Jiz, Slow Death Funnies, Snatch, Insect Fear and elsewhere. The interrelationship of violence and sexuality, a recurrent theme in the underground comics, was less central to Osborne's work than to

that of some other cartoonists, but he did draw sexually explicit
stories as well as violence-soaked ones—he just tended to keep
the themes separate.

There is little that is explicit in Osborne's illustrations for *Cocaine*, but there is much in them that shows his fine command of
the human form, his ability to accentuate and overemphasize so
as to render a character appealing, mysterious, jaded, emotionally
overcome, or in the throes of a deadly drug high. At its best—and
Osborne's work in *Cocaine* is some of his best—this is art that
beautifully limns a character, not so much simply illustrating
as actually enhancing the often-overheated prose by giving the
reader something visual and highly specific to which to attach his
or her perception.

Thus, Osborne offers an absolutely perfect portrait of "Maud,
cabaret dancer de luxe," arriving in Paris dressed to the nines,
attached by a leash to a dog that "gave the impression of being stuffed," with Maud's head tossed to the side in a display
of saucy artfulness that is something more than mere coquetry.
Readers will surely look again and again at Maud's portrait,
showing her rare beauty while hinting at her depravity, while
reading: "All great actresses, dancers and courtesans seem to
have come from some fourth floor or other, and as in every
saloon dishwasher there might be a potential Grand Hotel owner, so in every fourth floor maiden, who spends her time raising
potted sage and changing the water for her canaries, there might
also be some beautiful [courtesan Carolina 'La Belle'] Otero or
Cléo de Mérode [reputed 22-year-old mistress of the 61-year-old
king of Belgium] in the making."

The perversion and debauchery lurking just below even the
most attractive surface, and brought to the fore by incessant drug
use, are much of what *Cocaine* is about. But it is worth not-
ing that Tito, Pitigrilli's doomed anti-hero, comes to call Maud
herself "Cocaine." This seems to be a significant part of what

Osborne explores in his illustrations: Maud as personification of cocaine, and cocaine itself as encapsulation of all attempts to endure the unendurable in life – the worst element being not its pain but its ennui: "What boredom, life!" is Osborne's caption for one of the most telling portraits in the book.

Osborne had his own significant difficulties enduring life. He died in a boarding house in San Francisco. At his side were three bottles of vodka—and a comic book featuring Will Eisner's "The Spirit." Osborne's own spirit lives on as accompaniment to and intensification of Pitigrilli's prose.

—Mark J. Estren, PhD
Author of
A History of
Underground Comics
Fort Myers, Florida
January 2016

1

A at the Bamabite boarding school he learned Latin and was taught to serve mass and swear the false. Three things which are likely to come in handy any moment. But after leaving college he forsook all three.

He studied medicine for a few years; but at the special surgical pathology examination, they said to him:

"Look here, we will not examine you unless you first remove that monocle. You will either take that silly thing off your eye, or there will be no examination for you."

"Well, then, let there be no examination!" Tito flashed defiantly, starting for the door.

And he renounced his degree.

He smoked inexpensive cigarettes and chewed gum which a thoughtful uncle sent him from America, as a sort of advance payment against his inheritance.

Whenever a woman attracted him, he would jot her name down in line with the rest of his feminine conquests, and behind those he had liked before. When he wearied of the one with whom he was then enamored, he would consult his notebook and say: "Luisella is next." And he would call on Luisella.

"It's your turn, Luisella; make it snappy, now, because there's little Mariuccia who Is waiting to be next."

When he met Mariuccia on the street, he would say to her, "Sorry, honey; you'll have to be patient a while. Luisella is first."

Not having any moustaches to twirl, he stroked his eyebrows for fun.

"Why do you always twirl your eyebrows?" a young woman asked him one day.

"Well," he answered, "everyone will twirl whatever hair one has; that, of course, depends upon one's sex and age."

The young woman thought him very funny and became fond of him. She was his neighbor, that young woman of twenty. These, of course, are all trivial things that creep into the lives of both sexes when they have reached their nineteenth year and have not yet been ushered into the maturity of twenty-one.

Her name was Magdalena, and she was considered a good girl even though she went to a school for stenographers. Her unreproachable mother, when taking her for a stroll on Sundays, would stiffen her cuirass-shaped bosom as though this were a protection to the twenty-year-old virginity of her offspring.

The father, one of those old-fashioned types who are fond of spending evenings quiedy at home, counting banknotes and coins, their goggles propped across their wrinkled brows and a spent cigar between their lips, always waited up for Magdalena to come in at night, and if she happened to be ten minutes late, or even less, the old frazzle would srir into a moralizing tirade, and would rotate his clumsy, century-old watch in mid-air, like a glistening sabre.

The old man knew that nowadays young girls will start with being only five minutes late, but will gradually increase the habit until they are fifteen days late or more. All sexual morality tends, after all, to the avoidance in young girls of the habit of *delaying*.

The moral rigors of that father and of that mother were simply unyielding. One day, after Magdalena had been caught exchanging kisses with Tito, medical student and neighbor, there heaved forth from the motherly bosom all the smouldering villainies inspired by the comparative zoological terminology (degenerate, irresponsible, satyr), which spread like wildfire and echoed throughout the entire neighborhood. When her repertory was just about exhausted and her lungs thoroughly deflated, she clutched her brat by the arm and rushed her into the house, like a growling beast into a cage. The following day Magdalena was

immured in a school for erring young women, where she remained ten months, until she became of age, because her loving
mother, honest enough but poor, and her father, poor enough but
honest, were bent upon keeping their recalcitrant offspring from
losing track of that straight and narrow path.

At the Royal Reformatory her contacts with her depraved
companions were somewhat neutralized by the daily visits
of certain pious and aristocratic ladies whose presence, word
and example, were supposed to show the fallen ones the flow-
er-strewn path to righteousness. Alas, those distinguished ladies,
mummy-faced, bearded, and flat-breasted, threw the wayward
ranks into confusion and alarm, causing them to stray further
toward the pitfalls of vice. A very serious error, indeed, that of
entrusting to women who are as ugly and repulsive as that, the
task of safeguarding virtue. All reformatories for women should,
through adequate compensation, invite the most glamorous *cocottes* to call upon the inmates and make them believe that they
have become beautiful, attractive and alluring through the practicing of modest and chaste habits. The old, pious and aristocratic
viragoes, bilious and bearded, could on the other hand be profitably utilized as so many living exhibits of the appalling ending to
which dissipation and licentiousness have led them.

Her senior companions initiated Magdalena into all the artifi-
cies evolved by gallantry, from miscarriage to *entolage* robbery.
She went through her training course, preparatory to a successful
career; and when she left the reformatory and went back home
again, she forgave her parents the severe and undeserved correc-
tional measures which they had (for her own good) so cruelly
heaped upon her the year before.

Her parents in turn absolved her of her youthful escapade,
but reminded her that their rigorous moral standards would never
consent to a breach of decency.

A short time after her return to the paternal roof, Magdalena began calling herself Maud, for short, because during that time she had become the kept woman of a wealthy businessman and a very prosperous priest. Her parents, poor enough but honest, would not think of interfering with her career, especially after her mother had been granted permission to call every day to impart her maternal blessing and to stuff herself full with what was left in the kitchen.

The father, despite his, "no, I cannot accept," stopped pretending and accepted the banknotes given him, and helped himself to the businessman's own cigars and the priest's own liquor. The latter presented him with a sur-tout which the old man had had remodeled into a swanky tight one which he wore on all great occasions, or when he called upon his daughter to pay her his paternal respects. And since she discarded her shoes and hose when still almost new, the old man would gather everything together and would peddle them profitably, dividing the receipts into two equal parts, of course; one for himself and one for his wife.

When Tito heard that Magdalena had been placed in a reformatory, he had a fit of despair and entrained for France. He reached Paris after an eighteen-hour journey.

He had a few hundred lires in his pocket but no letters of recommendation. All successful men have reached then-goals without letters of recommendation. He called immediately on a printer from whom he ordered one hundred visiting cards, which were delivered to him that same day.

Dr. Prof. Tito Arnaudi.

Dr. Prof. Tito Arnaudi,

Dr. Prof. Tito Arnaudi . . .

He read them all, one by one. After reaching the hundredth card he felt really convinced that he was both doctor and professor; to convince others one must first convince oneself, of course. He sent the first of the lot to that pedantic idiot who had hindered him from getting his degree by ordering him to remove his monocle.

It was while pounding the asphalt of the boulevards, where he had been meandering for days brooding over his sad experiences, his eyes cast upward like one who searched for a convenient spot where to fasten a noose and hang, that he stumbled into a-former college chum.

"O, yes, I remember you quite well. You were the one who fulfilled all classroom requirements by memorizing all the dates in history like so many telephone numbers, Charlemagne's coronation, year eight naught naught; Discovery of America, year fourteen nine two. By the way, have you been here long? Where do you eat?"

"At the *Diners de Paris*" replied his friend "Come over, sometime. The meals there are excellent."

"You're there every day, I suppose?" inquired Tito.

"Every day."

"One must have a lot of confidence to be able to go every day to the same place."

"Not if you do as I do," replied his friend.

"What are you doing for a living?"

"I'm a waiter there."

Thereafter, Tito ate his meals at the *Diners de Paris.*

"What does one do in this country to get himself a girl?" he asked his waiter friend, one day.

"That's easy. You stop a woman and you offer her a drink, which she accepts; then a dinner, of course, which she doesn't refuse; then you offer to share your room with her, and if she has no other engagement to fulfill, she'll oblige you.

The following day Tito accosted a lady and offered her a drink, then dinner, then an appointment to meet again the morning after, in front of a theatre.

"I'll get the tickets."

"Get them."

"Will you be there?"

"Absolutely."

"Sure?"

"Positively."

She was a gorgeous creature, who worked as a *mannequin* for one of the large tailoring establishments located in the Opera district, Smartly attired, spicy, decorative, she was full of the glare and glitter which appealed to Tito. One cannot live long without a lover in a foreign land. The man who is not able to procure himself a lover after the first month or about that time, Tito ruminated, is compelled to husde back to his country of origin.

The moment a young bachelor enters a foreign country, he is taunted by a sense of brooding loneliness. His thoughts flash constantly to the town where he was born, to the streets and the home which he left behind.

But let him meet a woman who is ready to gratify his every wish, and it is to him like entering a new world, a, new homeland. Her tenderness, be it sincere or false, shields him like a protective hood.

It is a sort of extra-territonality, a right of refuge to the lonely. To the expatriated, woman is like a throbbing bit of homeland in a foreign land. The commissioner of emigration should furnish all boundaries with women-distributing stations to enable lonesome emigrants to pick them up as they journey along from one country into another.

Tito had every reason to feel happy. He had found his woman, and he would meet her again the following day. With exultation in his heart, or on his lips, rather—since he whispered it to himself now and then—he roamed the streets, window-shopping, Paris fascinated him. Woman is like a crystal prism through which one can gaze at the things surrounding one and find them eternally beautiful.

Three days later he met his friend who besieged him with questions: "Well, have you found her yet?"

Tito eyed him through narrowed lids.

"Quit talking about that!" he snapped, "I met her at a *cafe* and she cost me the price of two tickets at the *Pie Qui-Chante*. About half an hour before the performance started, I stood waiting for her near the theatre entrance, as we agreed. Nine o'clock and she wasn't around! The tickets cost me fifty francs comma seventy centimes. I couldn't think of going in alone. Believe it or not, but that empty seat alongside of mine would have embittered the whole show. And yet, how could I help not going? To walk off with a couple of bloomin' tickets still in my pocket would have stopped my blood from circulating. To settle this, I stood before the entrance and waited for someone to appear to whom I could sell them.

"Along comes an old gentleman, with wife and glasses tucked under his arm, I offered him the tickets which he bought without saying a word, and tipped me five francs, besides. He must have thought I was one of those ticket speculators, which got me very sore.

"I refused the tip, The old governor thought that perhaps five francs were not enough, so he offered me ten. It was then that I, gargling what little French I know, swept his hand aside like Curius Dentato did, when he refused the gifts of the Sannites. The other gritted his teeth and raised his bid to twenty francs, saying that I was a crook."

"What did you have to say to that?" asked the waiter friend.

"I became highly indignant."

"And I suppose you cracked him on the old snout with his twenty francs?"

"I did nothing of the kind. If it had been five or even ten, perhaps! But twenty! ... I pocketed them."

"That's the spirit." said the other cheerfully. "And what happened to the woman?"

"Never saw her again."

* * *

After the first few days, Tito became thoroughly adapted to his new environment, The woman whom for a moment he thought he had conquered, made him forget all about Magdalena, And now that he had forgotten her, he was unlikely to remember her. Stupid but true.

Women are to our hearts like so many billboards. Whenever you want to hide the poster that lies beneath, you paste another one on top of it, and the first one disappears completely underneath the second one, For a while, perhaps, while the paste is moist and the paper wet, you can still see, very vaguely, the color spots of the first poster transpiring through the second one. But in a short while, all traces will be gone forever. When you start tearing off the one on top, both posters are apt to peel off together, leaving both heart and memory as bare as the wall itself.

Every night, during his time off, the waiter friend took Tito around Paris.

"You'll have to step lively if you want to land a job," the waiter informed him; "you'll certainly not get one by applying to employment agencies. If you want to be a waiter like myself, I believe I can find you a place. It's not a hard job. All you have to do is to be polite to the customers. When you're in the kitchen you can handle things roughly, but the plate must be served clean, with a winning smile and a snappy bow. Every worker feels like proving to himself, once in a while, that he is nobody's fool; at least, that he has some kind of superiority over the person whom he serves. The humblest office clerk, burdened by a swarm of bosses, turns his wrath upon whoever happens to be below him; the most miserable of all laborers will sometimes wax malevolent toward the office boy, so as to have the feeling that he is not the humblest of the humble; the office boy will, in turn, insult the public. The most raggedy of tramps will sometimes behave viciously toward a child who happens to run between his legs, and the child will hurt the dog. So you can see, life is a series of cowardly actions. We need to console our vanity with the feeling that there is always someone beneath our level, someone weaker than we are. The waiter will purposely spit into the customer's plate in order to feel that by so doing he is humiliating whomever dares to treat him all too familiarly by tipping him. Perhaps to you, imbued as you are with prejudices, the idea of serving others may seem loathesome; but remember that we all must serve, at one time or another. Even a Supreme Court Judge serves on the bench; even the notorious courtesan, who earns five thousand francs for the privilege of letting someone loosen her chemise, serves; even the broker, when he picks up the receiver, makes a telephone call and pockets a cold half million, serves. The artist, the doctor, even the archbishop serve. . . Do you want to come along with me? In a few days I will show you how to balance eight full plates with your left hand and twelve more with your right, and I will teach you to repeat, though your mind be elsewhere, the name of twenty-five different viands."

Tito answered: "No, thanks, When I feel like spitting, I'll spit on the sidewalk."

* * *

Tito lived in a dingy Montmarte hotel, where the stairway, hall clogged by a compressed-air lift, was so narrow and steep that it was necessary to hoist all baggage to the upper floors from the outside of the building and bring it through a window.

The air fairly reeked with the scent of soap, tobacco, woman's perspiration, military leather and the cheap perfumes that invariably saturate all brothels catering to a clientele of small means.

The building itself was so tall and rickety that if someone in the street below cursed a trifle too loud, the rooms on the upper floors fairly oscillated like the hands of a seismograph, thereby causing Tito's bed, about thirty meters from the ground, to rock and quake.

The place was raided almost every night, and arrests were made sometimes. The hotel had no steady tenants outside of Tito and some mysterious man, about fifty, who had one of his legs cut off and supplanted by an awkward-looking and noisy wooden stump. His features were unmistakably those of the cattle broker, and the swarthy complexion of the boatswain. No one knew what the man did for a living. The hotel owner would shrug his shoulders and say: "What difference does it make? All I know is this: when his five days are up he pays his rent very promptly."

At four in the morning one could hear his blundering footfalls go hammering up the stairway to his lodgings.

The rest of the clientele were all transient customers who came in couples and seldom tarried over the half-hour period. Tito had already become used to hearing, four or five times each night, from either side of the two adjoining rooms, the repetition of those same overtures that accompanied the buying and selling of love. Here, a door slamming shut; there, one that opened; the snap of switches, stealthy footsteps through the room; then the voice of a man, then that of a woman, the smack of kisses, the heaving , and panting of lustful rhythm; the splash of rinsing water; then again the voice of a man and woman, the switching off of lights, the closing of a door, which would open again, a while later, to admit the series of identical and identically coordinated rumors.

"Love," thought Tito, "is true to itself at all times! The love which is sincere has always the same words; the love which is for sale, too, has always the same formula!"

"Where are you from?"

"Toulouse."

"What's your name?"

"Margot."

"Long in the business?"

"About a year."

"You're not diseased, are you?"

"Nonsense. You would say that, would you?"

"All right then; let's get on."

In another room, the one opposite, another man, with another woman, but the same silly chatter:

"What's your name, baby?"

"Louise."

"From Paris, I suppose?"

"No, Lyons."

"How long in the . . ."

"Eight months."

"How's your health?"

"Never been in bed before . . . alone."

"That's fine, take off your shirt.."

The doors communicating between Tito's and the two adjoining rooms were full of tiny holes which unknown curiosity seekers had drilled high and low to meet all requirements and heights, but which had been later plugged with bits of chewed paper by some expert hand.

During the first few days the voices of all those men and women who stole unseen into the nearby rooms to settle their affairs, and that maddening splashing of rinse water, drove Tito into such a frenzy as to induce him to spend a good part of the night peeping through the holes and stammering to himself.

Thus he learned that each performance was like the next one.

The most lustful exhibits, the clandestine forms, all the elaborate practices, were things which had been done over and over again before.

Every male fool thought that he was doing something really new, something truly exceptional, when in reality he did nothing else but re-enact with some other woman, or perhaps the same one, those very same acrobatics which had been admired in the male who preceded him, when he, too, believed that he was contributing something astoundingly rare to the lustful ceremony.

One night there came a Japanese youth with a girl of his own race, whom Tito had remembered seeing before along the boulevards.

The Jap and his female compatriot exchanged a few cursory phrases while the male removed his coat; The jabbering of Oriental chatter struck Tito's ears very clearly; it was a dull, broken, monotonous chatter, with all syllables detached and independent of each other, and sounding much like the clicking of a telegraphic key. The male spoke very slowly, his enigmatic lips sketched into a veil of a smile.

"Wonder what they are talking about?" said Tito to himself; then answered his own question:

"Yes, I know. He is probably asking her how long she's been a geisha, and she is maybe telling him that it all started a few months before, and that she was born in Yokohama, and that her real name is Haru or Springtime, or maybe Urni, cherry blossom.

* * *

Montmartre, this little patch of Paris, which, in the words of Rodolphe Salis, father of all Parisian funny sheets, has the good luck of protecting the brain of France; Montmartre, or better known as the Butte, this elevation of ground dominated by the Galette Mill, and underlined below by a network of boulevards and clasped down tight by two squares: Place Pigalle and Place Clichy; Montmartre, the modern Babylon, the gingerly Antioch, the litde Bagdad; dream of cosmopolitan nights; the dazzling nook, deafening, sordid toward which flow the dreams of the world's biases; the very spot where the most expert love concessionaires in the whole wide world come to fling their soiled handkerchiefs into the gutter, like many others who, like themselves, have nothing left to blow. Montmartre, the Sphinx, the Circe, the Medusa, venal, alluring, of the many poisons and the numerous tempting potions, that lure the traveller irresistibly onward with a fascination that outgrows the boundless. Every comedy, every book, every newspaper blows the fragrance of

Montmartre into the four corners of the earth: a scent which savors strongly of the bookish, of the literary, of the theatrical, of the jour-nalistic, to which every artist, every writer, has added a tiny contribution of his own making, Montmartre sends far and wide, scattering in every direction the glitter of its illustrious baldness, its granducal bareness, the sparkle of its royal gems, of its princely shirt-fronts, the spell of sharp-toothed and insatiable female devourers. Each of us has some time or other imagined, from far, a Montmartre which was fictitious, one that rested upon the framework of a few scattered thoroughfares, moulins, taba-rins and other nocturnal retreats.

When we get there we are met with grim disappointment, something which we would never dare confess to ourselves lest we put on the air of people who have lived too much. But deep in ourselves, each of us has said: "Why, is this all?"

"Why, is that all there is to it?" Tito inquired of his friend, the waiter, after they had rambled together through all of the quarter's famous and characteristic spots, "To be frank about it, I think that the Latin Quarter and Montparnasse are far more interesting; here people feign amusement; there they feign med-itation; between the two I prefer the false contemplative; at least they make less noise."

* * *

The owner of the cafe stood busily behind the counter, serving large glasses of beer to a group of taxi drivers, who smelled bad-ly of cheap tobacco and wet raincoats. The crystal shelves at his back were loaded with bottles of liquor held together in serried ranks by wreaths of tiny flags that scintillated merrily across, like a double row, into the mirror-paneled walls in front.

A large, round fish-bowl perched on the counter, formed an enclosure to the graceful evolutions of a few spleenetic fishes, red and gold, that looked like so many Chinese dragons, through the fantastic light effects, both natural and artificial, playing upon them.

"I know some people," began Tito, as he sipped his glass of sparkling Port at the counter, "who scurry to bed with rheumatic pains if a drop of rain so much as spatters them on the back, while the fish spend their whole life in water and do not even know what rheumatics feel like."

A burst of metallic laughter, shrill, piercing like a tray full of glasses colliding suddenly, rang through the place. "Get back there, you idiot!" bullied the owner.

And the girl with the glassy eye and the pale face, responsible for that outburst of laughter, drew back two or three steps as if she had been suddenly smitten at the throat, and disappeared behind the reddish curtains that barred the entrance to the other room.

"No roughhouse here!" warned the owner in Parisian slang; but seeing that Tito was a total stranger, he added a soft: "No noise here"

"Does he mean me?" Tito resented.

"I meant that for the girl", the owner explained.

After all the chauffeurs had gone, Tito's friend leaned over and whispered a few words to the owner who replied by drawing the curtains aside, with a deep bow.

"At your service, sir!"

Tito and his friend were then ushered into the next room like people crowding into a museum where wax figures are on exhibition, for men of eighteen or over.

Their ingress was greeted with signs of distrust. A pale, sickly light, yellowish and stagnant, poured upon the green-covered tables very much like those used for card games or at college examinations. The room was not large, and was encircled by a divan; a piano, eight tables, a few papers greasy with the touch of fingers and liquor, and a mirror scratched all over by a diamond chip, were the only furnishings.

Tito observed the surroundings even before he looked at the people, while, if he had followed his natural impulse, he should have done the opposite; but in order not to arouse suspicion and to make those about him think that he was an expert, long initiated into the mysteries of the alkaloid, he sat nonchalandy on the divan, side by side with his friend.

He picked up a paper. Three women eyed him suspiciously and hummed with subdued conversation, which Tito was unable to hear. But the girl who a moment before, while standing near the counter, laughed boisterously over some.remark he made, turned to the rest and, pointing to the newcomer, declared:

"He doesn't look so dumb!"

Tito turned his eyes full upon the withered forms, and studied them one by one. He noticed that all four wore clothes of very fine fabric, which were once very stylish, but had now grown shabby and old, and were wrinkled by many careless creases; the organdie white had turned yellowish; the leather ornaments were dented with cracks, the silk torn in more places than one, belts were twisted, their shoes still in fairly good shape were battered down by reckless walking. The neck of one of them was not very clean, while their finger-nails, polished but innocent of scouring and scrubbing, exhibited a sickening contrast of red enamel and black filth.

The women, huddled closely together in a lurid commingling of bodies, like sleeping birds in a crowded cage, and pressed tightly side by side to feel the warmth, rested their feet upon the horizontal metal bar beneath the table. One of them had her heels propped up against her seat, her legs folded across the thighs in jack-knife fashion, while she rested her chin upon her knees. All four had a vitreous look in their eyes. The pale lips, violently reddened by a thick layer of paint, throbbed with artificial life across semblances that were filled with ghastly pallor.

Those four sullen women sat in dread silence like so many culprits awaiting sentence to be passed upon them at any moment by some invisible court, sitting behind the curtains. One of the women, in fact, the least drowsy of the lot, turned her quizzical stare, now and then, in that direction, but no one appeared.

Beneath the huge mirror, two very thin-looking men shot dice with all the characteristic sluggishness of old employees put to work in some dusty office and paid for the time they wasted rather than for the work they turned out. One of them had raised the collar of his coat over a silken scarf, a substitute for his missing collar and tie. Of the other, Tito could only see the shoulders and the back of his neck, covered with locks of neglected hair that twirled in the middle like an embryo pigtail. But as he glanced up at the newcomers, Tito had a chance to see his face in full, One of those ugly faces which are very much in evidence during mob rioting. A face that was long and thin, almost devastated by erosion, and very much like that lean and bony cow's head, which architects call bucranium.

The girl who had been heard talking, got up and walked over to one of the men, rubbing his cheek gently with her ear as she leaned over him; but the male, in no wise affected by this move, continued his game of dice, Very slowly then, she lifted one end of his coat, and with serpentlike fingers crept into his hip-pocket from which she drew a cigarette-case. She lit one and walked back to her companions, raised one of her legs shoulder high and let it drop again with a significant bravado upon the table, amid a tinkling of falling glasses.

"Does it amuse you?'1 she chuckled, looking straight at Tito who sat ensconced the while, without uttering a single word. "Not so hot here, eh, stranger!"

"I grant you that," answered Tito. "The morgue is lots more cheerful."

"Go there, then!" she snarled quickly.

At this one of the men swung suddenly around, and his thick, coarse voice floated across the room: "Christine!" he admonished.

Tito's friend began conjecturing: "They probably mistook us for a couple of sleuths or something." Tito grinned, and turning to the more talkative of the lot, said: "Your girl friends and the gentlemen here must have formed a very bad opinion about us. Our presence seems to embarrass you all. But we are not what you suspect us to be. I am a reporter, and so is my friend. Nothing to fear, therefore, as you can see."

"Newspapermen?" chimed in one of the three silent women. "But what is it you want here?"

"What does one usually look for in such places as these?"

"But why pick on this joint when there are other cafís along the boulevards, where, at least, you can watch the grues and the shop-girls go by."

"Because this place suits me well enough for what I am looking for."

"And what is that?"

"Cocaine, of course!

The gamblers threw down their dice and walked over to Tito. One of them grabbed a chair and sat himself astride, his chin resting against the back. He pulled a small silver case out of his vest pocket, opened it, proffering it to Tito.

Four frenzied women swooped down upon him.

"You scoundrel!"

"Monster!"

"You scum!"

"He lied when he said he hadn't any more "

"He'd sooner see us dead with craving!"

One of the women brought her thumb and forefinger together and thrust them into the box, but the male, with a well aimed blow of his hand held out rigidly like a blade, pushed her rudely away.

"Hands off that stuff!" he roared. But the women refused to quiet down.

"The dope!"

"The drug!"

"Cocaine!"

With expanded nostrils and blazing eyes, they rushed forward, alternately pushing each other away, breathless with their mad desire to seize the magic venom case, very much like distraught, shipwrecked men, fighting for space in a life-boat.

For a brief moment Tito considered that confused mass of bodies blasting his eyesight; four fiends aroused by a single desire and fighting like maniacs around a small metal case. To Tito's mind each of the infuriated women represented the autonomous tentacle of some lurking monster curling avidly around its prey, which, from a lowly pharmaceutical origin, had suddenly soared to the dignity o£ a symbol. Tito stared and saw nothing but hands; strained, ghastly hands, they were, assailed by convulsive pains; bony, dead white but resolute, hooked like claws, or clenched into a fist with the finger-nails buried deep like blades into the flesh of their palms, either to stifle a groan or to assuage a craving, or perhaps to give a new outlet to their suffering, or maybe to localize elsewhere the spasmodic throbbing that wrecked their fast-decaying forms.

The hands of cocaine-addicts, once seen, are hard to forget. They appear to live a life all their own, and to die even before the rest of the body does; they seem to be always on the verge of some convulsion which is held in check with tremendous difficulty.

Their eyes, now blazing with desire, now faint with frightful brooding over the lack of drug, would the next moment take on a sinister pattern, which has something of the dying or of the already dead. Their nostrils become monstrously dilated to catch imaginary particles of cocaine hovering in mid-air.

Even before Tito had a chance to help himself, the four frenzied women dipped the fingers of one hand into the box and painstakingly cupped the other hand underneath, like a dish,

"The Dope! "The Drug!" "Cocaine!"

scurrying toward the corners as dogs with stolen bones would scamper for a place where they could hide and crush their prey undisturbed.

Every now and then they scanned their surroundings with deep distrust as they filled their hungry nostrils with the precious drug.

A man who is niggardly to the point of despair; a woman whose greed for jewelry spins her into delirium, do not worship their treasured possessions as much as the dope fiend does his dope. To him that glittering white substance, very bitter and very white, represents something avowedly sacred. He fondles it with the most lavish endearments, the most tender and sweet; he whispers into it like to an irretrievably lost love suddenly won back. That drug-filled case is to the addict something sacred, like a relic and worthy indeed of a religious monstrance, an altar, or even a shrine. He places it upon his table tremblingly, his eyes cast in ecstatic admiration; he would call forth to it for inspiration, or run a caressing hand over it, rubbing it softly and gently against his burning cheeks, or pressing it close to his throat, his heart.

One of the women, after she had inhaled her pinchful of powder, rushed up to the man who had proffered, it, and, just as he was making ready to bring what was left in the box to his nostrils, she seized his hand, held it firmly in her own, and brought it suddenly to her face, sniffing the contents with a deep shiver.

The man broke her grip with a jerk and brought the remnant to his nose, with vast voluptuousness. The woman retaliated by clutching his head between her palms (oh, the sight of those bloodless fingers curved like claws upon that black hair!) and with moistened lips, quivering and palpitating, flung herself at his mouth and licked his upper lip with gluttonous fury.

"Stop it! You're choking me!" stammered the man, his head thrown back and holding fast with outstretched hands upon the back of the chair; the veins of his neck swollen with painful effort, and his Adam's apple moving up and down rapidly with disconnected attempts at swallowing.

The frenzied woman acted very much like some little beast thoroughly aroused by the scent of flesh before commencing to devour it; she semed like some charming vampire with lips that adhered firmly to the man's face through the power of suction exercised by her greedy lips.

When she broke away finally, her eyes took on the veiled appearance of a cat peering drowsily while napping; and her drooping lips (they refused to stay closed, as if paralyzed) disclosed a set of grinning teeth, like the teeth of the dead, over a still mask.

She staggered across the room and sunk with a thud upon a piano stool, her head reclining over her forearm stretched along the ivory keyboard. The piano emitted a deafening sound.

The youth who had sat astride of the chair and had offered his cocaine to Tito, rose from his position like one alighting from a bicycle and paced briefly around the room. His black coat hung loosely from his thin shoulders as if suspended from a hook; his legs were curved into a circle like a couple of cherry stems put together. His partner, a blond youth, rather sickly-looking and very pale, sat himself on the chair which the other had left vacant, and turned to Tito:

"So the girls," he began, "refused to let you taste a mere pinchful of the drug. Those girls are a bunch of savages. Sorry that I haven't any left which I could offer you, but the cripple should come along any moment now."

"The cripple, you said?"

"Don't you know him?"

"Of course we do," intervened Tito's waiter friend. "He's the one who lives at your hotel."

"Well, he comes around every day at this hour. He never leaves his lodgings before five or five-thirty. In some calendars, I mean those that are a bit more educational than others, you will find written that the sun rises at 5,45',27": and it goes down at 6,9'12". . . . Well, one would almost believe that this cripple looks

the calendar over before going on his errands. At sunset, you can
see him toiling up the streets of Montmartre, without hurry, like
one who has neither goal nor pressing business to attend. You
can see him skimming along the tenement walls as if he always
fears being crushed by passing motor-busses. At times he meets
with strange faces, sneaks into a bar, or some cheap wine cellar,
or maybe behind some doorway, and presently they emerge like
perfect strangers, one after the other."

"But I saw him a little while ago at the counter, when I came
in," informed Tito.

"I know, but he didn't have the drug then. He had an appointment with a student in chemistry. He'll be here shortly."

"Here he is!" announced the man whose legs resembled two
cherry stems encroaching on one another. There was a low animal growl, and the four women rushed forward upon him like a
mob suddenly breaking loose.

The cripple frowned darkly, "Scram, you jackals!" he threat-
ened. "You will either calm down, or you'll get nothing"

"Five grams here!" hissed one.

"I want eight!" groaned another.

"This is awful, awful, awful!" screamed the third one, in a
rising voice. "I'm first! I'm first; didn't I pay you in advance
yesterday, huh?"

Before exhibiting his merchandise, the man with the wooden
leg glanced over at Tito to whom he said, by way of salutation:

"Oh, you're seventy-one!"

"Have you two met at the penitentiary before?" inquired his
friend.

"He means the number of my room over at the hotel."

One of the four women rested her hand upon the shoulders of
the skinny" man;

"Got any dough on you?"

"Not a cent!" he answered sharply.

"So much the worse," she resolved. "In that case I'll have to dispose of my bracelet."

"Money in hand!"

The girl who had asked for five grams drew a fifty franc note from her purse.

"Here," she said, "give me twenty-five francs change."

"I haven't any change."

"Then keep the fifty, and give me ten grams instead of five."

The peddler pocketed the note, ran his hand into a split that opened sidewise along his trousers, and drew out a small round box. The upper part of his wooden stump, too, provided a well furnished and unsuspected storehouse for his ware.

"One would almost say that he had his leg cut off for the purpose," commented Tito Arnaudi.

"How much will you give me for this gold bracelet?" asked the woman as she spun it right under his nose on her outstretched linger.

"That's cheap gold!" charged the cripple. "It must be from Naples."

"Maybe you're from Naples, you crook!" shouted the woman. "If it's money you want instead of the bracelet, I'll pay you tomorrow."

"Nothing doing; pay today and trust tomorrow," cut short the peddler. "Four grams, twenty francs, please," he said as he handed Tito a box.

Tito took it, threw him twenty francs, and read the label: *L'Universelle Idole!*

He then turned to the woman with the bracelet.

"May I?" he asked, offering it to her.

"For me?"

"I am offering it to you."

The woman did not hesitate long, but grabbed Tito's hand which held the box into her very white and thin hands, and, hold-

ing tightly on to everything, brought box and hand together up to
her lips and kissed them with famished impetuosity.

"Ah, the dear, the charming little powder; heaven of my life,
my love, my light . . ." she moaned wildly elated, raising the contents to her forehead, like one performing some weird ritual with
either relic or symbol.

She tore the wrapper open with the aid o£ a hairpin and lifted
the cover with infinite care, to avoid spilling any.

She then drifted toward some distant table where she lay the
precious packet, then knelt over the floor while her hand fum-
bled through her purse and drew forth a small turtle shell case
and a tiny spatula, of the size which druggists use when measur-
ing their prescriptions. Displaying the greatest care, and almost
holding her breath, she poured the drug out of its rough cardboard box into the more solid turtle shell case. When the former
had been thoroughly emptied of its contents, she turned it upside
down upon the palm of her hand, drummed away awhile with the
tip of her hard nails, and then brought the fallen residue to her
nostrils with deeply felt delight. Still exercising the most painstaking caution, she shook the precious shell case horizontally so
that the powder might lay smooth and even, Now and then her
blazing eyes would dart with feline suspicion.

As if it were so much radium, she took a pinchful and
brought it to her nose with great care. While she inhaled her
breast swelled and her eyes narrowed with inspired languor. She
took another pinchful arid sniffed again, plugging her nostrils
with her thumb, and that little which remained encased between
the nail and the flesh, she sucked avidly, driving her sharp teeth
into the ungual bed.

Tito had boasted to the thin man of his fondness for the drug.
Among vitiated people one feels ashamed not to know the taste
of this vice. Just as those in jail, when committed for a small
offense have the tendency to exaggerate it so as not to feel below

the rest of the hoodlums. Tito Arnaudi, though he had never scented the drug before, swore that he couldn't live without it.

And when the woman prevailed upon him to sniff some, he sniffed.

That white, crystal-like powder, stealing up his nostrils gave him a sensation of aromatic coolness, as if his throat had been filled with sweet cedarwood and thyme oils. A few particles, straying from his mouth into the throat, caused him a smarting sensation and a bitter taste on the tip of his tongue.

"More?"

And Tito sniffed once more. Then he quieted down. He became absorbed in a sort of meditation. "Ah, there, there, my nose is getting cold, a paralysing feeling at the center of the face; the nose has lost its sensitiveness; it's gone. . ."

The man with the storehouse-stump was busily engaged collecting more money and pulling out other boxes. All the women inhaled very quietly; the two men ordered some liquor and poured a full box of the dope into a tumbler.

"But why don't you inhale it?" asked Tito's friend, addressing the pair.

One of the two men simply thrust his head far back to show the nasal septum chewed away by an ugly ulcer.

"Cocaine, perhaps?" asked Tito.

"Cocaine," answered the youth. "It all starts with a little itching crust, which gets bigger and bigger as time goes on; it then becomes an ulcer which destroys the gristle around the septum, but fortunately it does not affect the bone."

"What do doctors say?"

"There is nothing they can do!"

"Is it possible?"

"Yeah. Give up cocaine, they say; but I would sooner lose the inside of my nose."

Tito grinned.

The man with the ulcer grinned, too. He laughed im moder-
ately, deliriously almost All four women, Tito and the Other man
joined in the chorus of laughter.

Tito's hand ran instinctively to his nose. It seemed to him that
he had lost it entirely, but at the same time, though he felt it was
missing, it felt exceedingly heavy.

"The weight of nothing."

And he laughed again.

All the rest joined.

"Goodbye, ladies and gentlemen!" waved the peddler as if he
were leaving.

"Ah, not yet!" shouted Tito, as he held him fast by the wood-
en stump. "Stick around and have a drink with us."

The peddler sat near Tito, stretched his wooden leg under the
table, and drew back the other.

"There's more money in this than panhandling," commented
the skeletric and yellow-faced youth.

"Sure," admitted the poison peddler, "but don't think that
panhandling is such a bad trade! It's true that one can make money anywhere, but there are places where you can make more than
in other places. Standing before a brothel doorway, for instance,
means a big haul generally! Of course, never as much as when
you stand before a church. But at any rate, enough to be well off,
I used to prefer standing before a church. Along the streets, on
the boule-vards, on the doorways of cafes, you watch the crowd
go by with its usual percentage of sharps and idiots; the percentage
is even higher near the churches; they are all idiots, ninety per cent
of them; you can't go wrong. Even the swindlers go to church, it's
true; I will even say that they are in the majority, but coming and
going from that home of God, they do not want to be thought impi-
ous and heartless, either before or after their vow of piety."

The man gulped down his drink, put down his tumbler and thanked everybody. Just as he was about to cross the threshold another woman rushed up to him and bought another box.

"Good luck to you all!"

Like the shrewd character he was he speculated upon the effect which his departure would have. In fact, as if their very savior were about to disappear from sight, all the other women surrounded him on every side, and handed him more money. Even Tito bought another box, opened it and sniffed.

"Where does reporting lead you to!" scolded the waiter friend. "To be able to learn all about cocaine you will have to become an addict yourself. . ."

"But what can one do?" answered Tito. "It could be worse. While travelling among the Egyptians, Pythagoras had to submit to circumcision before he was even admitted into their secret rites. . ."

"For what paper do you write?" queried the cadaverous one, confidentially.

"For a paper which is published in America," informed Tito. "And you," he asked, "what do you do for a living?"

"Not a thing," answered the pale-faced youth with great indifference. "Christine works for me. If I could work without getting tired, like Christine does, I would be the one to work for her. But since I cannot. . ."

Tito's friend could not conceal a shade of astonishment for the manner with which that egregious pander stated his occupation.

"Your friend," said the man, indicating the waiter, "your friend here seems astonished at what I am saying. But I don't see anything strange about this. Some time ago Christine and I worked together in a factory where five hundred women were employed. They were all becoming consump-tive. The boss exploited them all. Not being able to get them all out of that dump, I took Christine along. I am the one exploiting her, now. Yet, I see no reason why I should be judged more contemptible than that boss who exploited them five hundred at a time. Better still when you consider that the work she now does is far less tiresome, cleaner, and there's money in it. One may say that it smudges one's conscience. But what if it does? As long as the hands are clean,"

"What time is it?" asked Tito, making ready to leave.

"I haven't any watch, Man has shortened the days by inventing the watch, and the years by inventing the calendar. I have neither watch nor calendar."

"My calendar is right here," laughed Christine, with a gesture of the hand.

"And it never goes wrong," added her lover, grinning.
Tito turned to his friend and whispered, "Decency and will power are the two very first things cocaine destroys."

'They are beyond shame. But what decency is there left to lose in these people," chuckled his friend, "Why, they are worse than respectable women."

2

The article, which Tito wrote on cocaine and its addicts met with great success. Long before it made its sensational front-page appearance, the owner of the American paper had wired his nephew one hundred dollars. One hundred dollars meant unlimited financial power to Tito and the assurance that he was a great success in journalism. With this idea in his epigastrium (arrogance, conceit and haughtiness are all things which are located in the epigastrium), he hopped into a cab and drove back to his small and dingy Montmartre lodging, where he settled his bill, gathered his few belongings and moved into the Hotel Napoleon, in the Place Vendome, one of the swankiest hotels in town.

During that same afternoon he called upon the owner of a great Paris daily with a large circulation, *The Fleeting Moment.*

The owner was a man of very distinguished appearance, and he dressed well. Only old-fashioned college professors do not seem to understand that a man can be clever and yet be smartly attired. A fat ruby stone glittered on his finger like a small lantern; like one of those red lanterns which imaginative novelists very often compare to fat ruby stones.

"Yes, of course, I know your uncle," said the owner, as he rocked himself on his swivel chair of kingly comfort, with straight longitudinal and sidewise movements, very much like the conscience of a newspaper director, which must be kept clean and unspotted at all times, no matter how the wind blows.

"If you are as gifted in journalism as your uncle is," added the director as he ran a paper-knife up and down his thighs as if he wanted to sharpen it, "I say you will have a great future ahead of you. Where did you work in Italy?"

"I was with the *Corriere delta Sera*"

"And what were you doing there?"

"I was editor-in-chief."

"Do you hold any degrees?"

"Yes, law and medicine."

"What are your political views?"

"I have none."

"That's fine. To successfully defend an idea it is always best never to have any. But the trouble is this," proceeded the director, fumbling a pair of scissors which he jabbed into an English daily spread across his desk," all vacancies on the editorial staff are filled, and I really don't know what to offer you for the moment. At any rate, I will take your name and address, and will let you know when you can be of service to me. Where are you stopping now?"

Tito, figuring upon the sensational effect of his answer, let his words drop with studied emphasis:

"At the Hotel Napoleon."

At this, the director who had already pressed a button to have an usher escort Tito to the door, laid down pen and pad, dismissed the usher and turned to Tito again:

"I'll put you on for a month on trial," he proposed, "at one thousand five hundred francs. Tomorrow is the first. You can start tomorrow. I want to see you the moment you come in. I will have you meet your new colleagues. Goodbye." And he pressed the button again.

That night Tito dined at Poccurdi'ss and bought an orchestra ticket at the *Boite a Fursey*, where he learned the latest song hit. He whistled it softly to himself as he reentered the hotel.

The Hotel Napoleon.

The Napoleon Hotel.

Remember that you are now living at the Hotel Napoleon; on the fourth floor, where the rooms are without heating conveniences, it's true, but it is also true that you are living at . . .

The Napoleon Hotel, of course.

Back Into his room he began to unpack his things. He arranged his beautifying tools: combs, towels, hair-pluckers, etc., over the washstand. He spread his shirts, trousers and vests neatly into the various drawers, and hung his coats and jackets in the wardrobe. The room even had a telephone.

"What a pity," he thought, "not to have anyone to telephone to! To have one ready at hand, and yet not know to whom to speak. 'Tis sad. Still, simply because I have no one whom to telephone, is not a good enough reason why I shouldn't use it just the same." With this thought in mind, he picked up the receiver and gave the operator a number, the first that came to his mind.

He did not have to wait long. A woman's voice was heard on the other end of the wire.

"Is this you?" asked Tito. "But how is that? Why, madam . . . that's fine, you're just the one I want to speak to. I warn you that your husband knows everything that's going on, I can't tell you any more, now, and please do not insist. All you want to know is this: your husband knows everything. But no, no, please stop asking questions. No, I said! My name is not Jackie. . . . Well, all right, then. You've guessed it. . . I am Jackie himself. Good night."

And he hung up,

"Who the devil knows Jackie," he thought, smiling to himself. "I wonder who she is."

He darkened suddenly.

"Poor thing," he sighed with a pang of regret; "that sure was a dirty trick to play on her. She's going to have an awful night of it. . . Maybe she will be in trouble. I think I'll give her another ring and tell her that . . . but I forgot the number. O well, let it go for better or worse. Perhaps 1 did her some good by warning her."

And he laughed again.

He undressed and put his watch, money and a gold case upon a nearby table. He opened the case. It was almost empty; he recalled that during the intermissions at the theatre he had sniffed a few grams of it, to celebrate his ingress into a great newspaper, *The Fleeting Moment.* He had only a little over a gram left. Tito poured it out on the back of his hand and inhaled rapturously.

He cleared his valise of the few things still there: his pajamas, a Bible and a pistol. He donned the pajamas and lay the Bible upon his night-table.

He tucked himself into bed, pulled the quilts up to his mouth and turned off the light.

* * *

The cocaine he had sniffed sent its cooling and aromatic sensation clear across his lungs. "What cold feet in this hotel!" he grumbled as he coiled himself up in a ball.

The ear resting upon the pillow heard his heartbeats.

"My heart is rushing after something. Perhaps it's rushing after my nose that's run out on me. There's a great future ahead of me, alright, in that newspaper. I'll be a director in a year or so. Then I'll marry the daughter of the Minister of State. Then I'll be a member of Parliament . . . a member of Parliament at the Bordone Palace. And from there I will shout: "Believe me, Alcibiades, old scout, it is much better to deal with one of these peaceful youths than with any of those pleasure women from Athens. . ."

But how was it that he had to call back to mind a phrase that was reminiscent of the platonic feasting of yore, a phrase which he found, who knows how, who cares when, in the distant years of his Lyceum days? And how his poor legs froze under the quilts! His heart calmed a bit. But his fancy kept whirling. His brain reeled like a drunken revelry in an asylum for the insane; his eyes were shut tight and saw darkness; a background of bluish hue fired with exploding cold sparks. Each spark burst in twain, and from each, new sparks formed, which, in turn, spread into many particles, one of which sputtered into throbbing filaments that flashed with amoeboid undulations and flooded his entire field of vision, filling all surrounding darkness. His eyes though shut, were suddenly inundated with light.

And in this light there spun a circle, movable, elastic, that quickly took on the shape of a square, then a rectangle, then a parallelepiped, a black parallelepiped, with one, two, three edges of gold: a book . . . the Bible!

"The Genesis. . . What a clown, that good God; what a great humorist, that good God! . . .", thought Tito, while his heartbeats quickened and made the bed resound loudly like a music box. "What clown, what comedian, that good God! . . . He said:

"Let there be light,

Let us have the sky,

Let there be grass,

Let there be trees,

Let us have the sun,

And the stars when there is no gas,

And gas when there are no stars,

Let us have snakes, and birds,

Let us have cats in the alley and dogs in the backyard,

Let the zoos fill with wild beasts,

Let us have the male man,

Let us have the female man. . .'

"He then instructed the pair to go ahead and make children, and authorized them to hold sway over the fish in the ocean, the birds in the air, and over the animals that roamed the earth, He had only to say: 'Let us have stars, and crocodiles and guinea-hens; let us have rattlesnakes that creep, the smew, the porcupine and, lo and behold! all these animals sprung out of nowhere upon hearing their names mentioned.

"If this be true, then he had an easy job in creating the world.

"And yet on the seventh day, the wretch felt the need to lay down on the job and take a rest.

"How comical, that good God! It may be true that he was the one who regaled us with that blessing which is water to irrigate grass, grass to feed the cattle, cattle to feed man, man to feed woman, and the snake to annoy them both; the truffles to slice over lobsters, the sun to dry up the linen, the stars to inspire poets; the moon upon which to write Neapolitan songs. But it seems like a strange thing to me that all this should spring out of nothing by just calling it by name. I think that Almighty God was fond of parlour games and that he had everything arranged beforehand, and that he, like the clever magician he was, had glasses and double-compartment trick boxes ready for the game, and that during the first six days of his building tour bluffed his way by creating everything out of nothing, like Americans would, just to impress the folks.

"But there was a trick to it.

"To inject life into man he filled his nostrils with a vital breath.

"I don't think God did this to give him life, but to fill his mouth with some artistically assorted types of bacilli. The proof of the pudding is that Adam lived to be only 930, whereas he should have lived longer than that.

"He had commenced with a magnificent gesture, that good God, when he created the stars of the huge orbits, the sun to shed everlasting light, and all the plants and animals. Expenses meant nothing to him. But to make woman he did something beneath his dignity when he robbed poor Adam of one of his ribs.

"What a humorist, that old God!

"He knew through experience that when one reads the legend: *smoking forbidden*, one feels a fierce desire to puff at a cigarette. Regretting no doubt the many gifts he had showered upon Adam and wife, he wanted to get everything back without arousing suspicion, which would have made him look rather cheap, so he enlisted the support of the snake, the dear old snake, to whom he suggested that cleverly contrived apple trick, which we all know.

"The snake had an understanding with God.

"Everything had been arranged.

"The fruition of that fruit resulted in this: that the eyes of Adam and those of Eve opened suddenly, and both felt ashamed to see each other naked, so they got busy and stitched together a couple of wrappers the size of a fig's leaf. But how could they feel ashamed of their nakedness if they had never seen one another garbed before?

"The following morning the Lord called upon Adam who, like the gentleman he was, blamed everything on his wife.

"Thus God, slightly cowardly, retaliated by charging a stiff price for the stolen apple, and invented the spewing of pregnancy and the pangs of childbirth. Every woman whose womb is retroflexed should know whom to thank for that, considering that it was God, who said: Thou shalt give birth with pain; the Earth will bristle forth with thorns, and thou shalt eat thy bread by the sweat of thy brow and that of your baker, and you will pay a big price for it, too, because the currency exchange with America is now at a tremendous disadvantage.

"He then kicked both out of Eden, and he garrisoned the entrance with a swarm of bodyguards with flaming swords, and called them Cherubs. Briefly, the marriage between Adam and Eve was an unhappy one, like all settled affairs,

"But what really disgusts me is to see that good God playing the fool. He is all-seeing, all-knowing; it is he who plans the worst complications, and then sneaks over to Adam to ask him with simulated candour:

"What have you done with the apple?'

"Then scuttles over to Cain, and "What have you done with your brother?'

"If I were in Cain's place I would have socked him right in the eye.

"Yes, God's own eye.

"God's own eye that sees all . . . feels all, and maybe feels the sting of my curses, and is liable to smother me with a thunderbolt for that.

"But how cold my feet are!

"Still, if I should die right now, I feel that would make me almost happy. To kill myself is not what I have in mind. But to die peacefully, that's different. To step gracefully out of life like stepping out of a bathtub. What a beautiful thing to die! The corpses in the graveyard are the only ones who are happy, and the more advanced their dissolution, the greater their happiness. But if I cannot die, remain here, at least, in complete abandonment, inert, lifeless, like a mineral, void of will power, stripped of all initiative, without rebellion; let everything about me move at will; let everything crumble to pieces, with me never raising a finger to stay the ruinous tottering. Do like the respectable women of old, who grew in years and became ugly and disfigured without ever thinking of whitewashing, nor powder their faces. But what a queer feeling cocaine gives me! Cold feet, fireworks in the brain, a whirlwind of nonsense, my heart beating away like a sewing machine, and, on top of everything else, that serene adaptation to the state of inertia. And yet I would like to stay two days, three days in bed, till I hear the waiters come knocking at my door, and then the manager himself, and the police, and I would lay still, without uttering a sound, ever. I would let them carry me far away, wherever they want, however they please . . . but what funny sensation cocaine gives me, cocaine, the enchanting cocaine! . . ."

His heart continued to beat loudly and, subordinate, his whole body shook, trembled and quivered as would a parked car with the engine running.

By now, the drug had spent much of its frantic and depressing effect. Tito was slowly coming to himself again. Then he fell soundly asleep.

* * *

When he awoke the sun was already high, Tito, however, did not notice it because in Paris the sun is always very high, so high that you can scarcely see it. At ten he had to be at his desk. The boss spoke very plainly when he paraded those awesome, lion-tamer moustaches before his spirited eyes: "See me when you come,"

That meant that he had to show up with a clean-shaven face. Standing erect before the mirror, his safety razor skim ming softly across the lathered surface of his thin face, Tito thought:

"What a nuisance life is! What useless burden! To get up every morning, put on your shoes, shave, meet people, talk, keep looking at that same old clock and see those same old hands revolve around those same old points which we have seen millions of times before. Then eat. Eat chunks of dead meat; eat fruits that are decayed, or spoiled by cooking, which is worse. To pluck them nice and fresh off the tree and swallow them after they have been spoiled. To eat dead things, to use them and then destroy them that new things may rise upon their path of destruction. Everything that surrounds us is dead, with, here and there a tiny sparkle of life, but the rest all dead stuff: the wool in my clothes is something which is dead, the pearl adorning the neck of some young woman is but the bier of a worm. . . To have to smile to women; to force ourselves to be a little different from all other men. We too are trying to be different from the common lot and we give ourselves wide berth to avoid pursuing the high-ways of life, but end up with rubbing elbows with the mediocre, by journeying along the main thoroughfare. Life is like an arch extending from A to B. It is not a straight line, except for those who are born dead or are idiots from birth. For the slightly intelligent ones the curvature is small; for the real intelligent the curve reaches its maximum; for the simple ones the curve becomes almost rectilinear: they reach the B terminal by following a feeble curve. Those who suffer congestion of the brain, the eccentric, the bizarre, the queer ones, eternally searching for the new, the odd in life, and assume unnatural poses, get there with less speed, but, fatally, they too will reach the goal toward which the small people race, resolute and without hesitancy. The difference between the simple-minded indi vidual and the eccentric one lies in the amplitude of the arch itself. The one who has ridiculed matrimony and thirsted for liberty and adventure, will some day envy the man who has married and has children; whoever has planned a life of bright contingencies for himself, alternated between poverty and wealth, of superfluity and hunger, will some day regret that he has embarked on a government career, I think that deep in her heart the theatrical headliner envies the efficient housewife who bathes her snotty brats and whacks them when they do not stay still I believe that the big politician who is busy making history, too, will regret the lost opportunity of becoming either a country school teacher or a station-master.

"Mediocrity is truly the perfect thing. Perfect is the book-keeper who shaves himself every other day, who travels second class, aims at Purgatory, and is satisfied with a fifty thousand franc dowry; lives on the third floor, was non-commissioned officer in the army, wears shirts with detachable cuff links of gold-dipped silver.

"Mediocrity be praised!

"Why then do I go to work for a newspaper cherishing the hope that some-day I will be somebody? Nothing doing! Non-sense! Frankly, there is nothing I hope for. I have no ideals. I have very hard whiskers, though, and this darn razor is dull. But that will be all, now. I have grated myself enough for today. I am sure that the director of *The Fleeting Moment* will not want to kiss me or hug me. Nothing like that, I hope. I shall be a mere employee, a very humble employee, I shall never seek to be-come a matinee idol. The crowds love the man who amuses and serves them. But one must first love the crowd before serving it. I love nobody, and much less the crowd; mobs are very much like women; they betray those who love them."

Tito bent over the washstand and rinsed his face. The cooling sensation cleared his mind.

"What an idiotic pessimism mine is! Idiotic and untrue. I want to succeed. And I will."

He quickly descended the stairway, and when he was about to cross the threshold he hailed a bellboy, in a flaming red uniform which fitted him like a jersey: "Fetch me a cab," he said.

The director of *The Fleeting Moment* was at that minute in the fencing school, engaged in a few fencing rounds with the theatrical critic. But he had sent word that he would be in his office within three-quarters of an hour.

Tito Arnaudi removed his hat and coat. This is the first thing one does when he is about to take possession of an office.

"Are you the new reporter?" asked a gentleman who was dressed in black, who greeted him with extended hands. Everything was rigorously straight about him, the parting of his hair, the crease of his pants, the shape of his lips, the squaring of his shoulders, so that he seemed as if he had been drawn with ruler and India ink. "My name is Menier, and I'm the secretary here. Won't you please come in?"

And he led him through three immense halls, hung with tapestries and marblework and furnished with very light desks and huge armchairs, those soft armchairs that adhere caressingly to all the sinuosities and prominences of the body. The proportionated difference that existed between those slender-shaped desks and those huge and indeed hospitable armchairs was a just recognition of the uselessness of work before the right to idleness and sweet indolence, After having crossed the three halls along a strip of Oriental carpet, they finally reached the American bar.

The bartender, whose huge loins were wrapt in white cloth like some ancient Egyptian priest who, by sheer distraction, had donned a small black Spanish jacket of con-temporary style, was busy mixing some very complicated drinks for three or four reporters who sat, or rather, clambered all over their tall stools, which made them look like outposts on the lookout.

"Two cocktails, please!" ordered the secretary.

The bartender, with all the severe precision of the chemist engaged in erudite laboratory practices, poured three different liquors in what seemed like a large glass mixer, which he filled with cracked ice; from three other small bottles he poured out several drops of heaven knows what introduced a shaker, and immersed the brim of the glasses in a half lemon, then dipped them in sugar which adhered like frost, and filled the glasses.

The man of the somber and geometric-like cut of countenance, very polished, very austere and very solemn like a millionaire's funeral regarded the Italian quizzically for some signs of astonishment before the motley mixture. The French, and the Parisians especially, when dealing with an Italian, believe they unfold before him Lord knows what unsuspected horizons, and they expect him to look as astonished as those American savages were when Christopher Columbus showed them a cigar-lighter or a box of Valda tablets. Even the Paris cocottes, when undressing before an Italian, expect him to throw his hands into his hair when she discloses the fact that women are not shaped like men, Tito thought: "Cocktails are prepared the same way even in my country, and if you had imbibed all the cocktails I have, you'd have the delirium tremens by now."

"Meet Dr.----, who is in charge of the German political section; Prof.----, our Russian collaborator; Mr. ----, our medical writer."

Then he introduced them to Tito. The three gentlemen of whom Tito only heard the termination of their names (like *ein* for the German . . . *off* for the Russian, and . . . *ier* for the medical collaborator), leaped to their feet and shook hands with their new colleague.

"I'll now take you to your office," said the secretary, "and I would like to have you meet one of your countrymen, now our Italian correspondent. He's a charming fellow."

Tito laid his glass on the counter, shook hands with the Teuton, the Russian and the scientist, and the trio clambered back to their outposts.

Another room opened behind the bar; the billiard-room with two tables, and behind that, was the restaurant of *The Fleeting Moment*, for the convenience of reporters and their friends.

They thread their way through a long corridor; three or four ushers rose and sat at their passage. It looked like some hotel corridor, with doors to the left and to the right, and the only thing missing that would add to this resemblance, were the pairs of shoes in front of them, or the trousers hanging over door-posts. While passing before the various doors further on, one could hear very clearly the pounding of typewriters, all tuned to perfection after the same keynote; the shrill of bells, the ringing of tele-phones and women's voices.

The secretary knocked at a door. "Come in!" spoke a voice from the inside.

* * *

A flurry of cushions and pillows of the many different hues flour-ished upon a *dormeuse*, and atop that layer "of softness was a man." One of his legs stole quietly to the floor, and upon that leg, erect, stood Pietro Nocera.

"O, it's you, Tito Arnaudi?"

"O, look who's here . . . Pietro Nocera!"

"You, in Paris?"

"Sure, since last month—And you?"

"Since last year. Travelling?"

"No!"

"Stopping in Paris?"

"Better still; I've a job on the paper."

Pietro Nocera had not yet fully recovered from his as-tonishment at seeing his friend, when the secretary turned to Tito and added:

"Your office is next to your friend's. I'll have someone open the inter-communicating door, so you two will not have to step outside in the hall whenever you want to talk to one another,"

"Well, how come you're here?"

"I'll tell you all about it. And you?"

"I'll tell you all about it, too."

"Are you engaged for breakfast?"

"Not at all."

"We have a restaurant here "

"I saw it."

"So you'll have breakfast with me?"

"If you're responsible for what you're saying."

"Fully so."

"Then it's a go."

"I'll have you taste oysters that still smell like the ocean."

The secretary let the two friends expand their sentimental fumes, and walked away.

Pietro Nocera telephoned downstairs to the bar:

"Bring over a couple of *Turins.*"

He then turned to Tito:

"I offer you a *vermouth* for local coloring. Sit here, right before me, and let me take a good look at you. You've changed a bit in complexion, but you still have that boyish look about yourself. How come you're in Paris? And how's your old aunt?"

"Let's not talk filth at the table."

"So you're in the newpaper business, too?"

"As you can see."

"But how?"

"Simple enough: I am working as a reporter just as I would as a motion picture operator, or a boartswain, or a magician."

"You're right," approved Pietro Nocera. "We alll run for shelter to the journalistic profession, like people who wind up in the theatrical business after having worked at the most miscellaneous jobs; the priest, the dentist, the insurance agent, everybody. But newspaper people are not human beings who live through life. We stand upon its outskirts; we have to fight for opinions which we often lack, and inflict them upon the public like a punishment; we treat questions that we know little about and translate them into everyday language for mob consumption. We are not allowed to have an idea of our own; we have to take it from the boss, but not even the boss of the largest paper has a right to his own opinion and he has to swallow it when he is called before the Board of Directors, and approve whatever they decide doing, irrespective of all that he thinks . . . .

"But if you onnly know how miserable is the background of this great stage! You've just seen a lot of halls, lots of carpets, lots of lights; the bar, the fencing-school, the restaurant, but you don't know the people here yet; the atmosphere is so tenor-like! There are a lot of conceited saps who go around vocalising presumptuously through the halls; and there are many meglaomaniacs here who will boast of successes never achieved!

"Those who are not within our sphere believe that the journalist is some privileged character becasue they grant him free admission to the theatre, and governmental officials give him preference over prefects and senators, who are kept outside waiting, and all great artists treat him with cordiality. But the public doesn't know that all these people despise him secretly, although, on the surface of things, they deal kindly with him; from the porter over at the hospital who volunteers to tell him all about the samadh-up that has happened, to the President of the Republic who grants the scribe an interview. Everyone has the most dreadful opinion about newspapermen. They treat him gererously, of course, but that is only because they are afraid of having to pay himn ransom, or some other spiteful little trick. Very wittingly they give him the information he seeks, and sometimes even write it down black on white for him, or else dictate it to him textually, because, knowing of his frightful stupidity, they are afraid he might misquote them and charge them with, the Lord only knows, what beastly things. The great magician, the most popular among dramatic actors, the successful comedian, all treat the newspaper

critic royally, it's true, but deep in their hearts they know perfectly
well what a critic is. He is a man who, from the ages of eighteen
to twenty-five, began working for some local gazette just as he
might have entered the cod liver oil business or done bookkeeping
for some equestrian circus. The life he leads will naturally throw
him into constant contact with men of letters, comedians, artists,
painteres, sculptors, musicians. By rubbing elbows with them, day
in and day out, his meagre indeed, but well-nigh sufficient to jot
down a column full of vituperations and slander against men of
genius and decent people, and to heap apologetic praises upon a
nobody or the brow of a numbskull.

"Of course, I don't mean to say with this that journalism is a
mere typographical machine placed at the disposal of the irresponsible and the incompetent; in every editorial department you
will find two or three intelligent individuals, two or three upright
individuals, and sometimes one or two who are gifted with brain
and conscience.

"In this caravan-menagerie where you took shelter fifteen
minutes ago, you will also meet some admirable people: the
boss, the editor-in-chief, the theatrical critic, a very severe critic
indeed, who is also a writer of comedies. . . "

"Popular?"

"Not very. Then you have the stenographer, the German
collaborator. But the others ... all superficial people whose brain
is filled with a summary smearing of books they never read, and
who talk, talk and talk in fragments, using hackneyed, confused
phrases, and to hear them talk one would think that they had
a collection of newspaper clippings on hand, from which they
could read some phrase, some line, here and there, without thread
or purpose. There are others who never talk, and yet strike you as
if they were so many profound thinkers, because their heads hang
low as if hypnotized by the asphalt on which they walk; they
seem to be scanning every sputum they find, thinking perhaps

that they have struck a diamond or something. You believe them absorbed in the unraveling of some dark puzzle, while in reality they think about nothing; they are like those steeds of public vehicles standing at the curb who seem petrified by some tremendous problems, while they have in their brain, absolutely nothing. However, I believe you will feel quite at home here. Everybody here seems affected with a sort of *a-quoi-bonnisme*, that *"I-don't-give-damn"* air, and what happens in other places also happens here. Those who have made the grade will despise all newcomers, like those ladies who, having already found a husband, will mock those who are still on the look-out for one."

While Pietro Nocera spoke, Tito glanced around the room.

A huge window with frosted glass panes, a writing desk covered with newspapers, sheets of paper thrown disorderly about, a pair of yawning scissors, inkstand, liquid paste, a blazing lamp, an ash-tray filled with wax-tapers, the heads of which looked like so many tiny skulls mixed with shanks in a charming charnel-house (a remnant of cocaine still nestled in Tito's brain); then the telephone, newspaper clippings glued to the walls, a slender bookshelf with some books thrown there at random, which made it look as if the books had been flung there to please the shelf,

"Your office is just like mine," said Pietro Nocera, "They are all alike, like cabins in a liner."

Someone rapped at the door and a messenger entered.

"Let her come up," said Pietro to the messenger; then, turning to Tito, said:

"She's my temporary lover. Now you go and install yourself in your office. I'll call you in an hour."

"But how come? Do you receive women in your office?"

"Where would you expect me to receive them, you silly boy? In yours, perhaps?"

Tito walked out. The woman walked in.

3

There is a kind of free-masonry existing among cocaine-addicts, They recognize each other through some conventional signs which they alone understand; they have their lodges, it doesn't matter how democratic or aristocratic they be, since they invite each other mutually from one lodge to the next, from the cabarets at Montmartre to the villas of Porte Maillot, from the *boites a etudiants* of the Latin Quarter to the taverns at Montparnasse. In the span of a few months Tito learned all about the many cafes bound almost to history and legend; he became a familiar figure around the little show places of the Butte Sacree, the cordial shops, the underground retreats that echoed, from five in the evening till early dawn, with the rhythm of brass instruments and lust-provoking dances; he frequented all the half-tolerated, half-clandestine spots, meeting places for all the cocaine-addicts who made up fifty per cent of the *habitues*. He grew familiar with that small world bristling around the University: pathetic little women who, from the ages of fifteen to thirty-five fulfill the romantic role of friends of the students; little friends, they are, unencumbering, unobstrusive almost, who are well satisfied with a corner of a room, half a bed and a meal a day. They become attached to the student through the sentimental whim still persists, it holds out, everlastingly so; it continues to live on, it becomes transformed and a whole year will meanwhile go by, maybe two years, and youth will ebb away fast, but the staunch little girl friend will stick it out, faithful almost, and almost in love; then her youthful boy friend graduates and will leave her behind, and she will start crying, seriously perhaps, she grows sincerely desperate perhaps, and in her quest of consolation will cling to some other youth, younger than the one who had just left her, and she will guide him through college, setting the pace to his wisdom and folly alike, and through the several rooming houses, perhaps new to him, no longer new to her; she will lead him through the cafes where they play all sorts of games; and through the many little lunch counters, where for five francs you are given the illusion that you have been served with a dinner for two.

There will then come a day when some student in chemistry will come along and, through sheer bravado, will offer his friend a mere pinchful of white powder, pilfered from the university laboratory. The friend will accept it, either for the joke of it or perhaps because of snobbishness, but never for pleasure, because the first pinch proves disagreeable; then the time will also come when he can no longer go without it, and he will plunge, with his brain reeling in a veil of thick gloom, into utter degradation, down, down through the pit and toward final misery. The female companion who follows him through all the furnished rooms and the bars will also begin smiling as on the day when she first tried to powder her face, and then. . . .

Then these little women will meet, call and approach one another, recognize and understand one another; we see them in groups of two or three at a time in a bar, during the aperitif hour, looking very restless and sniffing about like many fox-terriers, until they disappear, two or three in a group behind wash-room doors, or telephone booths, and a minute or so later we see them emerge with eyes that seem brighter, their faces more serene looking, livelier in movement, more cheerful than ever, garrulous and exceedingly attractive. While in the washroom or in the telephone booths they have shared cocaine among themselves.

They are yet in the formative period of their intoxication; they still manage to retain a bit of self-respect; they guard themselves very carefully from admitting their hobby unless they are first convinced that the person spoken to is also a *renifleuse*; they poison themselves secretly, with a tinge of bashfulness, of shame almost; but within a few months' time we will see the wretches exhibiting their drug-boxes on the tables of bars, in full view, as though they were showing off some fancy cigarette-case emblazoned with a ducal crown. In their eyes one begins to see a dazed, wan look; their will power has waned.

And yet, if their will power were still in them, of what use would that be? Would it help them to keep off the drug? Of course not, never; the dope is absolutely indispensable to them by now. Not the lack of it, but the mere thought that they might have to go without it is enough to make them restless, to stir them, upset them, exasperate them. In such case they will sometimes take hold of your hand and press it against their heart to which a very thin breast acts like the outside of a music box.

"Listen, feel how it beats! Hear it clash suddenly . . . then slacken . . . looks as if it's going to stop . . . no it doesn't . . . hear it go again."

"My nights," they will tell you, "are agitated by dreadful shivering; insomnia tortures me; it's atrocious to be with out drug, but the thought of not knowing where to get it is far more atrocious."

They grow reckless, and take the most desperate chances to get it; seldom, however, will they do anything dishonest, because that would require courage and they haven't any. They begin, however, with dispensing with all useless expenditures, then they will cut down on the necessary ones, give up their apartments and rent furnished rooms, and from there move into an attic. They sell their furcoats and jewels at ridiculously low prices; then their clothes, and the body next. And they will keep on selling it until someday it will have become so shrunken and wasted that it will be impossible to find another buyer. Their coquetry, too, will begin to fade; they will lose all sense of cleanliness, although cleanliness and coquetry are the two indis-pensable things for the life they lead. . . . And this is the reason why you can meet certain women, poorly-clad and miserable, who just a few months before launched the styles for the well dressed, at Auteuil and at Longchamp.

And the furcoat?

Fifty grams of cocaine for it.

And the gold bracelets?

A box that big; but it was all bicarbonate of sodium and phenacetin, not cocaine. . . . .

And the woman will grin icily, to avoid crying, not to try weeping, because, maybe, she doesn't know how to cry anymore. Amidst all these human wrecks, half woman and half ghost, struts the peddler with his pockets filled with cardboard boxes of many makes: red, green, yellow; every color a cue to a motley that is more or less adulterated. He does not sell cocaine that is pure; the drug is mixed sparingly with all other ingredients: boric acid, carbonate of magnesia, lactosium. . . . The peddler knows that the addict is well satisfied with any kind of powder that re sembles, in a way, cocaine; the important thing for her is to have something to sniff; she does not stop to examine or analyze what she sniffs; during the last stages she won't be able to tell the dif-ference between cocaine and sugar, while during the first stages her interest centers more upon the ceremony attending the sniff-ing than on the drug itself; what concerns her then is the manner and the way to take it; with a pen-point of pure gold, perhaps? or an ivory nail-file or a small spade stolen from a salt box? or maybe the nail of her little finger, trimmed for the purpose?

And the peddler becomes fabulously wealthy in the space of a few months. With an ectar of cocaine he can buy ten thousand francs worth of jewelry, and when the clients offer to sell back their empty cocaine boxes, he pays them a cent for every ten.

* * *

The owner of *The Fleeting Moment* was quick in appreciating Tito's merits. In fact, only eight days after he took him on the staff, he telephoned to the general manager about him. And when Tito called to get his pay, he was agreeably surprised to find that he had been given a raise of five hundred francs.

"What does this mean?" he asked the boss.

"It proves you are a capable worker."

"But you never said anything to me about that."

"I never say it. I show it."

From that time on the boss treated him with every courtesy, and excused him from all bothersome duties.

"Would you like to go and 'report' for us this session of Congress?"

"No," answered Tito.

"But why not?"

"I won't get any kick out of that. Congresses are a collection of people who get together to discuss on how to conduct a discussion, and conclude by sending a congratulatory message to the Prime Minister?"

"Right you are. I'll assign someone else."

Even the editor-in-chief began to appreciate the fact that Tito was on the level, and he proposed that they treat each other with familiarity.

They became thick friends.

The editor-in-chief was not regarded as a very important person by the start, although the title—editor-in-chief—made one think of Lord knows what sublime heights in the journalistic hierarchy; but he was a good devil just the same, subdued and yielding before everyone. Our social scheme of things creates at times these consoling contrasts, these amusing contradictions the horse, for instance, after being worked to death, is nicknamed "the noble animal"; all deformations of the spinal chord, every hypertrophy of the bones, all signs of cretinism and other physical monstrosities are gaily designated, "freaks of nature"; the homes for the sick and ailing, are called "health resorts"; the places where people go to die are called sanatoriums; while the monk, after being condemned to a life of strict sexual abstinence, and forbidden to have children, is called Father. Pietro Nocera, his Italian friend, very cordially assisted Tito in his work, and during his first few months with the paper, he very affably initiated him into all journalistic performances.

"I can see the day coming when you will turn your back on me," said Tito one day. "As long as I am below you in position and salary, you will help and steer me along, and you will tell the boys that I have real talent; but the moment my salary, which is the true indication of merit where merit exists, is equal or perhaps above yours, then you will say that I am an idiot. That, after all, is something, which is perfectly human. The Almighty himself, after he had helped Adam to install his household in that terrestrial bliss of his own creation, regretted what he did and invented some pretext that would help him ruin the man."

"I can see where you've been sniffing again," said Pietro, in a tone of mild reproach. "When you begin drawing biblical comparisons, then I know that your nose is stuffed with a few grams of cocaine."

"Let's not evade this point," insisted Tito. "You'll turn your back on me yet."

"But no, my friend," continued Pietro, leaning against the back of a soft divan at the *Cafe Richelieu*. "You do not seem to understand that I have none of the stupid shortcomings other men have. I envy neither you nor the boss, nor the President of France, for that matter, nor Felix Potin, who is, by the way, the leading butcher in Paris. I work simply because it is necessary to have two thousand francs in my pocket every month, but far be it from me to idealize work with either enthusiasm, or envy, or emulation of others. Life is nothing but a brief stop that we

make while waiting to turn into nothing ourselves. Who wants to
work while sitting in a reception room? One talks there, glances
at the paintings on the wall, while waiting to be called in. But
work! I see no use in that if you are not able to look back at what
you did, after you have crossed the great beyond. I cannot see
why all these people should stir and quarrel, scuffle and argue.
That one will play the hero, while that other one will challenge
the people; still another will play the swaggerer, another will
come forth with new ideas, another will tear down systems, and
then still another will turn upside down the value of things. But
what is the purpose of all this, I ask? When you stop to think
that the victorious leader who today holds a race of people in
the hollow of his hand, might any moment enter a cafe", drink
out of some dirty glass, swallow two or three bacilli, less than a
thousandth of a milimeter in length, and he is on his way to meet
his Maker. But to get back to our point, if 1 should some day
tell anyone that you are an idiot, I will naturally have to believe
that all others are intelligent, first. Surrounding me, instead, I
see nothing but people who pretend to be what they are not, who
express ideas when they have none that are worth expressing, or
express beliefs which are not their own, or perhaps do something
which they think will arrest your attention, or maybe use flowery
phrases either to hide some fault or an inferiority complex. The
man who in the dead of winter will step out in the open without
an overcoat, alleging that it is a very healthy thing to do, would
even wear a furcoat in bed, provided he had one to wear. The
man who plays the misanthrope, the solitary, is, nine times out of
ten, an individual shunned by everybody. The man who makes it
his practice to be systematically silent and seeks to impress those
around him that his mind is absorbed In some ponderous philosophical problem, is never a man affected with congestion of the
brain, but a puppet, rather, whose cranium is filled with vacuum.
When a man tells me that he is afflicted with the *taedium vitae*,

and that he is tired of everything, and that the world sickens him, and that the only true happiness is in death, I shall only believe him after he has shot his brain out, and he is dead and buried. Not until he is six feet under the ground! Before then I shall keep on believing that he is merely pretending the part of the pessimist. . . ."

During Pietro's mental ramblings Tito kept looking at the crowded boulevard through the cafe window; a policeman, wielding a white baton, stood at the Intersection, directing the traffic of pedestrians and cars, amid a confused roar of voices and the mingling of deafening sounds.

Meanwhile, Tito thought:

"These are all things which you have already told me the first day we met. During the first half hour of conversation the man talking to you will have said all the interesting things he knows; after that, he will either repeat himself, or else will make some slight variations along the same subjects."

"What's on your mind?" asked Pietro.

"I think you're a very loyal friend. But how come that the editor-in-chief is not here yet. Wonder if he has forgotten?"

But just like in plays, Tito had hardly finished saying: "He's not coming anymore," when the person expected ap-peared on the threshold.

The editor-in-chief was one of those good old souls who would shower you with a variety of suggestions if something bothersome irked your eye (blow your nose, lift your eyes upward, walk waywardly, extract a square root, or something).

He was a man of forty, the most frightful age in one's life! An old man does not move you to pity because he is already old; the sight of a dead man does not pain you because he is already dead; the man who will grieve you is the one nearing old age, the one who is nearing death. Forty years old! In ail public amusement places, during popular celebrations, we see vehicles on rails

running up some very steep ascent, then down again, then up
again; at the pitch of the run, nay, a yard before that, the vehicle,
which has lost during the ascent all the speed it had gathered in
its downward plunge, will begin to waver and slacken in speed,
just as if the apex were something unsurmountable, and it seems
almost awed by the oncoming dash into the precipice that lies
ahead. The man who is forty finds himself precisely in that same
position of dis traught hesitancy, of breathless apprehension; his
speed slackens, and that steep plunge, which he cannot yet fath-
om, but guesses must be there, paralyses him with fear.

The editor-in-chief was forty!

"I hate *tabarins*." he said as he emptied his fourth cognac
tumbler. "All these people who spend their lives dancing in
underground retreats, believing they are having a grand time
by tickling the ends of one another's nerves, do not see, in their
frenzy, that they are simply a series of passive tools in nature's
own hands, which provides them with the necessary excitement
of the dance and causes them to reproduce the species."

And he gulped down another tumbler.

"I only laugh to appear polite," he resumed presently, "and
while I laugh I try to conceal my sadness. And since I am unable,
despite my laughter, to hide it from myself or from others. I
drink, that I may at least hide it from myself; I drink to smoothen
the wrinkles in my soul; but the wrinkles in one's soul cannot be
smoothened—they will perhaps vanish for a few moments, like
the wrinkles of the face will when you massage it briskly; but
they disappear only for an hour, and will then come back deeper
than before"

And he drank again.

"By force of living in newspaper pressrooms, I have trained
myself to read the other way around, to see things turned upside
down. What a sad heritage, mine! Because of this, I have lost
faith in a friend once dear to me; through this I have been able to

discover that the woman who feigned to love me, despised and betrayed me instead,

"So I drink now.

"I drink, and I go to the devil I know it. I am going to pieces, but everything around me looks rosy just the same. I am satisfied when I can see rosy around me. Looking at the world this way, I begin to believe that optimists axe right when they tell me that the world is rosy."

"How does it look when you're sober?" asked Tito.

"When I am sober . . . but let's first distinguish: the devout and the mystic do not see beautiful and alluring women when they gaze at the world, nor do they see men who are cheerful and gay; they see skeletons instead; they see skulls with hallowed eye-sockets, mandibles without tongue, teeth without gums, heads that are ignominiously bald, feet that look like shapeless dice, hands that are long and thin, with fingers that resemble many pipe stems strung together at one end. But when I look at men, I see many spinal cords, many spinal marrows branching out into nerve ramifications."

"That may be all right for me," said Tito, "But how about women?"

"Women? A lot of swarming wombs, they are. Nothing more, nothing less, I see nothing but wandering wombs surrounding me, with men in hot pursuit after them; all hypnotized they seem, and mumbling disordinately of glory, of ideals, of humanity. , , ,

"Thus I drink again!"

Through the glass panes veiled by the fumes one could see two distinct currents of people moving, dense and endless. The hubbub of the hurrying throngs, the uproar, the quick patter of feet, the waving of the crowd, struck one's fancy with some idea of color; the color of bitumen, mixed with yellow-gray, evenly spread, over which the occasional shrill cackling of a *camelot* would rise suddenly; the shrill laughter of a *gavroche*, the warbling of a woman's voice all seemed like many spots of crimson, gushes of white, a sprinkling of purple, allegories tinged with silver, spouting of sapphire effects, flashes of green, a whirlwind of yellow and blue. Through that gloom-laden monotony strut ted, slipped in quick succession, elastic women's limbs; they were all long and slender, muscular and nimble, pink-colored and wrapt in silk like a thread spiral twisted around their calves and ankles, which brought to mind the grooveing of a phonograph record.

The modern Venus lacks the plump, chubby graces that our grandfathers used to look for (with their hands); the modern Venus, instead, reminds one of the androgynal female with a troupe of English acrobats.

"So I drink," continued the man who grinned out of politeness.

"Love would perhaps be the only thing left to me. But I have learned what love is like. It is a subtle poisoning which the woman you love injects into your system. After a while, all the poison you have absorbed becomes habit forming, and all the sweet venom fed into you thereafter becomes harmless and leaves you cold and indifferent.

"There was a time when I got a great thrill out of my enemies and rivals alike, whom I strove to fight openly; but now that I am editor-in-chief of a newspaper, now that I have made the grade, I am also through, I am finished. And the joy of combat is gone from me because, now, I have no more enemies to fight and would never fight them if I had any left, I have come to the conclusion that enemies are very necessary to one's life, if one wants to go ahead. Opposition is indispensable to a career. Since the very beginning of our embryonal life, we should have understood the wisdom of this elemental truth; the semen must swim against current when flowing into the ovaries."

"This is a paradox," broke in Tito.

"I never utter anything that's paradoxical," returned the editor-in-chief, "because paradoxes are more often a lot of nonsense

**"She is an Armenian . . .and is very
famous for her white orgies."**

skillfully set forth. I maintain that enemies are most useful, but
you must first know how to handle them shrewdly. In medicine,
and you who are a doctor can very well teach me all about this;
in medicine, as I was saying, don't they use bacilli to combat
those same ailments which they themselves have caused? All
serumtherapy is based upon the exploitation of our own enemies,
to further our own welfare. Is not the leech man's own parasite?
And yet it becomes a most useful thing In the hands of a skillful
man, the doctor.

"Enmity is a force; contrary, negative, if you will; but nevertheless a force; and all forces of nature are there for man to
exploit. What have you to say about it?"

It was Pietro Nocera who answered:

"I say it's a pity that a brain like yours . . . "

Tito interrupted:

". . . should be ruined by alcohol"

The editor-in-chief, turning to Tito:

"You remind me of those who say that it is foolish to believe
in the influence of number seventeen; seventeen is, after all, a
number like any other; but thirteen brings hard luck, they say,
while seventeen doesn't. You, Arnaudi, act very much the same
way, You kill yourself with cocaine, and it seems like a stupid
thing to you that I should kill myself with alcohol. Somehow,
you do not seem to understand that the reason why we get along
nicely together is because there is an affinity of poisons between
ourselves, and that creates also an affinity of ideas.

"You and I have the same *forma mentis* (state of mind),
which is also that of Pietro Nocera. We three agree to perfection
on everything, because we are tuned to the same keynote. We
three men are simply the products of our own times; not merely
three exceptional types who have come together for the purpose
of forming a singular triangle. Am I not speaking the truth when I
say that poisons have made us what we are today; or is it per-

haps 'our being that way,' which makes us so heroically willing
to swim and drown in suave venoms? In every way, however, I
consider myself very fortunate to be able to poison myself. And
it would be folly not to keep it up, after you've realized that it
is the only way to enjoy yourself a little. Should a half liter of
alcohol be all that would be required to drown my sorrows away,
to change and beautify this filthy world before my very eyes, and
all that I would have to do to get it would be to press an electric
button, why should I then deny myself this? If the experience
were one difficult to live through, then I would understand one's
reluctance. To overcome all the griefs caused by love one could
submit to a surgical operation; but that is something painful;
moreover an operation may not be always successful, while
alcohol is something which I regulate myself, as I see fit; it is an
instrument which I use upon myself, as I like. I know perfectly
well that people disagree with what I do, but I will drink on just
the same, because these five or six shots of good liquor give me
the relief I seek. Through this, all the slights done me will seem
like so many courtesies; all my pains and griefs change, if not
altogether to joys, at least to indifference, and thus I am carried
beyond the surface and reality of things, and see them through
that distorted prospective that constitutes the foundation of irony.
What could be sweeter than to pass by your own neighbor and
yet not recognize him; to live on forever in a sort of unconscious
inebriety? The imbecile and feebleminded will say that all I do
is ungodly, and that I will go to the dogs. To my way of thinking
imbeciles are those who cling on to that worthless and despis-
able thing which is life. Even our boss, who has such a clear and
intelligent understanding of things, deals with me very kindly
when he bids me sit before him and tries to soften the austerity of
his huge moustaches, and with a voice made sweeter and ringing
with true sympathy, he begs me to quit drinking. But the poor
devil doesn't know that I become serviceable, docile and easy to

handle only when I drink! He could then even order me to polish up the floor, and I would do it."

A pale and thin lady, all clad in somber black, entered suddenly, glanced briefly around and sat before a writing desk.

"Some writing paper and a Grand Marnier, please," she ordered.

A waiter quickly brought her the drink and some writing paper. "That's Madam Ter-Gregorianz," said Pietro Nocera, nodding in the direction of the beautiful visitor, "She is an Armenian who lives at the Porte Maillot, and is very famous for her white orgies."

She wore a hat of black veil through which shone her wavy and beautifully black hair; a bird of paradise, also very black, slanted down along one of her temples, caressed her neck and sloped under her throat and beneath the chin. The effect was such that her face seemed enshrouded in a soft and voluptuous frame, the shape of a question mark, turned upside down.

When she had finished writing, she called over a bellboy, all green and gold; enameled and shiny he was, and handed him a letter. The boy's right hand snapped in salute with a vertical motion, palm stretched outwardly, to his green, cylinder-shaped, vizorless cap, cocked to a stiff angle by a close fitting throat-band. He rushed out into the boulevard, slipped amongst the passing motor-busses and vanished from view.

"Allow me, Madam, to present my friends to you!" spoke Pietro Nocera, after he had approached her and invited her to join them at their table.

The lady regarded him quietly through her question mark and smiled; she had a very pale face, and her mouth was thin and straight, as if it had been cut with a chisel. To smile prettily, she lengthened and stretched it a centimeter each side, without curving it.

The editor-in-chief had been newspaper correspondent in Armenia. There was a double current of mutual cordiality existing between the beautiful Armenian and himself. The lady launched into a discussion of the traditions in her country; reminisced upon the martyrdom of her people, the color of its mountains, the sensuality of its women.

While the pair evoked and reminisced, Tito Arnaudi turned to Pietro Nocera and whispered, in Italian:

"What marvelous slanting eyes!"

"Try and tell her so," answered Nocera, "and see how quickly shell set them working. She is the woman I spoke to you about yesterday. The one who keeps a beautiful ebony coffin in her room, stuffed with feathers and lined luxuriously with old damask."

"But is it true that ..."

"Ask her,"

"Really!"

"She won't mind your asking her that question,"

And turning toward her:

"Isn't it true, Madam, that you own a coffin of very black wood and. . . ."

"It's true," she confirmed.

"And that. . . ." hazarded Tito.

"And that I use it for love making? Certainly! It's comfortable, it's delicious. When I am dead I will rest in there forever, and within it I will find the sweetest memories of all my life, , , "

"Well, if that's the case—" granted Tito,

"Who is her lover now?" asked Tito of Nocera, "Some painter. But a woman like that is never without a reserve of five or six spare males on hand."

* * *

The following night Tito Arnaudi and Pietro Nocera were invited to the villa of Madam Kalantan Ter-Grego-rianz, which glittered beautifully white between the Etoile and the Porte Maillot, between the Champs Elysees and the Bois, in that mundane quarter where the cocaine aristocrats dwell in security. Within the many sumptuous villas where often gather the various *tout Paris* (the *tout Paris* political, the *tout Paris* mundane, the *tout Paris* artistic), one sees many organized parties, who meet and share together the gay ebriety afforded by the drug. You can find there the youthful turf and theatrical snobs, the not yet fully pubescent or hardly pubescent gentlemen who deem themselves duty-bound to exhibit upon their shelves the latest poems launched in the book market, and in their beds the adolescent debutante; and the youthful Parisian boys who have their pajamas designed by artists of the *Vie Parisienne.* They feed themselves with congealed tropical fowl and inject between conversations all the poisons a la mode, the extravagant exaltations, the etheromania, the chlorotomania and the hallucinating white powder from Bolivia, So they get together and decide to give it a test. Thus, from one day to the next, they turn the home of a perfectly normal family into a den of cocaine-addicts. Men and women invite each other to "cocaine parties" just as they would to a dinner. In some families the infection extends itself from the nephew of fifteen to the grandfather of seventy; cocaine mania for two in many cases; the conjugal toxicomania is also very frequent, and if the practice would not make the male sexually helpless and the woman sterile, I believe their progeny would be reaching for that white powder the moment they are born. The alcoholized, at least, has still the strength to judge the harm he does to himself and can still advise the uninitiated to steer clear of the liquor venom. The cocaine-addict, instead, likes to surround himself with proselytes and followers; thus, every victim made by the fatal drug, instead of constituting tangible warning, becomes a veritable hotbed of infection to the novice.

4

The villa of Madam Kalantan Ter-Gregorianz glimmered
white as a charnel-house, and was built round like an ancient Grecian temple, surrounded on one side by a triangu-
lar garden of everlasting green, which made it seem like a huge
leaf clasped to a nuptial blossom.

It could have been called the alcove of a Fairy unknown to
this day in current tales, but who should be introduced: Dame
Libertine.

Tito Arnaudi and Pietro Nocera reached the place at night,
by open cab. From a perfecdy round moon there streamed forth
a ribbon-shaped cloud, like some outstretched arm supporting
a lantern across the face of heaven. Here and there, confusedly,
bouquets of stars twinkled in the firmament like platinum dust
blown yonder by a gust of wind.

Beneath that pale moon, playing upon the darkest recesses
of the garden, between bowers of restful intimacy and the hedge,
glittered two enamel shirtfronts. The breeze was scented with the
fragrance of night, that eternally beautiful young enchantress. The
two men alighted with nonchalant ease, and strolled into the villa.

The vestibule was a Roman copy, the walls were hung with
mythological frescoes upon a background of bright vermilion,
like those Pompeian exhibits which young and bashful English
misses would call shocking. The temperature inside was that of a
tapidarium.

The two Italians deposed of their silk hats and, led by a
servant, trimmed like a Turkish admiral, they stepped gingerly
across a semicircular theatrical corridor and were ushered into a
large hall. It was the penguin hall.

Polar landscapes figured across the walls over the many huge mirrors encircling the hall: boundless snows, sparkling glaciers, blocks of ice, giant icebergs that provided a platform to a swarm of penguin gatherings. Only the lower part of the mirrors were painted, while the upper, bare and cold, reflected to infinity the scenic effects and landscapes of the mirror in front.

The penguins looked like so many thoughtful gentlemen in frock coats, with hands behind their backs.

A broad carpet with hieroglyphics of green, white and blue stretched across the whole width of the hall. Tiger-skins and pillows of brocade were spread over semicircular divans. No lamps or windows were in sight. Only a ceiling of celestial glass panes through which filtered the misty glow of invisible but easily divined colored lamps.

"We were just admiring the enchantress's den," said Tito, moving in the direction of Kalantan, who had just then entered and greeted them with outstretched hands.

"We have been the first to arrive. Is it perhaps too early?"

"Not at all. Somebody has got to be first."

The servant had hardly let fall the skin, woolly as a royal cape, that acted as a portiere, when he pulled it up again, announcing the arrival of three rides and three names.

Three gentlemen entered.

One was tall, thin and clean-shaven, with very white hair and side-whiskers, which were also white, and which gave him that austerity of brow typical of the maitre d'hotel.

Madam Kalantan introduced them:

"Meet Professor Cassiopea, director of the Observatory; he owns the world's most powerful telescope."

Bows.

She then introduced the two Italians,

"Meet Doctor *Moonlight;* Professor *Orange Blossoms*; both editors of a Paris newspaper."

More bows.

Two other gentlemen had entered with the astronomer. *"Triple Sec*, the painter."

Very blond, very young, very thin, he was, three times thin.

Some more bows.

Beckoned by the hostess the five gentlemen headed toward a divan; the two Italians were invited to lead the way for the three Frenchmen.

The divan was of such soft and elastic material that, once seated, the knees reached as high as the shoulders. To avoid assuming postures that were ridiculous, one had either to rise or else stretch one's self out lengthwise.

Meanwhile, the servant announced the arrival of new guests.

A wealthy industrialist; an antiquarian who boasted of a few dispossessed kings among his clientele; a blonde female of deceiving age, between thirty and sixty; a *cocotte* of recent distilling; then other men and other women.

One of the latter informed the guests that Mr.— would join them later as he was performing at the theatre in one of Corneille's tragedies.

Some old gendeman apologized for his colleague who had to absent himself from Paris as he had an important surgical operation to perform at Marseilles. The painter was quick to grasp the meaning of that Marseillaise errand, and knew what the operation was all about. The surgeon, Master of an important Masonic Lodge, was never free on Thursdays.

New guests kept coming; introductions, bows; nobody exhibited any sign of surprise in meeting each other again.

Four servants brought one hundred pillows of many different hues, with dazzling color spots, into the room, and began heaping them around the ladies sitting on divans. Toward the background, within the larger area of the circular hall, another and smaller circle formed; a gathering of bodies, men, women, cushions, heads of hair, pink-hued shoulders of women, threads of smoke from cigarettes. The soft glow coming from above tinged everything with roseate and blue colorings, while all shadows seemed to dissolve into green and purple effects.

An impressive restraint lent a touch of refinement to the promiscuous display of pillows, of leg encroachments, to that rubbing of austere and senile dress coats, side by side with revelatory feminine tunics.

Kalantan, the beautiful Armenian siren, stood erect and motionless in the shadow; her very somber gray garment, rich with green and blue reflexes, tensely girdled her shapely form. There were no trimmings or seams that pressed the silken gown against the hollow parts of her body. She looked like some bronze nude. Before one's eyes she bore an impressive resemblance to a basalt statue, but to touch her, one felt that she must have had all the adhesive softness of the vampire. Not even a silken chemise between her gown and flesh. A green cordon looped her around the waistline, with tassels terminating into two thick emerald studs, knotted over the abdomen. She wore green slippers of satin, green hose, and even her nails were enameled green.

A solemn hush subsided. Then, something resembling a trapdoor was flung suddenly open. A weazened, pale-faced youth emerged timidly through the opening with a fiddle in one hand and a bow in the other. The lady motioned to him and he disappeared again. The trap-door folded over him.

Through the floor (it was only then that one could detect the thinness of the floor), came gushes of soft and slow music, which reverberated hallowly and solemn, as if from an unfathomable depth.

"This is not the first time that we meet," said *Triple Sec*, the painter, to a man sitting next to him. "Yesterday, during my exhibition at the Grand Palais you remarked that one of my paintings was full of sublime falsehood. I was struck by what you said."

"How is that?" asked the gentleman with the austere brow of the maitre d'hotel, the one with the white whiskers. "Were you that near your painting?"

"Of course he was," smiled a woman with metallic blonde hair. "The author will always stand next to his masterpiece, just as you will always find relatives behind a hearse bearing their departed kinsman. When speaking ill of either painting or deceased it is always best to step aside a little."

"Do you like the false in art?" asked the artist.

The Astronomer: "Certainly: it is only in the false that you can find real beauty. All crazy deformations, the dazzling contortions, the exasperating contrasts are about the only things with which an artist can hope to give us some emotion. We are weary of the truth, of what is human, of what is likely and probable. I would like some artist to give me the illusion of walking through streets that are paved with stars, with a pair of galoshes over my head with which to slush across firmament pud dies, while rain and light poured over me from below. Instead of admiring the blossoms of trees I would like to bury them altogether and dissolve the roots to the wind. Everything inverted; the causes instead of the products; instead of the consequences, the origins; the roots of daisies are far more interesting than their corollas."

The Surgeon: "That's a trifle too strong, I should judge, for an astronomer of your calibre."

The Astronomer: "Why so. We astronomers are poets with mistaken judgment, that's all. Rather than attempt the study of deformation in qualities, we dabble in the analysis of quantities, which is very stupid."

Kalantan, the beautiful Armenian siren: "Still, astronomers are held in such high esteem. . . ."

The Astronomer: "I know, but that's because we use giant telescopes, we juggle with numbers of thirty figures, and we calculate by the fraction of a split second and by sextillions and then write formulae that are positively undecipherable. Truthfully speaking, of what practical use is it to measure the distance of stars?"

Kalantan, the beautiful Armenian siren: "If your judgment in measurement and calculation were at least mistaken; but, unfortunately, you are burdened with an exactness most disconcerting! . . ."

Entered a gentleman with the face of the born cuckold, Like the rest, he went through the usual formalities and then sat himself upon the floor and fell soundly asleep, hugging a pillow between his legs, like emigrants do with their baggage.

Kalantan, the beautiful Armenian siren: "The fool always sleeps "

A cocotte recently retired from business: "But who is he?"

Kalantan, the beautiful Armenian siren: "Some big business-man."

Tito Arnaudi: "But how does he manage his business if he sleeps."

Kalantan: "His partner looks after that."

The Surgeon: "Lord only knows how he fleeces him."

Kalantan: "Hardly so. The partner is his wife's lover, and the wife, with a keen eye upon the business, prevents him from doing anything that's dirty, at least in the business. . ."

A half-complacent, half-wicked snicker shot through the gathering.

A servant tarried before each guest, bearing twenty champagne glasses filled with fruits, upon a silver tray.

Another servant provided each guest with a tiny spoon of gold.

"A fruit preserve, Macedonian style," explained Pietro Nocera to Tito Arnaudi, as he brought an ice-crystal led strawberry, soaked in champagne and ether, to his lips.

The whiff of ether had inundated the hall; the outer part of the glasses had become frosted with the congealed ambiental fumes.

A third servant made the rounds, bearing a small cube sieved with holes on one side, through which he poured some white powder Into each glass, where it quickly dissolved.

The invisible fiddler continued to weep his pathetic lament like some troubadour entombed beneath an ominous tower, charged with crimes of love. The dim, quivering light raining from above, the soft and luxurious rugs, the carpets, the cushions, the circular walls, all those men clad in somber blacky and the taciturn women, lent a touch of solemnity to the pagan ceremony. Squatted like Turks over the floor, the men held their glasses—enervating source of brilliant hallucinations—between their encroached legs, and sipped with measured slowness the cleverly alcoholized motley of aphrodisiac and very sweet fruits.

A bouquet of purple carnations and black roses in a Chinese vase, perched atop a tripod taller than a man (clever wrought iron workmanship, it seemed), and carnally scented with gray amber, shrieked with picturesque impurity.

The notes from the invisible fiddle fell like slipping dewdrops on the silky threads of a web spun in the sun.

Tito Arnaudi: "And who is that convalescing-looking cuckold over there?"

Pieiro Nocera: "An antiquarian. He and those other two of the incurably romantic faces were once the lovers of our hostess. They are known as the mummy gallery, because their former volcanic lover literally snuffed the life out of them and made them useless in love matters. It seems as if our hostess was heard saying; "What do I care if a man, after he has served my purpose, is unable to gratify other women?"

Tito Arnaudi: "Nonsense, Do you really believe that sexual abuse will lead. . . . "

Surgeon: "Of course it will. Look at the turtles, for instance. They live to be a hundred and love only once a year."

Painter: "I don't envy the turtle a bit. To me there's only one thing worse than abuse."

Surgeon: "And that is?"

Painter: "Complete abstinence."

The man who always sleeps, awakening*:* I've heard what you said about me; you've accused me of being a cuckold; cuckold, wench. . . . Just words! I say, it's all a matter of words. The cuckold is ridiculous only because we have a word that expresses him. Even a woman who has been double-crossed in love would look just as ridiculous if we had a word like cuckold in the feminine terminology. The unfaithful woman is a bitch. The man who is unfaithful is nothing but an unfaithful man and that's because we have never thought of coining the masculine of bitch. But why worry over that? I spend my time between a nap and a dream. When my veins are full of morphine, I just dream. When they are not, I just sleep."

And with a shrug of the shoulders he rolled over and went back to sleep.

Tito Arnaudi: "But why does he always sleep?"

Surgeon: "Morphine"

The portiere suddenly rose; two servants came forward holding the two ends up, to admit two dancers.

"Darjse Polynfaienne!" announced the dancer, seizing his partner by the waistline.

The fiddler struck off into a barbaric music.

But no one seemed interested. The surgeon drew a gold box out of his pocket and sniffed a generous pinchful of cocaine, while a servant, at a sign made by Kalantan, the beautiful Armenian siren, began filling cups and glasses with more champagne and ether.

The Armenian siren knelt upon the floor and bent her head over a cup of champagne, whence she drank as if it were so much lake water.

While she was thus engaged, Tito Arnaudi thrust his face close to hers and rubbed her raven black hair, odorous with the scent of musk like India ink, with his lips.

**A flight of butterflies . . . burst suddenly
into the hall . . . .**

The dancers withdrew, and the servants reappeared with small white cups, like those which Arabs use when sipping their coffee.

"Strawberries preserved in chloroform," explained a slender woman with a green peruke.

"Who is she?" whispered Tito,

"Just another ether of recent distilling. One would think she lived and was born in some imperial court, and she was only a police commissioner's servant, last year. These women offer the most sensational phenomena in the world. Only last year they had dirty feet, but now they hold out their gracefully arched hand and feel insulted if you don't kiss it for them. Only last year they didn't know whether numbers were counted from left to right or vice versa, but will now talk to you about stocks of the Senegal and Zanzibar through Lake Tanganika Railroad, and treat, learnedly, they think, of the latest Goncourt Prize or the paintings of Cezanne."

A flight of butterflies, eager for freedom and frightened, burst suddenly into the hall; some fluttered despondently against the mirrors, while others strayed carelessly among the guests, with the most absurd evolutions. Their wings were like dazzling fabrics woven in purple and metal, gold and crystal, silver and ice, air and copper. They soared and whirred frantically about, then rested upside down upon the luminous ceiling, or flitted to the floor: one of them, with wings spread and the huge eyes gazing in astonishment, lingered across the moire cuff of a dress coat.

It then broke away and fluttered waveringly, between a red-headed woman and a cup, into which it fell, vanquished by the mingling ether and chloroform fumes, and almost covering the brim with brightly extended wings, like a paten spread over a chalice.

"A friend of mine from Brazil sends them to me. They are the most beautiful butterflies in the whole world. I get a small cage

full of them with every steamer coming from Rio de Janeiro. I
should love to possess some marvelous jungle beasts and toss my
servants to be devoured by them for your own entertainment, but,
alas, in the way of exotic fauna, these beautiful butterflies are all
I can offer you."

Tito eyed her intently. "She's a sweet scoundrel, that woman," he whispered to Nocera. "If they are all like that where she
comes from, I don't blame the Curds a bit, nor do I disapprove of
Armenian pogroms."

"I offer you all the spectacle of the butterflies' death. They
die intoxicated by the delicate venomous fumes and the scent of
perfume. Butterflies, like gems, suffer before perfumes. Did you
not know that gems suffer before perfumes? A most enviable
death, theirs, because even in death they keep all the beauty they
had in life. You see them pierced by a pin in the insectars, and yet
they seem alive, because of that very fine, multicolored dust they
have. When I am dead you will all come to powder and paint my
face, as if I were making ready for a dress rehearsal at the *Come-
die?* And she paused to note the effect of her words.

"Poor butterflies!" sighed the incurable sentimentalist.

"Enough from you!" she admonished with queenlike haughtiness. "After all, I regard my home well worthy of being a butterfly's tomb. A home," she went on in biting tones, "where illustrious people like yourself come to die, drop by drop."

"But where do you keep your coffin?" asked Tito.

"Surely, you would not want me to parade it around you,"
answered Kalantan, "As the ancient Egyptians did during their
feasting."

"And why not?" remanded Tito. "There is no one who is
afraid of death among us."

"I, especially, have a certain familiarity with hearses," narrated the skeleton painter. "During my Bohemian days, when
times were hard, I had been allowed to spend the night sleeping

over a pile of hay, in a casket factory near the custom house, down at Bercy, The first night, I could not sleep a wink. I tried to chide myself along by imagining that those coffins were used for packing fruits or ladies' lingerie, but that peculiar shape belied me. The second night, I managed to snatch a little sleep, while, on the third night, I slept well. Although no longer troubled by nightmares, however, the dampness of the surroundings soaked my bones through and through, and the hay-stalks pierced my flesh.

"One night they prepared a swell coffin for a, bishop who was to use it the following day as a permanent abode. In comfort and ornamentation, it was a masterpiece! It was furnished with a cushion upon which would rest the episcopal feet, and a cushion for the episcopal cranium. The only thing missing was the episcopal corpse itself.

* * *

"It even had an umbrella-stand for the pastoral staff.

"That a living artist like myself should be compelled to sleep on straw, and a dead body to decompose in a. coffin as comfortable as all that, was not fair, I thought. So, after I had made sure that the watchman had gone to bed, I stole into the coffin and went to sleep.

"In that bishop's coffin I rested like a Pope. They carted it away the next day. But they had a coffin ready every night. Of course, none as beautiful as the first. One like that could only be had whenever a bishop died; but, anyhow, they were all too good for a pauper like myself. I admit that during the first few nights, it was a trifle uncomfortable to change beds, to keep shifting from one coffin to the next. But like everything else, one gets used to it in time, and after that one would never think of swapping it with the bed of King Soleil himself, now at the Versailles Museum.

"For two long months I slept in that factory. But came a dark day when somebody started making serious remonstrances. They complained that the coffins had already been used."

Who complained? The dead?"

Their relatives did."

What numbskulls I When one is dead, what difference does it make if the coffin is a second hand one . . ." said the Armenian siren.

"But the relatives' piety," noted the astronomer, "the cult of the dead . . ."

That had nothing to do with it," explained the painter. The boss refused to let me sleep anymore in his shop, not because his customers complained in the name of the dead, but simply because they shrewdly seized their chance to ask for a reduction in price."

The dancers reappeared, announcing: "Aridalusian dance!"

"Where did you sleep after that?"

There was a sharp resounding of castanets.

"I rented an attic and started selling some of my paintings. Since that time, my success seemed assured. Remember"—and he turned toward the woman with the yellow hair—"remember the great receptions I gave at my boite, up yonder, in the Butte? Why, I even had silverware."

"I remember," affirmed the woman with the red hot hair, "what your silverware looked like; Restaurant Duval written over a fork and Station Depot over a teaspoon."

"But that was only to express a kind thought toward you," explained the painter. "You see, I wanted my guests to feel that they were in a fashionable rendez-vous."

"I was then a student at the Lyceum Voltaire," recalled a gentleman who had not yet spoken.

"You're wrong; that was the Lyceum Louis-le-Grand," corrected the painter.

"No it wasn't. It was the Lyceum Voltaire."

"You're mistaken. I say it was the Lyceum Louis-le-Grand."

"*Triple Sec,* the painter, is right," confirmed a friend of the gentleman. "You were then going to the Lyceum Louis-le-Grand."

The surgeon turned to Tito: "It's already a good start; loss of memory."

"Cocaine?" asked Tito.

"Morphine," informed the surgeon."

The gentleman remained with his mouth open and the eyes staring fixedly away, as if hypnotized by some chance detail in the rug.

His hand shot toward the inside pocket of his dresscoat and drew out a metal case. He plunged a needle into his thigh, clear through the cloth, and a moment later he exclaimed, enlightened:

"Right you are! It was the Lyceum-le-Grand, and Ivan the Terrible and Scipio Africanus were my school chums."

The butterflies dazed by the fumes of ether flapped wearil about and fell prostrate over the floor. One of them was crushed beneath the dancers' feet. Another had bent over a rose and drooped pathetically over in death while gazing with coquettish grace into a dewdrop.

Still another, of the very white wings, slumped over the edge of an ash-tray and seemed intent upon strewing itself with humility before dying.

The Armenian siren dipped her little finger into a champagne cup, and a drop of moisture descended upon the butterfly's head. It rolled over, fulminated by the venom, and lay motionless in death.

"No, Kalantan, stop that! It's a stupid cruelty!" shrieked the blonde woman just as if she had been pierced with a hatpin.

"It's a fiendish cruelty. You're mean and bad, Kalantan!"

The woman's voice had a woody sound, and it crackled sharply like water gurgling in her throat. Her eyes took on a glassy look, her fingers stiffened, as if ready to clutch at someone
. . . .

The violin sobbed in agony.

The frenzied woman slumped supinely, overcome by a spell of exasperation. Her breath came short and fast. The Armenian snatched the cocaine box out of the surgeon's hand and filled the nostrils of the writhing woman who, "With wrinkled forehead and terrified eyes, kept hissing: "Wicked! Wicked!"

Tito Arnaudi rose and peered through the trap-door left ajar; neither fiddler nor instrument could be seen through the opening; only the bow flashed, from time to time.

"She's coming to herself," said Kalantan, the beautiful Armenian siren, quietly, as she returned the gold box to its owner. The venom reanimated her, for the moment; the brow cleared of wrinkles, her fingers relaxed, her eyes became serene again.

* * *

You're kind, my petite Kalantan!" she murmured. Forgive me." And she broke into tears.

Kalantan seized her under the armpits, bare and moist, and, lifting her like a child, sat her at her side.

"You poor monkey! Your cute little face is all messed up now! Stop crying, and, above all, don't laugh!"

She knew perfectly well, Kalantan did, what these out-bursts were like. She knew that a convulsive fit of laughter would follow the crying spell. A fit infinitely more spasmodic than despair; a laughter filled with sobs. The woman laughed and cried with all her body. Her mouth was livid, ana contracted into an ugly grimace. A terrified merriment, a lugubrious kind of hilarity, as if her eyes had been suddenly blasted by the sight of a corpse dressed like a clown playing a fierce pantomime with a green-eyed lizard.

The man who always slept did not stir.

The astronomer had plucked a rose from the bunch and dipped it in ether. He inhaled voluptuously through admiring eyes. His left leg, stretched over the floor quivered rapidly as if

by some electromagnetic phenomenon. The mummy gallery sat
hushed; one of them had jabbed himself with a Pravaz syringe
and now lacked strength to put it back again, so readily had he
been transfixed by the stupefying bliss. The surgeon, in wanting
to impress others that a residue of self-respect was still left in
him, and that his mind preserved its lucidity, began talking about
paintings.

"A certain Norwegian-like touch I perceive in Van Dongen;
to my way of thinking, his colors are too rich and he uses too
much ceruse; moreover his figures lack stereoscopic blending.
Don't you agree?"

"I say, my illustrious Doctor," replied the artist, "that the
latest method used in curing arteriosclerosis is all right with me:
to graft a horse's kidney into the patient's ear and make some hot
vitriol inhalations into his eyes; I would also advise, however, a
chlorate of potassium and ipecacuanha injection between the first
and second rib."

"But what beastly things are you saying?" exploded the surgeon, angrily.

"I merely wanted to even up the score for what you said a
while ago about painting." And he rose.

"The Bengal dance," announced the male dancer. He wore
a white silken turban topped by a luxurious aigrette clasped to a
thick brilliant stud. The woman, completely naked, wore a gold
tiara with two flaps flowing down her cheeks to accentuate her
oval features. The bronze yellow and the glistening moisture
of her flesh, squirmed and trembled with frenzied feline movements. Her body was full of supple rhythm, interpolated with the
insidious and brief perplexity spells of the young jaguar, crouch-
ing before the leap. Vastly dilated by antimony applications, the
eyes shone with opiate languor. An ambiguous yet tenaciously
pungent mingling of saffron, sandal-wood and benzoin scents exhaled from her flesh. The snowy whiteness of the teeth across her

dusky face? alternately tinged by greenish reflexes, glimmered like an ivory paperknife held rigidly between crimson lips, while the arms, flexible and nimble twisted and entwined with springy suppless-ness about the neck, down her flanks and crept sinuous-ly along the abdomen, to turn the next moment like two snakes with heads simulated by distended and curved fingers, adorned with two fascinatingly cold chalcedonias, like two magnetic eyes. The youthful jaguar-like form squirmed desperately between the winding coils, and the enamel white grin settled into a pre-ago-nistic grimace.

That agony full of spasmodic and arid erotism re-enacted the fabled jungle mysteries like a miracle, and with greater force than those wearisome and unending lectures on India, accompa-nied by picture projections.

Raptured by the dancer's limbs, Tito exclaimed: "Look at those slender ankles! What excites me most in a woman is the ankle. The breast, the hips, the sex can hardly satisfy a young sophisticate."

The music died away; the dancers disappeared. A rectangle in the crystal ceiling was thrown open to let the foul venomous air out. The pungent morning breeze rushed through the opening, flashing with the indigo of the cloudless sky overhead. From the garden, a bird warbled a song that was brief and gay, ironic and concise, like an epigram.

The dormants awoke with a start: Kalantan, the beautiful Armenian siren, sprawled over a carpet, with mouth between her hands, whined:

"Shut that!"

Someone moved to close it.

Tito Arnaudi and the painter were the only two who lay awakened, with faces almost serene.

"I have the highest regard for your art," said Tito, "and it makes me very happy to know that the public takes to you."

"It is not the public who takes to us," replied the painter; "rather we are the ones who take to the public unknowingly, despite appearances to the contrary. Were you ever in those tents where fleas are trained to pull small aluminum cars? It looks as though the fleas are doing the pulling, right? But, in reality, it's the little car that pushes the flea before it as it slides down the slightly inclined bankment. I never would have thought that someday I would come to paint portraits of presidents and Asiatic potentates. I thought perhaps I would remain a mere funny sheet cartoonist or magazine illustrator or a cabaret painter for the rest of my life. That's why I have patched upon myself that ridiculous *Triple Sec* nickname. A nickname, you know, is something like tattooing; you begin by applying it sort of lightheartedly, and then you're stuck with it for the rest of your natural days. I have many friends among newspapermen and, if I have made any appreciable progress, I should be thankful to them for the publicity they gave me. Merit alone is not enough, if you're not properly publicized."

"I know," replied Tito, who was beginning to see all things in a distorted way. "Publicity is absolutely necessary if Jesus Christ has become famous he can thank his Apostles, his twelve big publicity agents, for that."

Pietro Nocera, upon hearing the name of Jesus Christ mentioned, gathered what little strength he had left, and walked up to Tito:

"Look here," he said, "when you start picking on religion, it means you've got more cocaine than gray matter in your cranium. Sit down!"

And with a shove more forceful than gentle he quietly tossed him across two piles of cushions like a bale of rags.

The whir of an invisible ventilator broke the silence, The astronomer looked about in a daze, wondering whether that buzzing could be an hallucination of his hearing; but the man who always slept awoke suddenly and, speaking about that uniform noise, said to him:

"Those butterflies would have been better off if they had stayed home, on the Orenoco."

The painter knelt alongside of Tito.

"Even the women have been of great help to me," he resumed. "Women as a rule will greatly facilitate your success. When you are faced with some extremely difficult task, just turn to a woman for assistance—she'll help you."

"I know it," answered Tito, munching his words and skipping a few syllables, and switching from a low undertone to the shrillest *falsetto*: "I know it. From the chimes of high treason In which international drug addicts succeed in robbing opposing generals of their carefully guarded war plans, down to the days of Eve, who acted as the intermediary between snake and man, woman has always succeeded in her dirty schemes. I am not, therefore, surprised to know that they have even helped a dog of a painter like yourself."

The artist did not stir. He would have lacked the strength. Besides euphoria, cocaine gave him a sense of grand optimism, a special receptivity toward abuses, which became so many enticing courtesies before his eyes.

He smiled.

Everything about had assumed appearances and meanings that savored strongly of the fantastic: the voice would produce sounds that were not human; the light effect, generated from various sources and the manifold opposing reflexes would grow faint with the fluid transparent undulation of light playing in aquariums; a straight line would become a curve; an unsettled fluctuation would succeed to the fixity of the things about like some faint throbbing that reanimated all chill immobility; all those men of the sluggish and slow movements, who slumped, spilled and writhed over the floor amid a flurry of multicolored cushions, and that flowing women's hair, all those moist nudities and crushed champagne cups, were like so much fauna flourishing in aquariums, in which the ambiental fluid would soften every movement and slacken every rhythm.

The green-hued carpet, moist with spilled liquor, was like the slimy bottom of an ocean, where the pillows and cushions wallowed like comely seashells, and the loose flowing hair of women resembled filamentous tufts of byssus, much like the fabled growth of abyssal landscapes.

And the music went on, exasperated and exasperating; it was like some melancholy gipsy song, created by the whim of a blind fiddler who did not know that he played before a host of corpses. Everyone had ceased talking. From time to time, a sinister creaking would sway the hush; the clash of a surgeon's knife over an anatomical marble slab, and the feeble moaning of a voice, barely perceptible. Was anyone dying in that room? The woolly curtains hung like portieres throbbed faintly with dark mystery; the thin, flimsy floor, separating the hall from the one underneath, seemed to heave and roll as if moved by the slow and rhythmic breathing- of low sounds that swayed it down-wardly and the sharp notes that made it rise in endless undulations.

If for some unknown reason the lights had gone out in that moment, all those people would have turned insane; and when the light returned, those huge mirrors would have perhaps glowed with the gush of blood.

Kalantan lay stretched over the floor, with face, breast, abdomen, hips, knees and one foot upon the carpet. Her other foot lay distended across the other ankle. Her posture was perfectly symmetrical as if composed by a lover of equilibrium in poise. The slender ankles and lovely calves, were superb in their beauty and muscular sturdiness; if seized by your hands those calves, exquisite calves, must have crackled no doubt like oven-hot bread.

Tito lay nearby, his face resting against her graceful limbs and his eyes flooded with green—the silken green hue radiating from her hose. The exceedingly blunt visual angle caused by the proximity of the eye to the silken and fleshy objects, altered the image to a fantastic degree. That sheer, emerald-green thing, suffused by a halo, warm and rich with the scent of woman, seemed like a gentle cyclopic slope, odorous with the flesh of youth.

The woman lay immersed in a sleep that was almost cataleptic. With hesitating fingers, wilderingly, Tito raised her garment, very slowly, to savor gradually the disclosure unfolding before his bewildered eyes; his hand had reached mid-way across the thigh; the stockings were supported by a small chain of platinum and pearls, clasped to a buckle friezed with Armenian motifs. Stealthily, religiously almost, like peeling an almond, like uncovering a relic, he forced the hose down the calf, then tarried in ecstatic wonderment.

It was a magnificent chalice.

A cup filled with champagne stood humbly nearby; a layer of flaccid foam had settled around the edge, and a few spare bubbles gurgled out of the bottom and dissolved upon the surface. Tito seized the slender stem with trembling fingers, and drank greedily.

"Kalantan!" groaned Tito.

Aroused to a frenzied pitch by that mouth of white flesh, Tito bent over with lips parched with fever, and began sipping with eyes shut.

"Kalantan!"

It was like drinking out of a magnolia,

"Kalantan, my beautiful, my wonderful Kalantan!"

Never a shiver came from the woman, not even when Tito, faint with daze, drooped listlessly beside her.

Someone moved to open the window rectangle. It was almost daybreak. Across the sky the color of absynthium dripped the fast-receding twinkle of stars lingering behind to meet the on-coming sweep of day.

An automobile rolling softly along the Avenue des Champs Elysees honked with a loud blare. Today Dame Aurora is no longer satisfied to ride her steeds, Lightning and Phaeton, To sound the dawn reveille she now needs the eighty horse-power of a swift *torpedo* skimming upon soft pneumatic tires, while she herself sits at the wheel with "rose-hued fingers", made still rosier by the enameling of a skilled manicurist.

5

KALANTAN . , . Kalantan . . . Kalantan . . " Tito Arnaudi,
stunned and dazed by sleep, moaned, while the car of the
beautiful Armenian siren carried him swiftly from the
glimmering white villa, built like a small Grecian temple, across
the Place de la Concord and the rue Royale, toward his hotel in
the Place Vendome.

In that shadowy morning hour, Paris teemed with a motley
crowd of sullen-visaged banlieue workers heading in the direction of the San Lazarre, d'Orleans and the des Invalides depots,
to catch their trains; shop girls with freshly washed faces who
sprinted hurriedly about, like people anxious to encircle the globe
with the sun. A pauper, with a stray dog stationed at his elbow,
rummaged without rivalry through a motley heap of oyster-shells
and lemon peels before Maxims place.

"Kalantan . , . Kalantan , . ,, Kalantan . , ." Tito kept murmuring, with lips buried deep into the collar of his coat, which
was raised up to his nose, while the car swung briskly in the gray
fresh breeze of the rue San Honore, outlined in shadows; Kalantan, a lovely name for a lover who is unblemished and sweet,
but never for one who is perfidious and wanton, both poisoned
and poisoning . . . Kalantan . . . Kalantan, a slow spoken name,
ethereal, unresisting, falling caressingly upon one's ears, like a
tremor, uttered softly by a soul without a single twitch of one's
lips; a name that was made to be repeated a thousand times over,
very slowly, very tenderly, over the brow of a woman who is
very pale and very sweet. Kalantan, a name that has the musical

sound of that verse by Dante Gabriel Rossetti: "Ye gentle hand
in lover's hand . . . Kalantan; in lover's hand . . . Kalantan . . .
Kalantan."

The car halted noiselessly as if it had been stayed by a puff
of wind. The bellboy of the Hotel Napoleon rushed to open the
carriage door and Tito alighted, tossing a fifty franc note into the
chauffeur's hand. The man refused to accept it.

"Keep it," he jested; "a sentimentalist like myself offers it to
you; I know: in lover's hand . . . I'm a sentimentalist . . . disgust-
ingly so. But take it, anyhow."

Dignified and stiff, the chauffeur pocketed the note and drove
off, blaring his horn with insinuating mockery.

Two letters awaited Tito, One from Italy; the other from his
office.

He read the latter, first. It was from the boss himself:

"Tomorrow at 4 a.m, Marius Amphossy, sledge-hammer
killer of Jamaica governesses, will be guillotined in Boulevard
Arago. I want a detailed account, that is also colorful. We haven't had any executions in France since seven years ago, The
new President has discontinued pardoning the doomed. I am
depending on you. The story must be in the pressroom by 6 A.
M. tomorrow. At 8 we'll have a special edition out in the streets.
Regards."

He rolled up the first letter into a ball and proceeded with the
next.

"Dear Friend:

I have your postal card. You are being wonderful! Do
you still remember me, Magdalena? But I am not Magdalena
anymore. They now call me Maud. After leav-ing the reformatory where I spent ten months, I met several influential men, a
cabaret owner among them, who, realizing that my legs would
take me very far, taught me dancing and secured many profitable

engage-ments for me with the leading vaudeville houses in Italy.
I'll be hitting Paris and playing the Petit Casino in a month or so,

> Will you be glad to see me?

> —Maud"

Tito ordered a linden decoction with a few drops of orange blossom from the elevatorman who had taken him up to his quarters on the fourth floor.

The waiter who brought the beverage had to knock many times before entering the room because Tito was sound asleep in bed.

When he awoke the decoction had cooled eighty degrees; the orange blossom drops had evaporated while his watch had brought all of its organs to an irremovable stop,

He rang the bell.

"Waiter," he called,
"What time is it?"
"Four in the morning, sir."
"What's that?"
"Four in the morning, sir."
"Which day is it?"
"Thursday, sir."
"What time did I get home?"
"At seven in the morning, sir,"
"Of which day?"
"Wednesday, sir."
"And what day is today?"
"Thursday."
"What time?"
"Four in the morning, sir."
"That's altogether . . ."
"Twenty-one hours, sir. "
"That's a lot."

"Evidently, sir. But there have been cases more serious than yours, sir. Shall I take the tray away? I see where the drink has done the gentleman a lot of good."

"What makes you say that?"

"The gentleman has slept."

"But I haven't even tasted it."

"It wasn't necessary to taste it. It's a specialty of the house."

"All right. You may take your specialty along with you."

The tray hopped a foot ahead of the waiter, out of the door.

"By now," thought Tito, as, without flinching, he read the boss's letter over again, "I should be at the Boulevard Arago to watch them behead Marius Amphossy. But is my presence there really necessary? The article must be written, I agree; but to go there . . . But wasn't that Armenian siren strikingly beautiful; Kalantan! A name sounding like a distant bell knolling . . . the melancholy dirge of the dead . . . the death knoll of Marius Amphossy, the Jamaica sledge-hammer killer, whose specialty was butchering governesses, But even if I should go there, what would I be able to see in this pitch darkness? Still, an order is an order, and I must write something about it. There's a special edition for the beheading ceremony . . . at 6 a.m. the manuscript must be in the pressroom . . . ."

With this cast of mind he rose from his bed and slumped into a chair, half of his frame leaning on his elbows over the writing desk.

Large sheets of ghastly white paper waited to be filled. He resembled a suicide preparing to scribble his last wishes.

I have never been able to understand, he thought, why they should execute people this early. What a nuisance to have to bother the executioner, the priest, the doomed one at an hour when sleep is a pleasure to them! Wouldn't the lunch hour have been better? He wrote:

THE DECAPITATION OF MARIUS AMPHOSSY
THE JAMAICA SLEDGE-HAMMER
KILLER OF GOVERNESSES

But instead of unfolding (in detail the gruesome ceremony),
he mused: What a dreadful thing it is to be a newspaperman in
the summer, when all members of Parliament are vacationing,
the theatre folks move to their country homes, and all Criminal Courts are closed. One doesn't know what to write . . . but
the boss nevertheless orders you to fill a double column with
smears of no particular importance, like this one. Still, it would
be worse in Italy. Over there, when there is a penury of writing
material they scribble long articles on the death of Giovanni
Orth; elaborate minutely upon the brain faculty of the ants, and
give you a detailed account of the birth of triplets (a Calabrian
specialty); or else will tell you all about the plague in Manchuria,
or the freaks of a thunderbolt, or the theft of a necklace (North
American specialty); if not that, they will overwhelm you with a
dissertation over the habitability of the planet Mars, or upon the
age of the earth, or maybe upon the real name of D'Annunzio (is
it D'Annunzio or Rapagnetta?); and if that weren't enough, they
will describe the angling of some "giant cetaceanx", even though
it is only a shark or maybe a swordfish. In a newspaper there the
belief is rampant that all fairly good-sized fish are likely to be
cetaceans. What idiots!

His watch registered a quarter past four. He re-read the tide.
But ideas refused to germinate, They were closed, stilted, they
were lifeless and as tightly pressed as a box of sardines. Gastro-
nomic comparison how nauseating at four in the morning, after
sleeping twenty hours! The ideas were as closed as that box of
cocaine, that enchanting, bewitching metal case lying there, right
under his eyes, next to the inkstand, O you—the satanic conspiracy of cocaine and ink!—but to try it.

He knew that under the invigorating spell of cocaine his ideas would sprout like flowers in the sun; they would spread and unfold like dry tea leaves under a splurge of boiling water. He, sniffed. Then wrote:

He wrote uninterruptedly—one, two, three pages in quick succession, without wavering, without stopping to revise, without distracting. His fancy began to color the tragedy enacted before his eyes. Bits of reminiscences from former executions intertwined and intercalated with biting and pitying comment. The blade of that horrid death instrument sparkled with a livid glimmering in that drizzling dusk. A few passersby, attracted to the spot, tarried to watch the grisly executioner and his helpers preparing for the coming execution. The gray prison cells, solemn with grim setting; the soldiers of the Republican Guard forming a cordon around the scaffold, were all told with glowing detail.

When those seven mute figures in black halted before the cell, Marius Amphossy was immersed in deep slumber. He had been hoping for a pardon, Upon seeing those seven grim, solemn-looking gentlemen in *redingote* and cylindrical hats, who bade him follow, he abandoned all hope.

"Marius Amphossy," chanted weirdly one of the seven men. "Have courage! Executive clemency has been denied you. The time to expiate your sins has arrived. Be brave, therefore."

There was a moment of tense, dramatic suspense.

"I will be brave," answered the doomed man, with a mocking grin.

Behind the prosecuting attorney trailed the prison warden and the attorney for the defense. The other gentlemen could not conceal their intense emotion.

The prison clock clanged mournfully the hour of four. The gentleman who had spoken before, read the death notice. When he finished reading, two assistants of the executioner took the prisoner in charge. All others got out of the way, and assembled to the right and to the left, in two silent arrays.

Marius Amphossy, not wholly destitute of courage, walked briskly with a sure and steady step. He darted ironic glances in direction of the group of newspapermen who watched, sullen and grim, from a dark corner of the vast and bleak corridor, flanked by blocks of cells. Many terrified eyes watched through the many peeping holes—were they wretches doomed to the same fate? They stared fascinated, livid-faced, hatred shut in their hearts.

The executioner led the way through the long and narrow corridor.

Behind him walked the condemned and the two assistants.

Then came the attorney for the defense, the prison warden; other officials and then the reporters.

We descended a few steps, and trod our way through a gallery. The sound of footfalls echoed mournfully along the vast and sepulchral stillness, to halt, a moment later before a hall, which we entered.

A clergyman, crucifix in hand, waited there. Displayed over a table, were champagne bottles and other strong drinks.

The priest embraced the doomed, while one of the guards poured champagne for him.

The wretch then asked for a cigarette. They gave him one already lit.

The two helpers cut the shirt collar off and shaved the back of his neck summarily. They seized his hands and arms and tied them behind him.

The procession got under way. Suddenly, while descending the ramp of stairs, Am-phossy hesitated; his knees sagged under the terrific strain, and nearly toppled over in a dead faint but for the assistants who grasped him firmly and quickly under the armpits, steadying him.

The prison yard yawned with myriads of cold, gray windows, with the glare of evil eyes. We crossed the court-yard rapidly. In the bleak dawn, a large police wagon had pulled up alongside the entrance. It was drawn by two white steeds. It was the famous punier a salade. A small ladder is drawn up. The doomed climbs it with the executioner, the two assistants and the attorney.

About one hundred meters beyond, the scaffold reared its menacing arms to the sky, voracious and eager for prey. The steeds trotted along at a gentle and peaceful pace, indifferently cold, as when driving a bride.

The wagon swerved, then came to a stop. The assistants forced the doors open and lowered the ladder. The ex-ecutioner jumped off the vehicle. Marius Amphossy followed falteringly, terrified. The attorney remained motion ess, as if he were paralyzed, nailed to the spot. He watched in silence across the purplish shadows.

The assistants seized the shrunken figure under the armpits; as the police vehicle moved out of his sight, his eyes fell upon the wide, deserted square; a deadly stillness hovered about; uniforms and weapons dazzled everywhere; the Republican Guard unsheathed their swords while civilians doffed their hats. All murmurs hushed; every eye was fixed with an anxious stare.

The condemned, awestruck and puzzled, was pale with a ghastly pallor, His mouth, distorted with fiendish terror, muttered unintelligible words demanding pity from men, from the day just dawning, from life which still throbbed about him.

But could the wretch still see? No, no, his eyes could not see anything, although chilled into a stare toward that machine looming skywardly with cold, glimmering flashes of steel through the boulevard green; a contrivance tall and slender: three beams of which two were straight and the other laid transversally across—a startling, nightmarish vision!

Two beads of cold sweat flowed down his temples and bathed his cheek; the chin was pearled with moisture; his mouth opened wide to emit a shout of terror, but the voice choked in his throat.

He is now standing about a foot from the guillotine; his life measured by a few split seconds; the ears strained vainly for the sound of a human voice, the rustling of a single leaf, the flutter of wings; even the fine, sharp drizzle seemed to fall with a soft patter, more gentle, more religious . . .

He mounted the scaffold without moving his limbs; it seemed as if death had already seized him and picked him bodily off the ground, to raise and elevate him high above all other men. He did not walk, in fact. His feet, long dead, floundered along like a couple of tin cans which street urchins pull after them with a thread. The hands, tied behind his back, writhed spasmodically; his chest swelled as if it were bursting, his neck grew turgid.

The axe glimmered in the shadow; a round, gaping hole blasted his eyesight; it was ready to open still wider, to enable his head and neck to slip through, to clasp the next moment firmly around him. Beyond that, stood the hamper into which his head would roll in the next second or two.

He struggled stoutly to pull away from that terrifying vision of the infernal machine. But he could not pull back; he then arched his back and thrust his head forward as if propping it against some imaginary stronghold that would enable him to break away. The air throbbed with cruel dismay.

The assistants, however, resolute and grim, bent his head forward with a savage thrust, tripping him, and he fell headlong like a dead body, his head jamming the *bascule*. The executioner adjusted his head beneath the *lunette*; it clasped him tightly, like an iron fist.

The flash of a moment; a moment filled with grim savagery; a moment, which lasted an eternity. That vanquished form flung across the *bascule*, with hands tied behind the back and the head held firm in that pincher, gazed into the hamper that yawned like a black cavity under his frightened eyes.

One rending stroke. A plunging noise. The head rolls; the blood gushes with a semicircular splurge, bathing the surroundings.

Justice was done. We reporters were permitted to draw near. The dismembered body, still palpitating, was thrown into a spruce casket. The head stared with wide open eyes; the tongue thrust out of his mouth moved perceptibly, bathing the disfigured features with a greenish foam. A helper held that gory visage by the hair and flung it into the casket, with the body, which was rushed by truck to the physiological institute for the vivisection.

The square, very slowly, filled with sunlight. The Re-publican Guard had left for the barracks, while the ex-ecutioner and his associates, the outrage perpetrated, began to dismount the scaffold. It was all over.

At the institute where we drove a few moments later, we were told that the heart was still beating and the retina throbbed with unmistakable signs of life, O ye ruthless, vindictive, ill-tempered human laws, ye students of law, does that mean that . . .

But Tito's story did not yet fill the double column which he had been assigned to cover. To remedy this, he diffused into endless Tolstoian comments on the right to judge, upon the power to kill, but still it was not enough to fill all blank space; so he added a few dissertations upon the guillotine, and placed it at the very beginning of his narrative.

He recalled the last words spoken by the fleshy and raven-ous-looking Louis XVI, who shouted: *"Frenchmen, I die innocent of everything"*; he evoked Marie Antoinette, grayed in a single night, who, having stumbled inadvert-ently into the executioner, murmured a soft and apologetic: "Pardon, Monsieur!" He spoke of Elizabeth, sister to Louis XVI, who, noticing that her shoulders lay bare, turned sup-plicantly to the executioner and entreated him to cover them. He also quoted old Bailly, whose teeth chattered with cold under the sharp November drizzle: "You're shivering, old man!" someone called out to him. *"It's the cold,"* came his pathetic retort. Then he made mention of Charlotte Corday, crimson with shame, too, because her shoulders were bared; Danton (You'll show my head to the people; it is well worth it!); Desmoulins, who entreated the executioner to deliver a lock of his hair to his graying mother; Adam Lux, who kissed Charlotte Corday before death; Jourdan Coupe-Tete, who ascended the scaffold with a twig of lilac blossoms between his lips.

But not yet having been able to cover the double column, he launched into a recapitulation of Marius Amphossy's crimes; the fiendish Jamaica killer, whose specialty con-sisted in battering governesses to death, with a sledge-hammer.

He spoke of Jamaica and its rum; explained why its government refused extradition, although the international laws . . . .

He elaborated painstakingly over the imperfections of international laws. He then described the executioner, and even rehearsed an interview he was supposed to have had with that most ludicrous and grisly personage who, after all, was a good devil, but times being what they are and money scarce, he had to do something in order to live . . . . He recited how the guillotine worked, added here and there a few colorful notes upon the cast of mind of the doomed, and told how he, only one among all other Paris reporters, stole unseen into the prisoner's cell, a few hours before the carnage, by practicing a little deception.

"But why did you murder all those women?" I asked the killer.

"Because I despised them," he replied with a smile of naturalness. "If it is all right to kill the man who attempts to take your life, or enjoys your wife, or enters your home to steal, why shouldn't it be all right to kill the man you don't like? Isn't the fact that you despise someone a good enough reason to kill?"

Sensing, however, that the prisoner's demeanor before the axe was not sufficiently described, he flavored it by quoting his last words:

"I'm innocent. Before God and man, I swear that I have not butchered those twenty-seven women!"

But the phrase seemed a trifle too flowery, and did not ring true. He erased briskly and wrote all over again:

"Sure, I've killed them all, and I'm glad of it. I would do it all over again tomorrow, if I had the chance."

But Tito felt that before a confession as heinous as that the mob would have vent its wrathful anger. If this be the case, he would naturally have to re-write a few parts in the story.

He erased again the words of the condemned and sub-stituted:

"Mother, Mother, you save me!"

But the head rolled in the basket just the same because mother could not hear in that far off Jamaica graveyard, where pineapples blossomed.

It was six o'clock by Tito's watch. He had thirty sheets of paper crowded with dense scribbling. He did not bother reading, but sealed everything hurriedly in an envelope, upon which he wrote: "Urgent. Rush to pressroom," and rang for the waiter.

"Waiter, have someone deliver this at my paper, but hurry, tell him to take a cab if he must!

As the waiter was leaving the room, Tito jumped back into bed. The bed sheets were still warm from before.

* * *

Six hours later the telephone roused him from his slumber.

"Yes, it's me," he yawned.

"You fool . . . This is the boss."

"O, good morning, boss."

"What have you done. You're ruining the paper. They never went through with that execution." His voice rang with alarm.

"Well . . . boss."

"They pardoned him at the very last moment"

"Very well . . . boss."

"But what did you mean by submitting that . . . ."

"You needn't print it."

"You needn't print, eh? It's been printed already, and the paper has been on sale for four hours."

"Take it off the stands."

"But it's all sold out around Paris."

"Well, if that's the case . . . . But what time is it now?"

"Noon time sharp."

"That's funny," he continued intrepidly. "But what's wrong with it, anyway. He's been pardoned this morning at three by the President? . . . But hasn't the President anything more import- ant to do at three in the morning? As far as we are concerned, we have fulfilled our journalistic duty remarkably well, almost to the point of sacrifice. It would not have been fair to deprive our faithful readers of a story as interesting as that, because of a stupid incident having to do with fickle executive clemency. According to the modern conception of the criminal law capital punishment sets the example to the wayward. We, in rehearsing the facts as if they had happened, did the duty of men who are conscious of their mission, fulfilled by the press."

On this whimwham he proceeded, but there came no answer from the other side of the wire. Tito kept raving and never fal- tered when he became aware that the boss had hung up on him.

Down the street, hawkers shouted shrilly into his ears, on the fourth floor of the Hotel Napoleon. He recognized the familiar name of the paper, drawn up in a special edition with the grue- some details of the decapitation of Marius Amphossy, the Jamai- ca sledge-hammer killer.

* * *

Madam Kalantan Ter-Gregorianz had a husband who was the proprietor of tremendous and profitable oil wells.

"I want you to meet Doctor Tito Arnaudi, a most interesting person."

"You will stay with us for dinner," smiled the husband. The husband was extremely bald, though still young, and fabulously rich.

He did not like Paris very well, and liked his wife even less. He was fond of travel and shuttled between foreign cities and different women, but would interrupt his peregrinations, now and then, and tarry with the vices of Paris and those of his wife. But the beautiful Armenian siren could not please him indefinitely, because she was too slender and nervous. He only liked fat women; the fatter they were, the more they attracted him. In all matters of love he obeyed that famous physical dictum: *attraction is proportioned to the mass,* (the greater the body, the greater its magnetic pull).

The wife attracted him as a side dish. "Tomorrow my wife and I will leave for Deauville, by the sea. If you like the sea, we can have them reserve a small apartment for you, as our guest."

Tito accepted. The following day, after the boss had turned down his request for a month's leave of absence, Tito took it just the same and left with the Ter-Gregorianz folks for the fashionable seashore.

The two men agreed to perfection in speaking ill of the Turks (Tito didn't care a button), and in praising the vegetarian diet, (this time, it was the Armenian who didn't care a button). They played bridge and cannon, took long automobile trips along the shore, harkened to the sound of the waves that whispered in hexameter and pentameter prosody, while Tito, at times more sentimental than a *Pierrot*, would say, with Verlaine, that the sea was more beautiful than cathedrals. They spent their nights playing at baccarat or swimming. Tito swam well, but the husband couldn't, Tito helped him, if not to compete in a race across the English Channel, at least enough to save him from drowning altogether. But there was one thing Tito had never been able to teach him, and this was probably due to the extreme thinness of his pupil—to play the *"dead man's float"*.

Tito would hold him by the arm and would order him to plunge his head four or five inches underwater, and keep the body stiff and his arms extended. He explained to him Archimedes' principle by which the displacement of water caused by a body immersed. . . . But when Tito left him all to himself, the Armenian would submerge entirely.

"How are you progressing with your swimming lessons?" Madam Kalantan would ask every morning, when the two men appeared in sponge pajamas at the hotel.

"I've learned to swim underwater and can paddle twelve meters a minute; but I haven't yet learned the dead man's float."

One day Mr. Ter-Gregorianz sneaked out for a swim alone, and selected a quiet water inlet for the experiment. But an angry billow surged against him and he was swept off to sea. He tried to shout, but the water poured into his mouth. A pair of limbs were seen for a moment signaling for help, but were wiped off the surface in the flicker of an eyelid.

"Well?" asked Madam Kalantan as she greeted Tito, with her hands thrust manfully into her pockets, Tito had walked in alone.

"Has my husband learned the 'dead man's float,' yet?"

Tito answered: "He has."

* * *

They buried him in Paris, in the Armenian Gregorian cemetery, after he had been fished out of the water. In the cortege that accompanied the deceased to his resting abode, figured all the former lovers of his wife as well as the future ones.

Among these, Tito stood forth very conspicuously, and marched intrepidly in the first rank.

How Tito ever became the lover of the Armenian siren, the reader will find amply described in any other novel, but not in this. I would especially recommend those certain novels that describe in proper sequence all the phases leading up to the climax and conclude exactly when the hero and heroine, after enduring some three hundred faultless pages of unconclusive grimacing, finally rush into each other's arms to exchange the first kiss that has got some punch to it. This is the point where every book should start, not end, I believe. And since we have already come to the middle of the book, and the heroine (who is not the Armenian, but the Italian), has not yet been ushered into the scene, let us get her started at once.

COVER OF THE RARE ORIGINAL EDITION

6

Maud, cabaret dancer de luxe, strode into Paris with a
small dog and eight trunks.

She wore a light gray suit, dapper, sartorially
perfect, with cuffs trimmed with monkey fur, fluent and flow-
ing-like Leonardo da Vinci's beard. Maud, dress coat dancer de
luxe, alighted at the Hotel Napoleon, because Tito not only came
to greet her arrival at the station, but also reserved a suite at his
hotel for her, a sitting room and bathroom.

Whereas stuffed dogs sometimes resemble live dogs to perfection, Maud's dog, on the other hand, gave the im-pression of being
stuffed; when one pressed a caressing hand across its back one
was in danger of getting a bristle stuck thru his finger. Its hidden
eyes, peering beneath a thick, flowing fringe, proved Darwin's
contention on the uselessness of looking, caused by the habit of
being pulled about by the will of another and by a leash. Very tiny
in-deed, small enough to slip into one's pocket, and charmingly
dumb. Only on nearer approach, and after careful consideration,
was one able to distinguish which end was the tail and which the
head; that dog impersonated the beauty of homeliness.

"What's the dog's name?" asked Tito.

Maud pursed her deeply red lips into a small circle, with
a tiny opening in the centre (very much like a cherry with-out
a pit), and gave a long drawn whistle, which penetrated the ears
like a musical *sol.*

"That's the name."

"Very charming, indeed!"

From Italy, Maud brought a maid, experienced in dress-mak-ing, hairdressing and men. A very moody sort of per-son, though, who gave her name as Pierina, whenever she felt like it.

Pierina, never having been in Paris before, gazed at every-thing she saw with astonished eyebrows.

Her mistress, Maud, although in Paris for the first time, too, seemed astonished at nothing. . . .

In that woman Tito quickly detected the embryo of the inter-national adventuress, transoceanic, irresistible, one easily accus-tomed to masculine hides of all races.

That Maud, cabaret dancer de luxe, could never have been taken for the crude Magdalena, upright pupil of a corrupt school for stenography of two years before; that the charming and electrifying creature could no longer be mistaken for the meek and subdued middle-class girl, who lived on the fourth floor with windows overlooking the garden, was so obvious a thing that it seems unnecessary for me to say it. All great actresses, dancers and courtesans seem to have come from some fourth floor or other, and as in every saloon dishwasher there might be a po-tential Grand Hotel owner, so in every fourth floor maiden, who spends her time raising potted sage and changing the water for her canaries, there might also be some beautiful Otero or Cleo de Merode in the making.

Tito had been wise enough not to inquire about her parents. He could still remember the incorruptible and stiffly upright mother who scowled upon her daughter over her dauntless breasts, as she ran through a rapid-fire discourse on morality; he also recalled the fierce and unflinching father whose one absorbing interest was the counting of dollars and cents (when he had them), and who would brandish the old timepiece like a fencing tournament if his daugh-ter happened to come home a few minutes late.

He remembered the old homestead, humble though honest, bedecked, however, with all those ornamental trifles which all

"Maude, cabaret dancer delux, strode into Paris. . . . "

charity lotteries (sewers of bad taste) peddle around from house to house, until they find one like Magdalena's where they stay put. But the day that Magdalena became Maud, they moved back to another charity lottery.

Maud was to Tito nothing more than a creature in whom he noticed many points of resemblance to a girl almost ugly and dumb, whom he had met on a balcony two years before.

Yet today that woman wore kangaroo skin gloves and used words as difficult as "idiosyncrasy," "eurythmy," "tetragon," and said *cattiveria* with the accent upon the "i" instead of the "e", and *separa*, with accent upon the "e", instead of the "a", as is taught by pedants and dictionaries.

Maud would laugh of Magdaleha as of some distant friend. What was known of her past began from the first day she . . . in short, from the first time she . . . .

'Til tell you how it happened", she explained one day to Tito, while the maid busied herself with the trunks in the next room. "This is how it happened", and meanwhile she kept her eyes focused upon the Vendome column sur-mounted by a Napoleon in bronze, while Tito, leaning against the window, had his back turned to the street. "It happened one summer day when I was all alone in the house; mother used to rent a room to a bank teller. It was very hat that day; there was something in me which made me gasp with craving; a sort of melting sensation which swept hot as fire through my body. We were all alone in the house; mother, of course, had the key and could have come in if she so wanted. The man began to kiss me all over, then seized me suddenly and stood me against the door where he possessed me without stirring, without noise, just quietly, as when you pierce a sun-dazed butterfly with a pin. Not much left for me to do, was there?"

"But did you like the man? Did you love him?" She gave a short laugh, her eyes still riveted on the Vendome column, which shone with the fluid transparence of porphyry in the sun.

"No," she answered; "that moment I yearned for a man. I didn't even know who he was; I didn't like him; but he was a male, and that alone mattered. The blood had surged to my head and I burned with craving, and he had the wherewithal to satisfy me. When this became known there was hell to pay. Still I have never been able to understand to this day why all this commotion had to happen. Just because in that moment—August, imagine! I yearned for a man, I have had to endure the screamings of mother, the insults of father, the curses of both."

"And what happened to that man?"

"Never heard from him again. Before yielding to him I had turned down two or three other men who said they loved me."

"You're always the same. You refuse the men who love you, and yet you will yield to a man who is perhaps unworthy of yourself." She smiled faintly.

"Unworthy, did you say? What has that to do? I have never yielded to anyone unless I wanted to; we women never offer our body as a premium to anyone; we never give ourselves up to compensate a man for heaven knows what merits. We give ourselves up simply because we feel the need to. . . ."

"Miss!" called the maid. "In that big trunk over there I found. . . ."

"Excuse me a moment!" said Maud as she hastened into the adjoining room.

When alone, Tito thrust his face between his elbows as his fingers interlocked behind the back of his head. He stood meditative before the window and without moving a single muscle of his face, watched the automobiles wheel past the gray square through the rue de la Paix and out on the rue Castiglione at the other end, causing the asphalt to whiz with the familiar noise which scissors make when cutting silk.

He thought: "What an extraordinary woman. With what nonchalance, with what engaging ease did she relate to me all that happened in that distant summer's day!" He had heard the whole story. "It was hot," she had said, "and there was a man nearby, ready to satisfy me." "I was excited," she had also said; "I yearned, and I yielded without stirring, without pretending, without fainting. . . ." Of this, she spoke.

Another woman in her place would have said, somewhat dismayed: "I met a coward. I was a mere child, sweet, innocent . . . I didn't know a thing; didn't know what it was all about; he took me by force, he abused me . . . the brute!"

Or else: "He gave, me something to drink . . . I don't know what. I fell asleep, and when I awoke. . . ."

Or else: "Poor mother was dying. We didn't have any money in the house to buy medicines, to pay the doctor, to buy the coffin; so I had to yield to a wealthy. . . ."

Then they would add: "O, if you only know how I despise that man; how he nauseated me for all that he was worth . . . and how I hated myself for what I did."

But that delightful Maud was different. She speaks of that fateful event as she would speak about her first communion, if that's anything worth telling about. She doesn't attach any too great importance to that physical episode, to that harmless, simple and quiet happening, around which has rallied the screams of poets down through the centuries, and inflamed into fits of frenzy the moralists, the judges: that unimportant, nerve-thrilling little matter which has provoked so much fanatical wrath and stirred so many imbecile philosophical marmalades in defense of prejudice; that most natural approach of two bodies drawn to each other, which seems so different according to whether it happens before or after the trip to the marriage bureau, and is considered godly if performed in one bed and sinful when performed in another.

Maud had related with charming frankness that which is today called wrong. And because of that unvarnished and simple accounting, she emerges clean and admirable from the slush of putrified morality.

The erroneous valuation of that act—the attraction of two bodies yielding to an impulse—serves no other purpose except a criminal one. The day when it will no longer be regarded sinful for a young woman to yield before the man she loves, that day, abortion and infanticide will be wiped out forever, because then a child will cease to be the fruit of a wrong act; then it will be no longer necessary to hide the fact.

The Jews used to stone the young woman who surrendered to a man before marriage. The people themselves did the killing, And perhaps among those who tossed stones at her was the man whose wishes she had gratified. He, too, helped to suppress her.

In every case of procured abortion or infanticide, it should not be the girl who has either aborted or committed infanticide who suffers punishment, but we should behead her father, her mother, her big brothers, the neighbors and all those rattling tongues who, with their tittle-tattle, prejudice and training have led her to believe that to be pregnant without first informing the Mayor of the town, constitutes a serious crime. We would then have the satisfaction, at least, of seeing in the streets many young mothers revered like archbishops and kings. And that would be only fair. The unmarried girl who brings a child into the world is the only mother who is worthy of admiration. She is the one who has sacrificed everything to become a Volunteer in Motherhood.

Wherein lies the merit of those who are married? They know that to make a child, or to promise to make one, will create for them a position in life, the family. They know beforehand that somebody is going to assist them during their vomiting and child-birth periods, and will continue with elaborate care to look after their welfare until forty days after the manufacturing or-gans will have settled down to their original places. They know, further, that a midwife, a physician, the mother, the husband, the mother-in-law, the wet-nurse and many others will be there to bear with them during the pangs of child-birth, during the accouchement and suckling periods; they know that the "blessed event" will be celebrated like a glorification.

But a girl who is in a family way and unmarried, cannot look forward to all of this, except in very few cases. Little does she expect of those who claim to love her. On the contrary! The seducer will turn his back on her; her parents will shower her with invective and abuse; she is turned adrift, an outcast, harassed by mournful presages, gloomy, hopeless; she will have to provide alone for the support and well-being of her love creature; she knows that someday her infant will turn bitterly against her for having made a bastard of him. Yet, she will face all this for love's own sake, for her noble maternal instinct! She, and only she, is the real mother, worthy of that name! All others are the gossips of motherhood. All others have no merits, compared to these. These others will create a child with all possible guarantee and safety! They are like those warriors who engage in battle after they have learned that the foe will use paper bullets. How bold!

* * *

It was five o'clock. The square was quickly filling to overflowing with merry people. This is about the most thrilling hour in Paris: from five to seven. Parisians have a reputation for being night owls. I would much rather call them lovers of the twilight hour.

"Pardon me," said Maud, with her bare arms encircled about Tito's neck. "That Pierina can fill the trunks very well, but as to emptying them. . . I, however. . . . "

"You don't know how to fill nor empty them," chirped Tito. "But to go on with your story, what happened then? When did you leave your home?"

"Does it interest you to know? I had met two or three men who were very kind to me; one was a magistrate who spoke ill of all priests; another a priest who spoke ill of all magistrates, and a landlord who rented furnished rooms by the hour and spoke well of priests and magistrates alike, because they were his best customers. Then I took to dancing; I travelled through Italy. At Naples I became acquainted with an American; his uncle was the owner of the Metropolitan Opera House in New York."

"I must have met at least twenty-five Americans of either sex who claimed themselves related to that Metropolitan owner. The brothers and sisters of that man must be blessed with a fecundity that savors of the miraculous. In America they manufacture even the children in series, like everything else."

"But this one was really the nephew of. . ."

"Yes, yes, I believe it. It seems to be a specialty with all Americans in foreign countries to boast they have an uncle who is the proprietor of some theatre or other. The same thing happens to all the Russians outside of Russia. They all claim Maxim Gorki as their friend. The Spaniards, no less, treat the Quintero brothers like friends of the family; the Norwegians claim to have been held at the baptismal font by Ibsen himself. . . ."

A waiter and a porter, very cringing of manner, entered (every hotel waiter is our cringing enemy) to take the bed apart and cart it away.

"All I want is a couple of mattresses;" explained Maud to her friend. "I spread my rugs, my Turkish shawls and the chinchilla fur I brought from Italy, over them."

"Will you have dinner with me?" asked Tito who had just pocketed his watch.

"No, thanks; I'm too tired for that. I'll have them bring me something up to the room.' But you can go, if you like. When will we see each other again?"

"Tomorrow."

"Why not tonight?"

'Til not be home till quite late."

She nodded assent.

"Tomorrow, then. . ."

"I suppose you will want to see your impresarios? When will you start performing?"

"In three days."

"I am *going to* chaperon you around Paris during my time off. . . ."

Maud, in extending her hand in a parting greeting, gently reclined her head backward and let Tito kiss her on her throat, while a shudder of delight ran through her.

She then slipped into the next room.

* * *

While Tito stood before the mirror, unable to make up his mind between a black suit and a gray one, someone arrived with a message.

Then, between the two suits, he quickly decided for the *smoking* one, because the message came from Kalantan, the beautiful Armenian siren, who sent for "him because she was then very lonely and very sad.

As always, Madam Kalantan's car waked for him outside the hotel's entrance. Tito got in. He ordered the driver to stop a moment before a flowershop on the rue de la Paix, from which he emerged displaying a white gardenia fastened to his buttonhole, and walked back to the car.

The delicately soft gardenia petals smelled like the languishing scent of the Cote d'Azur.

The air throbbed with those delightfully fa.int waves which, although not registered by laboratory instruments, are nevertheless detected by our nerve-centres as we step gingerly down the Champs Elysees shadows, toward the dusk of evening, haunted with waves of love and adultery. Loving couples everywhere, But where were they coming from? From cafes, tearooms, from the art galleries of the Grand Palais, perhaps; or maybe from the Seine waterfront. But there was something pathetically languished in their manner of walking, in their faces; the very atmosphere surrounding them had something of the exhausted, of the extenuated, of the weary. . . .

Loving couples. . . .

Lovers.

Lovers. The most beautiful word in the world.

Lovers.

The automobile sped along the straight tracks made upon the moist asphalt by countless cars ahead of it. Beyond that, loomed the Arc de Triomphe like some white dreaminess against the black curtain of night.

The arched lamps sparkled with a bluish brilliance.

The car drove through the full-foliaged grove. The leaves tipped caressingly over the tonneau, glossy as Japanese shellac, releasing drops of moisture.

A servant rushed inside to inform Kalantan that the gentleman had arrived.

When a man ceases being called Mr. Arnaudi by the servants, but merely the gentleman, then it means that he is officially recognized as the only, or at least, the favorite lover of their mistress.

"You may go, Csaky," said the beautiful Armenian siren, as she moved forward with extended hands to greet her guest.

Csaky stood stiffly at attention, veered suddenly around his heels and, with a great sparkle and creaking of boots, strode out of the room in grand stand fashion.

Kalantan threw herself into the arms of Tito who held her pressed to his chest. Even before he spoke, he clutched her into one long, trembling caress which slipped softly along her hips, her thighs, her shoulders and back. The body of the woman writhed with serpent-like movements under the sensuous touch of his hand.

Over her flesh she wore an easy fitting Grecian tunic fastened at the shoulder with a green cameo, into which floated many

narrow folds. Her arms and limbs were completely bare, and
her tiny feet peeped through very light *taphia* sandals, while her
lustrously black hair lay tossed across her back fastened to a bow
in the simple, graceful and modest manner of a romping child.
Encircling the peplum (tunic) and belted toward the bottom, like
a hem, was a girdle embroidered with large fret-work stitches of
wool dyed in brilliant vegetable and conchineal extracts.

Poisoned until now by morbidity and artifice, she now felt, in
a love, which was pure and untarnished, the need to drape herself
in the mythological simplicity of a Grecian garment.

It had been designed for her by Raymond Duncan, that half
dreamer and half merchant, whose twenty years of residence in
Paris had not yet changed his American accent. He is the brother
of Isadora Duncan, the celebrated classic dancer who, adorned
with flowing black veils and necklaces strung around her white
neck, would sometimes moan over her children's grave, and
would raise to God her motherly prayers.

Raymond Duncan has founded a monastery of very strange
regulations and stranger practices in the Latin Quarter, near the
Saint-Germain-des-Pres church. He and his followers wear very-
long hair, cloaks, sandals, etc., and in that queer habiliment they
go their way, now singly, now in groups, unmindful of the sting-
ing sallies of the boulevards, where they are called, with a slight
shade of malice, the *back to nature people.*

Theirs is the uniform, which one should wear in his quest of
the ideal, they say. The monastery does not hide any secret rituals
behind its walls. Through many huge windows opening on the
rue Jacob one can see many healthy and flourishing young girls,
busy spreading out fabrics and, with arms bared to their pits,
wind the blond woolen threads into skeins. From looms operating
with the haste of a carpenter's plane flow fabrics of many hues,
cotton cloths, raw canvases and dark woolens like those worn by
shepherds. Along jambs decorated with primitive Grecian archi-

tecture, clusters of woolen clews hang like so many giant fruits, which have been ripened in honor of Vertumne, Proserpina and Pomona.

Thick masses of golden woolens interwoven like tresses of distant mythological pattern, flowed unceasingly along the looms at which a girl, working at the shuttle, made her sturdy leg and arm muscles quiver and flash.

An Andromache in *décolleté,* Kalantan seemed.

In that humble monastery devoid of crosses, idols and altars, Madam Kalantan Ter-Gregorianz had found the very thing which all famous tailors along the rue de la Paix had not been able to offer her in the way of styles; a richly flowing and loose garment, keyed deftly to that simple and indeed primitive love which, after the many years spent in chaotic complications and turbulent chemical excitements and artificial exaltations, had finally found its shelter in the arms of Tito, the youthful Italian, of the very pale face and the very deep blue eyes.

Up to a few weeks before, Kalantan had been surrounded by many strange lovers, who had a very strange conception of what love was. In her former delirious frenzy she had surrendered to morphine and musical savagery; she had lain in that coffin in the grip of death and love, shuddering beneath the weight of crazed and greedy men; her emotional arteries flushed with the most maddening poisons and the most fearful cerebral exaltations. Since five thousand six hundred and eighty-two (Jewish calendar) woman has been taken in the usual, traditional way by man, Kalantan struggled desperately for some new form to satisfy her inordinate sexual hunger. But the more she reveled in the fictitious, the more she seemed to drift away from genuine voluptuousness.

A deep distaste of life was beginning to take possession of her, when along came Tito, Tito, whom she had met during a night of white orgy, during one of those cocaine orgies which had made her famous throughout Paris; Tito, at last, who had come with ail his simple youth to lay it before her like some luscious offering on the naked palms of one's hands.

Tito, the youthful cocaine-addict, to whom cocaine still gave an exceptional sense of merriment.

"You're still in time," said Kalantan to him. "I know the workings of that dreadful and deadly powder. You have not yet reached the stage of frightful depressions, the period of brooding and destructive melancholy. You still can smile though your blood be filled with venom. You are in the first stages yet, when one again becomes a mere boy."

She had spoken to him as she would to a child, and yet both were of the same age. Cocaine performs the cruel miracle of distorting time and age.

Csaky, the steward, had prepared a small dinner-table of a diameter so small that the mouths of the two table-companions could join with ease across it.

"Csaky!" said Kalantan, simply.

And Csaky brought out a silver platter with large pink fish cuts, and slices of aquamarine-hued pineapple placed between them.

In a plain decanter like that used for water, champagne sparkled and sizzled. To bring a labeled champagne bottle to the table, would be like offering a gift with the price tag still on.

A Siamese cat rubbed against one of Tito's legs, with voluptuous purring.

Kalantan leaned her bare arms across the table, and ran her fingers caressingly through his hair, and then stole softly down his pale cheeks. His faint smile grew melancholy. The caress was so soft that it might have been that of a ghost.

And instead of experiencing a shudder of delight, Tito felt a suave shiver run through his frame.

Since falling in love with Tito, the Armenian siren had refused to see all erstwhile lovers. Her period of mourning over her husband's death gave her an excellent excuse to justify her voluntary retirement. Banned now were the orgies where wanton madness and venom once held sway to the tune of Stravinsky's music and the flutter of enamel-white butterflies from the Rio Amazon, She was now resting in the serene security of a love which was to her as pure as a hand shorn of jewels; as simple and as unadorned as flowing tresses.

Her whole being now clamored for that illusion. Her whole soul was now invested in the budding romance. And she offered herself to Tito without artifice of scent and powder, in all the smiling perplexity of a nymph slipping gracefully out of a bath-tub; and in her offering one could still detect the scent of her fiery flesh, slightly savage, no longer western, and not wholly Asiatic. It savored faintly of salt, just as if it had been permeated by the rock-salt breezes of her faraway homeland.

Kalantan!

A name that sounded as deep and as vast and as somber as the slow winds that howl through the Caucasian gorges.

Kalantan!

Tito felt the warmth of Kalantan's knees against his own. One of his hands shot underneath the table and caressed something round, smooth, soft, and fresh like the velvety coolness of a child's face.

The steward returned several times; but vanished entirely after serving caffeinized coffee and liquors. Propped against a paneled wall of the little room, enam eled white like a liner's cabin, was a low-decked parallel-epipedon, deep and wide, constructed of three or four superimposed mattresses hidden beneath a large rug. It was the *takhta*, that sort of Asiatic shrine dedicated to the glorification of feminine laziness, where Oriental women sit with legs encroached, greedily crunching sweet-meats and spending their worthless time weaving fanciful arabesques around decrepit legends.

"I don't blame them for being that way!" intoned Tito,
joining Kalantan who lay squatted between two pillows and had
indicated a place beside her. "Why, after all, excite yourself?
We are like those kids who strain their backs pulling a toy cart
up a slope, for the absurd and short-lived enjoyment, which the
downhill slide will provide. But you, Kalantan, you who said that
I am still in the merry stage oj my poisoning. You think I can still
laugh. But it's long since I stopped laughing, Kalantan. I am sad
most of the time. We cannot have anything destroyed in ourselves without suffering. I have quit believing that every cloud
has a silver lining. There is a certain ailment called *caligo*. Like
a dim veil thrown across your eyes, *caligo* prevents you from
seeing a certain color. I am now suffering with a sort of *spiritual
caligo*, I cannot see the pink, anymore! My dear, my petite Kalantan, cocaine does not only weaken your lungs and disturb your
heart, as all hygienists seem to believe. Its real damage is mainly
a psychical one. There is no escape from it. Cocaine literally un-
couples and splits your individuality in twain; it accomplishes the
almost electrolytic destruction of one's own conscience. In every
intelligent man there are two inner beings of opposing views and
different tastes: of differences absolutely irreconcilable; and I
believe he is an artist at heart, that man in whom these two conflicting individualities are so cleverly and clearly delineated that
one can criticize the other with impunity; suggest remedies and
cultivate habits, when they are desirable, and cultivate virtues, if
they are not too boring. Through cocaine, the splitting of individuality occurs like an explosion of long-repressed aversions;
the two individualities within myself criticize each other and
wage a continual warfare, which is bound to create, within myself, hatred against myself. Then is the time when one begins to
feel how useless everything is, I feel my heart beat, but to what
purpose? To send my blood through my lungs; but for what?
To charge it with oxygen; but for what? So that along with the

oxygen it may burn my .tissues inside, to flow the next moment
back into the lungs to discharge all combustible materials. And
then? Then it goes on like that forever; even when I sleep, even
when I walk, even when I am between your arms, even when my
thoughts are far away. Tell me, O, tell me, Kalantan, why does
my heart beat? If you only knew how many are the times when I
feel tempted to speed a messenger of lead in its direction, and say
to it: 'Quit beating! You'll have to stop, anyway, someday. Don't
bother wearing yourself out until then.' " Here his voice faltered.

"You silly boy!" said Kalantan. And she smiled, vaguely,
tolerantly. And then, instead of saying those words which every
woman uses to assuage our griefs; instead of throwing open the
emergency kit of common sense; instead of plastering his brows
with the packs of verbal tenderness and sympathy; instead of
proving that he was wrong, she comforted him with the sweetest
of all known cordials, the only one that is really invigorating and
lifts us high above the mournful workings of a sick fancy.

She used no other word but this:

"Boy!"

But in murmuring it between clenched teeth, she seized him
softly by the cheeks and drew him after her as she sank voluptuously over the pillows, and when his face lay over her white,
firm bosom, she smothered the bitter lips with a panting breast.

7

Th article written by Tito Arnaudi on the execution which was never staged, had a sensational repercussion throughout the entire capital. The edition featuring the story sold out in a few hours; all out-of-town dealers wired for more copies; three editions had to be printed to meet the rush of the widespread demand. All other Paris newspapers, those carrying the news of the executive pardon, were hopelessly scored, while *The Fleeting Moment* became, in a few hours, the best read and most informed newspaper in all France.

A fiery polemic ensued between *The Fleeting Moment* and *The T. S. F.,* with the latter sustaining that all the institutions of the Republic should be kept above board, and then went on to protest with all the voice at its command against the false rumor of the Presidential grace, which had been communicated to fool all newspapers so that they should refrain from sending their reporters to the place of execution. It stated, in other words, that all capital executions should be made public, so that every citizen could witness them at will, and not conceal them under the pretense of a false executive pardon. Other papers, to excuse the inadequacy of their news service which had not functioned properly that day, claimed that they had been informed of the execution taking place, but that they refrained from featuring the grim event through a sense of humaneness, and to the noble purpose of uplifting the spirits.

And when, two days after, the Department of Justice communicated to the papers the confirmation of Marius Amphossy's pardon, everybody refused to believe it, because the description given by *The Fleeting Moment* had been so glowingly rich in detail that it could never have been written unless borrowed from actual reality.

Even the executioner came pretty near believing that Tito Arnaudi wrote the truth.

"As a mystifier, you are hard to beat", the Chief told Tito. "You're so marvelous that I want to take you off the chronicling and let you handle our home-policy section. Later on, I will promote you to our foreign-policy section. But first I want to ask a favor of you".

"I'll be glad to do it, Chief.

"Our Bordeaux correspondent just died and I want you to take his place for a day or two, or three, in which time I hope to be able to get someone to take his place permanently".

"But I have never been in Bordeaux".

"It doesn't matter. Every morning you will scan the local press for news of great interest and you will relay it to our paper".

The following day, Tito Arnaudi was in Bordeaux, angered beyond measure that he had to leave his two loves behind him in Paris: the Armenian siren of the many charming vices, and Maud, dress coat dancer de luxe.

The first thing he did was to buy three or four papers; then he reached for the telephone and put in a call for Paris: *The Fleeting Moment*.

"An Entire Family Poisoned by Mushrooms", read the title of a news item on the third page; and, with his mouth close to the telephone, his eyes focused upon the paper and his mind on the Armenian siren and on Maud, both of them his incomparable loves, he began dictating the story to a re-write man who, at a distance of eight hundred kilometers, began taking the news down. It was all a gruesome story of a middle-class family who, to celebrate the grandparents' golden wedding, had gathered around a delicious dish of mushrooms, picked, no doubt, by some

"I know the workings of that dreadful and deadly powder."

inexperienced hand, and were suddenly overcome with terrific pains in the stomach; and when the grandparents, their elders, the children, the nephews and nieces, and even the wet-nurse of one of the tots were just about ready to meet their Maker. . . .

But the news item ended with a eulogy upon certain olive oil preserves (guaranteed pure by chemical test), which a well-known Bordeaux firm put on the market. The story of that mushroom poisoning was nothing but a cleverly done bit of advertising.

Tito was dumbfounded.

He had telephoned his paper an advertisement which he mistook for a news item.

"Well?", urged the re-write man on the other end of the wire, "What happened then? Why the interruption?"

His self-respect kept him from admitting his blunder.

So he continued: "Despite the prompt intervention of doctors, none of the stricken could be saved".

"How many dead altogether?", recapitulated the re-write man.

"Twenty-one dead", he replied, with determination.

In its afternoon edition, *The Fleeting Moment* gave a three-column spread to a news item which no other paper could boast of having.

The title ran: "GOLDEN WEDDING ENDS TRAGICALLY AT BORDEAUX. TWENTY-ONE DIE OF MUSHROOM POISONING, OFFICIAL INVESTIGATION TO PROVE WHETHER TRAGEDY WAS WHOLESALE SUICIDE OR MURDER".

If the thought of those two women he left behind did not haunt him with a relentless agitation, Tito Arnaudi would have been well of? at Bordeaux, Bordeaux is a city that—to hear the natives talk—has no reason to envy the capital; even the elegant ladies there speak the Parisian argot. At Bordeaux, the famous Bordeaux wine is held in very low esteem; and no one ever uses the Bordeaux mustard, which, incidentally, is world famous. There the Atlantic Ocean breathes with its scent of infinity.

But it did not give him his Maud, nor his Kalantan, the Armenian widow of the many charming sins and of the many oil wells.

The news assignment at Bordeaux was a difficult one to handle, not because of the excess of news material, but because of the lack of it.

Nothing really important ever happened. Never a scandal, Never an interesting crime committed. No prominent man ever died. And yet his Chief had wired: "Your service very unsatisfactory. Must communicate sensational news only".

"But if nothing ever happens here, Chief, that's sensational", poor Tito writhed with clenched teeth close to the telephone, while his fingers thumbed through the faded and dry papers, as he scanned for something really sensational that would please his Chief.

"The boss", said the rewrite man, "orders you, through me, to transmit news; but it must be all news of great interest."

"What's that?" Tito roared. "All right, then, take this down: A big sausage manufacturer in Southern France, whose name we cannot print at this very moment, having learned that his wife betrayed him with a Valdeian shepherd and that two children had been born to them, killed his wife and the two infants, and then, to hide his crime, he ground them to pieces during the night in his deserted factory, and then filled the hash into hundreds of sausages which were sold all over France. By tomorrow, we believe, we will be able to furnish more details anent the gruesome discovery. But the following morning the French minced meat products market crashed ruinously. Everybody stopped selling sausages; the grocers and the dealers refused to accept their sausages when they arrived, and suspended all new orders and all payments.

A Toulouse manufacturer whose business had been bad on account of his sterling honesty, fearing that he might not be much longer able to weather the storm, with bankruptcy threatening, ended his worries by sending a bullet into his heart.

The biggest shareholder in *The Fleeting Moment*, a great exporter of minced meat products himself, called the Board of Directors into a hurried conference to decide upon the measures to be taken, and demanded the immediate removal of the General Manager.

All sausage consumers insisted upon knowing the trade mark of the heinous sausages.

The dealers, too, insisted on knowing the name of the criminal manufacturer who had filled human minced meat into the sausages instead of using donkey hash.

The Chief recalled Tito to Paris.

Tito Arnaudi rushed back by first train.

"I'm ruined", the Chief sobbed, "they want me to print the name of the sausage manufacturer."

"Go ahead and print it", Tito replied.

"But what name shall I invent?"

"You needn't invent it. Some big Toulouse salt-meat packer committed suicide the other day. Let's tell the folks that he is the guilty one; his suicide reads like a confession. His name is Thomas Salmatre."

The Chief, beaming with joy, sparkled with a radiance of his own. The evening edition of *The Fleeting Moment* brought the climax when it printed in big black letters the honorable name of the suicide: Thomas Salmatre.

The account rang true, and the situation was saved. Inasmuch as the sausages of this man bore no trademark, it developed that none had been consumed. The Board of Directors retained the Chief in his office, but he had to pledge himself to settle a life pension upon the widow of Thomas Salmatre and to look after the future and education of nine little tots, left fatherless.

Tito was never again sent to Bordeaux. He could therefore go back into the arms of his beautiful Armenian siren and into those of the no less beautiful Italian dancer, his neighbor at the Napoleon Hotel.

He had begun loving Maud since the first day of her arrival in Paris. "Day" is yet too vague an expression. The beginning and the end of a romance can be determined with an almost astronomic precision in hours, in minutes and even in seconds. His love started when Maud, with arms resting upon the sill of the window overlooking the Square (the day when the Vendome column shone with the fluid transparence of porphyry in the sun) had related circumstantially what happened that mid-summer day. How it all came back to him! "I hardly knew the man. He was just a plain sort of a man, but that was what I wanted. It was August; imagine!—A hot summer afternoon, too. He propped me up against the door and without stirring,without noise, just quietly, nailed me like a sun-dazed butterfly pierced by a pin".

And from that obscure and inexplicable reaction which is caused in us by learning how one had yielded to another before us, Tito felt a sizzling surge searing through his frame. Men are even jealous of the woman they have not yet begun to love.

He had met her when she was only Magdalena, a shy and unsullied sort of a girl, who someday would have had to endure the love of some distrustful and fussy old bookkeeper, or perhaps the ungallant aggressions of some prolific, quarrelsome metallurgist, a member of the ruling party of the country.

She was a good girl; the Royal Reformatory had not yet made an accomplished prostitute of her. She still washed her kid gloves with benzine, over the balcony, and threw coins at peripatetic organ-grinders and street-singers who tarried in her backyard, so that they might repeat to infinity the latest hits.

The kitchen on the first floors oozed with the smell of meat cooked in Port wine, and the odor of burnished vanilla sugar. Maud was as sturdy and firm as a rivet guarding an enclosure. She breakfasted standing before a Venetian blind, with a cup in one hand and biscuits in the other.

She ate cherries at the window and tossed the pits over the neighbors balconies. When she hit a pane, she would run into the house, amused.

But now she has ceased being the sturdy and firm rivet which guarded the untarnished enclosure. Tito found in her a flower, he had found in her a flower that, having passed from one button-hole into an alcove or into a furnished apartment, had its petals soiled with the finger prints of too many males.

That much sufficed to stir in Tito a feeling of growing jealousy of her past; the regret of not having been the first to be gratified, of not having been the only one; the keen hatred against all the men who had already possessed her, and hatred against her for having yielded to them; hatred against time, that crystallized reality, hatred against reality itself, which could never be changed nor denied; hatred above all against the past which he could never reclaim.

Oh, the grief of not being able to reclaim the past! This is the most excruciating of all known anguishes, if we wish the miracle accomplished of reaching far back into the days of one's youth and if we wish for the virginity of a woman whom we began loving after she had become old and had already been ill-used by too many hands.

And then with both hands we hang on to time that flies, as if it were the last coach of a speeding express train. Together, we fly through what is left of the road ahead; we swear to cover it all; not being able to redeem the past, we try at least to insure the future.

Nevertheless, in our torment, we feel that a future of ten years, or all that is left of one's life, is not worth the few months of the youth that she offered to someone else before us. The photographs of her past show us that she was not beautiful, we gather that she was not refined, that she was not as alluring as today; and yet it is one of the old photographs that we desire most to have had. The lover (the one who is in love) of the most beautiful and best known of all actresses, would like to turn back the tide of time to the days when she was just a plain trouper, drifting from one small town theatre to the next, with small wardrobe trunks and the charm of a concealed virginity.

In that late spring or mid-summer day, Tito fell in love with Maud, while she, at the window of the Hotel Napoleon, stared at the automobiles that sped in droves along the rue Castiglione and the rue de la Faix, with the rustle of fingernails over silk, confided to him the little story of that memorable mid-summer day.

And when, a short time after, he left her, with all her trunks still unopened and dashed to the villa of Kalantan, the beautiful Armenian, he might have become suddenly aware of his love for Maud, had he not alighted in the rue de Rivoli, to have a gardenia fastened in his buttonhole; a gardenia in which the soft petals breathed with the languishing scent of the Cote d'Azur.

His love bloomed and blossomed because he did not tarry to watch it sprout. A mountaineer from Slovenia once told me that the little mushrooms should be picked off the ground the moment they begin to open; because they will not grow anymore after you have taken a peep at them. Little use going back the next day and expect them to be bigger and riper.

Even love, if you halt to watch it grow, will stop. Some-times the ground swallows it up.

Tito did not stop to peep while love grew because he had to hurry to the villa that glimmered white like a channel-house and was built round like a small Grecian temple, where Kalantan, completely naked under the peplum, and all aquiver underneath her quasi-chaste nudity, waited for him with open arms.

That same night, after a very delicious repast had been served hurriedly as it is done in station buffets, Kalantan lay upon the parallelepipedon berth and harkened to the voice of Tito, who, with legs crossed, narrated his melancholy to her.

Kalantan listened to him tamely, with her face bent over her knees, in that tender posture of self-loving tenderness of which cats and women are so fond.

Then they moved beyond, into Kalantan's bedchamber. The morning after, when Madam Kalantan's car carried the gentleman back to his lodging, the gentleman had the unhealthy appearance of one who had just come through a long illness; Kalantan had that night lavished herself upon him with delicious fever.

"You see", she confided almost blushingly, "tonight . . . during these days I desire you more than ever, because , . . please listen to me, for I will tell you; there are days, certain days, when women desire with a greater fierceness, and we cannot appease our craving, because those are the days in which we. , . Oh, It is so difficult to explain. Forgive me. I stammer like an idiot Remember Marguerite Gauthier, the Lady of the Camelias, who used to adorn herself with white camelias every day, except for two or three days out of each month, when she would exhibit herself in public wearing a red flower fastened to her bodice or between her hair? That red flower meant that those were the days when she. . . Well, I will never again be able to wear red camelias, I have lived those days through, Morphine has made me this way.

"Marguerite Gauthier tonight would not be able to receive you in her boudoir. But I can. These are the days when love is strongest and greedier than ever".

So spoke to him, the somber Armenian siren, heaving in tumultuous and unquenchable sensual yearnings.

Tito drove back to his hotel like a convalescent just released by a hospital on his first day out; the sexual abuse killed the male in him.

Despite this, when he entered the room and found Maud buttoning the kangaroo skin gloves over her slender wrists, he felt a vague uneasiness stealing over him.

He watched her in silence. "How did you sleep, little one?"

She looked up at him with thoughtfully knitted brows.

"Quite well. And you?"

"I spent the night at the club", Tito answered.

Maud, of course, meant nothing to him. He did not love her. There was no love between the two. There was nothing in common between them to indicate some future bond. And yet, despite all this, Tito lacked the courage to say that he had spent the night with another woman, as he feared that the confession would be like admitting that he had been unfaithful to her.

Because of this virtuous reaction, because of this foolish, needless, and yet instinctively felt and spontaneous little lie, Tito became for the first time aware of the fact that he was in love, that he loved his petite Maud very much.

8

aud, cabaret dancer deluxe, met with meagre success at her debut at the Petit Casino, She was applauded like Talanki, trainer of lazy and shortsighted Pekingese dogs; like Kerry, the negro boxer; like Sibemol, the musical comedian, allegedly Irish, who, walking on his hands, played with his feet upon a bell keyboard. She took two bows, and obliged with an encore. She would have obliged with a second, but that part of the audience occupying low-priced seats growlingly excused her from the unnecessary trouble.

She agreed nevertheless to a month's engagement; for the month following that she was engaged as first ballet-dancer with the *Folies Montmartroise*.

She was not in the least perturbed by her mediocre success in Paris, because she never pretended to add new laurels to the Villa Lumiere, which is Paris. There was nothing original about her work; dancers like herself could be seen by the dozens; the music was the music of Paris which, transplanted into Italy, had been restored to its city of origin by Maud herself; her beauty was not alluring enough to attract the attention of that unappeasable metropolis. All those things she knew very well.

The night of her debut, therefore, she returned to her hotel without feeling discouraged, without sadness, because she had gathered exacdy the scant laurels she had antici-pated and nothing more.

Tito Arnaudi, however, reporter for *The Fleeting Moment*, did not share her views upon that particular point, The dog trainer, a chink who also peddled opium and cocaine, sold him a box of powder, which Tito hastened to open. And tinder the inebriating spell he detected in Maud's dancing many pleasurable revelations of a new art; the manifestation of universal energy; beauty expressed in motion; the divine sparkling of rhythm.

Tumultuous with admiration, he followed her evolutions from a front row seat and lavished himself frantically in applause whenever she appeared to take a bow; but his applause remained isolated and was met with a spasm of ironic reaction when a light laughter of scorn pervaded the audience.

Her black dress coat shone before his eyes with a multitude of gaudy effects, sparkling with animation, as if it had been fabric dipped in phosphorus. Before the hallucinatory effect of cocaine, Maud's hair flowed like glittering wires of metal.

The music seemed to come from some invisible distance, and the background of the stage unfolded before his eyes like a landscape flooded with sunshine and lashed by the wind.

And when he met her after the debut, he exclaimed with heartfelt glee: "Why, Maud, your interpretations disclose many new worlds, beautiful, sunlit marvels".

And he kept on repeating this right along up to the time they entered the suite at the Napoleon Hotel.

And he kept this up all night long, while the moist blue that gushed from the sky above the sleepless metropolis, dripped across their naked steaming bodies through the open window.

The following day Tito had to leave for Bordeaux on business. After an eight-day stop-over, he came back to Paris.

After a conference with the Boss, dramatic and determined like a scene in one of Bernstein's plays, he rushed to the Hotel Napoleon and found Maud in bed with a stranger. His face darkened momentarily as he neared collapse.

"Forty", shouted the stranger as he sat on the bed, his eyes riveted on Tito in a steady stare, and without attempting to conceal his indecently exposed body.

"What does that number mean?", Maud asked, sharply.

"Your fortieth husband calling this afternoon".

"But he is not my husband".

"Well, who is he then?"

"My lover".

He leaned over and whispered:

"Seventy-six, then!"

Tito quickly recognized the stranger. Repugnance smote him. It was Kerry, the negro boxer. A type never to be forgotten once seen.

The three lapsed into an awkward silence, Tito's lips were set awry, as he surveyed that massive, thick and lustrously black hide in which he thought he detected the faint scent of the savage. Even a bullet would have rebounded from his back. Therefore he might well spare himself the trouble of shooting him.

Tito sauntered out of the room with great dignity, muttering pathetic reproaches against the door locks of hotels which are never bolted from the inside.

He hurriedly changed his clothes, put on a new purple necktie over a sandy-colored suit, and directed his steps in the direction of the beautiful Kalantan's villa, built round like a small Grecian temple blown yonder by goodness knows what historical mischance, on the Avenue des Champs Elysees.

I do not wish to eulogize bigamy, but one cannot help admitting that Tito lived in a state of perfect balance be-tween those two women. He loved neither Maud nor Kalantan, and yet he believed that he loved them both. When one of them made him suffer, he would find solace and virtuous reaction in the arms of the other. If Maud remained faithful and loyal to him for any length of rime he, having been fed to satiety, and his jealousy no longer teased, he would give her up and run to Kalantan. But the moment Maud threatened to yield to someone else, his jealousy flared up again, then he would forsake Kalantan to enwrap himself with all his burning passion around Maud. With his passionate outbursts he built a protective love enclosure around her against the assaults of other casual males; but the moment he saw other males overcome his resistance, he would go storming into Kalantan's and there, upon the Turkish rug and pillowed parallelepipedon, he would seek a momentary escape from his confusion. The lines would then disappear from his troubled face, and his placid smile would return.

Poor Maud earned the fifth part of what she needed for her living expenses at the Petit Casino.

But a few wealthy friends gave her in cash ten times the amount she spent.

One asks: How much did Maud earn? And how much did she spend? How much money did she receive from her gentlemen friends? What a sorry figure that half-kept Tito cut in the eyes of others. What a feeling of growing embarrassment!

These are problems, which need not be solved with the logarithm tables, but can indeed be figured with a method far more simple, if one did what Tito did. He would knock at Maud's door. If her response was: "You can't come in now", he would say "pardon me", and after apologizing for the intrusion he would go his way and come back three hours later.

Oh, how many times did poor, patient Tito wait outside for three hours before he was admitted into the room!

But he could fool away those three hours by putting on his soft purple necktie and his sandy-colored suit and sneak over to the beautiful Armenian siren, who was always willing to soothe his pent-up feelings, because every day she could adorn her musk-scented tresses with camelias that were as white as snow.

When he tiptoed back into Maud's room and attempted some shy reprimand of her conduct, she soothed him by throwing her arms around his neck and hugging him tightly to her breasts, and she would rattle off in the most delightful manner:

"Please don't talk that way, honey! Now, I am all yours. The other men, even the one who left just as you came, constitute the past. The past doesn't belong to us anymore; but the future does. Come now, come, let's patch it up!"

When two men want to patch up a quarrel, they usually go to dinner together.

A man and woman, instead, will celebrate in bed. Tito and Maud had almost daily some quarrel to patch up, for the sake of their past, near and remote.

Even Kalantan's home held a past.

This past had penetrated silently into her nuptial chamber, now converted into a widow's chamber through an accident at sea.

That past was constituted by an ancient coffer of velvet and pewter, a very fine specimen of Caucasian craftsmanship.

"What's in there?" Tito asked suddenly one night, as he undid the knot of his soft purple necktie.

"Someday I will tell you", Kalantan promised, letting one of her gold laminated slippers fall over the carpet.

Tito blinked. "But can that be today?" he insisted as he removed his sandy-colored coat.

"Not yet", Kalantan decided, as she unlaced her girdle,

"And why not?", Tito insisted, unbuttoning his vest.

"Because today I have things more important than that to tell you", jested Kalantan, with a smack o£ her green garter against her full thigh.

* * *

"What is it you want to tell me?"

"That I am liable to lose myself in this big bed if you don't come over quickly. Never mind winding that clock. Put it down",

"And if it should stop?"

"That's it. Wait until it stops before winding it". And so Tito had not been able that day to extort the secret contained in that velvet and pewter coffer, rare specimen of Caucasian art, which guarded Kalantan's glamorous past.

Maud, the Italian dancer, met a prefecture official of very high standing but of short build, who held his chest out and his head back so that when seen in profile he looked like a tablespoon.

He was attached to the Custom House Guards.

She was also introduced to a young surgeon who aimed at a doctorship at the Sorbonne University, and was, more over, the author of a very worthy treatise on medicine and surgical therapy.

The young specialist would not visit the charming dancer for scientific reasons, but as an amateur, rather, and after his tapering white fingers had examined minutely every tissue in her body, he would turn with an ingratiating smirk and assure her that everything was in perfect shape. In fact, he even ventured that with the exercise of a little will-power, or indiscretion, rather, she would have become an excellent mother of a family.

But dancing and motherhood are two things which have never, save on rare occasions, been on speaking terms with each other.

The high prefecture official who looked like 2 tablespoon when seen in profile, being a man who was very fond of peace and quiet, haunted with the prospect of scandal, wrung his hands in supplication as he begged Maud not to become compromised in a family way. He sighed with relief when she assured him that the deft little surgeon, also author of a worthy treatise on medicine and surgical therapy, would always be ready for an emergency of that sort.

He was so astonishingly adroit and cute, that little doctor!

He had specialized himself in a certain operation which is practiced with unscrupulous frequency in Vienna, Berlin, Paris and lately even in Italy. A small operation which the little doctor of the lastingly downcast eyes did without aids or assistants in one hour or less, which, of course, included the sterilization of tools and hands. And for this operation of little import, indeed, he

would be satisfied with a mere pittance of ten thousand francs—
which is very small. In Maud's case, he was satisfied with twice
that amount, because he knew that the fee would have been paid
by the high prefecture official, Maud's own lover and a lover of
peace and quiet as well, who could not bear the thought of disturbing the repose of his progeny dozing in the blue of a far off
future, and would have been happy to disburse an extra one thousand franc note for the security of letting them sleep indefinitely.

The young doctor was very decorously satisfied with a paltry
sum, a few elaborate bows and the grateful patronage of so eminent and influential personage as the prefecture official, connect-
ed especially with the Custom House Guards.

But when Tito learned that his little Maud had stoically
submitted to the surgeon's knife, he felt himself collapsing, as
though his very heart had been yanked out by the surgeon's lan-
cet. He caught his breath like a child who is trying to keep itself
from crying.

His not too far removed studies on physiology had left him
with some recollection of the days when he frequented the gy-
necology clinic, to witness with a sinking of the heart the fate of
some women, who because of some pathological reasons, had to
be operated upon as Maud did.

He still remembered certain young creatures who, after being
discharged by the clinic, seemed to have lost something in their
voice, in their smile, in their charms and, one by one, all their
signs of womanhood. Something very harsh survived in their
voice, something stern about their eyes, something pathetically
asexual, hermaphroditical almost, something prematurely aged
about their faces that become rapidly mantled with masculine
hair, while their bodies swelled into an unpleasant plumpness,

Tito foresaw all of this in Maud!

"Poor, poor Maud!" he said, with tears choking his throat.
And since Maud could not understand, and he lacked the nerve to

disclose to her the dreadful glandular travail, he had no other alternative except that which is taught in fiction. So he slumped on his knees with clasped hands, and with something akin to a sob, cried: "Maud, what have you done, what have you done, Maud!"

Maud quietly begged him to wipe the tears from his eyes and leave the room immediately, because the high prefecture official was due to arrive at any moment.

Before she broke from Tito, she asked:

"Why did you cry?"

And he: "I was just pretending".

"But your eyes were red with tears".

And Tito, very bitterly: "We sentimental fools, when pretending to cry, we cry in earnest".

He lacked the courage to tell her the dreadful truth, but bid her a curt goodbye and left.

The very young but very deft specialist was awarded the Legion of Honor.

For a few days Tito roamed the streets of Paris, discon-solate and miserable, like any other madman would have done in his place, and remembering now and then that he was still a reporter for *The Fleeting Moment*, made a brief excursion to the newspaper's office, to see if there were any assignments for him.

As flaccidly as a corpse in advanced dissolution who still. managed to drag himself about, he floundered wearily through the corridor and into the editorial room.

His face was as pale as if it had been soaked in gum ammonia. In the editorial room he met the Man of whom nobody knows anything about, who greeted him with his right hand extended and a cordial smile suffused throughout his whole person.

The Man of whom nobody knows anything about, is that person who is seen roaming around every newspaper office; no one knows what he is doing there, nor why he is tolerated around, but who is greeted just the same by manager and porter alike with various deferential degrees. He is not a reporter, nor is he on the payroll; he has no special duties to discharge, but will nevertheless sit before any desk, use the telephone, keep his hat on, read the papers, use the newspaper's own letter heads, and order the porter about.

The Man of whom nobody knows anything about, said to Tito, abruptly: "Young man, you're leading a life that is too irregular a sort of thing to last! Isn't it so, Nocera?"

Nocera: "The gentleman is right! It seems all very clear that you are letting those two women ruin your life, my dear Tito."

Editor-in-chief: "You should get yourself a wife."

Tito: "Burst!"

Editor-in-chief: "A devoted wife who would compensate you for the many griefs caused you by your two loves".

Nocera: "We can help you find one like that, if you say so".

Tito: "I believe you're right. I should take refuge in matrimony as one does in castration".

The Man of whom nobody knows anything about: "Marriage provides a diversion for one who wants to change from one bore to another."

Editor-in chief: "You should marry a widow. To me, a widow is the ideal woman. But, of course, I don't mean your Armenian siren. Just a delectable little widow whose voluptuous ardours have been decorously appeased long ago. A neat, quiet subdued woman, ready on hand for you. A perfect match!"

Tito gave a short laugh.

"It isn't easy to guess my likes and dislikes", he .said. "I, for one, would prefer a wife who is gifted with that dumb, foppish domesticity of the walrus; and as to her figure . . ."

Nocera: "Fat or thin?"

"Neither too Amazonian nor too ravenously thin."

Editor-in-chief: "I know of a little widow who is very pretty and very wealthy. Some widow, by Jove! A real bargain of a

woman. But she's as good as new. She ceased her marital func-
tioning only six months ago. After all, I believe that where wom-
en are concerned, one should do like Brummel, who let his butler
wear all his new clothes first, so he could break them in for him.
But she is a virtuous sort of a person, though, who goes in for
economy in a big way, and when her period of mourning is over,
she will store her weeds away in moth balls in the belief that they
would do well for a second husband."

Nocera: "I would rather advise you to marry a prostitute;
I don't mean a regular whore, understand me right. But one of
those glittering strumpets who will never consider anything less
than two hundred francs per private consultation. Facts hereto-
fore have proven that they make the best wives. If you should
marry a respectable girl, one, who because she brings you as
dowry some stocks, expects to monopolize you throughout your
natural life and have you around, and have you worship her at
her feet. If you marry a prostitute, she will have an apartment,
furnished with all the modern improvements, that her long career
has suggested. She will also bring you as dowry a chest stuffed
with gems and a good dose of shekels, besides, wisely set aside
for rainy days."

Editor-in-chief: "Prostitutes never save their money".

Nocera: "But they are very thrifty I tell you, almost niggardly, they are. They'll have the male squander thousands of francs
on mere trifles, like a *corbeille*, but if they, the prostitutes, of
course, receive a letter with a stamp that is still unmarked by a
postal seal, they detach it with painstaking care, and use it again
the first chance they have."

Tito: "But this is something that even respectable women do.
Four cents, when ever it is a woman who has to spend them, are
always four cents; but the hundred francs which men spend on
them, are worth to them less than car fare in a trolley, I have had
occasion to notice that the most serious cases of niggardliness
exist among women".

"Yes, go on".

Nocera: "The prostitute you will marry will bring you money which you are not compelled to donate, to soothe your pride, to the parish poor. You may at first feel tempted to part with some of the money just the same, but when urged to do so, you will resist, and the temptation will go while the money will stay. Money smears your hands when you have too little of it; but it washes them both clean, when you have plenty. Luckily, on bank-notes there are no other signatures except those of the Director General and the Chief Cashier, and you do not have to add your signature to theirs when paying a woman off, and your self-respect is saved. Having earned her money with some effort, she will most naturally feel that what is left in your pocket is all yours and should be respected as such. Something, which a respectable woman never seems able to understand.

"Your wife, moreover (provided, of course, that you marry the one I have in mind), will have tasted all the flimsy joys which luxury provided; her craziest whims will have been satisfied: the villa on Lake Lucerne, and the Yacht at Nice, and the duplex car, will no longer tempt her. She will feel instead all the nostalgic simplicity of a Cincinnatus.

"And instead of saying to you everyday: 'You know, dear, what you should buy for me?', she will say, I don't want you to squander your money on trifles, honey'.

"Both the respectable young woman and the prostitute are likely to make a cuckold out of you in time to come. The curse of marital unhappiness will visit upon you, to be sure. But there is a difference in technique: the respectable miss will deceive you in a boisterous, pyrotechnical way, which will naturally attract to your unhappiness the attention of others, if not your own.

"Her experience with men being necessarily a limited one, she will think that the imbecile who then happens to be her lover (she will no doubt fall in love with an imbecile), is a superior sort of a man. And if the latter will tell her that her husband is an idiot, she will take his word for granted and treat him as such by holding him up to the ridicule of friends and neighbors alike.

"The prostitute, instead, will be true to her former pro-fes-sion; she will, therefore, deceive you with elegance, with meth-od, with a display of parsimony, with zest, with re-serve, with style; tact and honesty. She will be able to draw a balance sheet, scrupulously exact and fair, between your merits and those of the other men competing for her favors, because she knows what all men are worth, while the wife who has been drafted from the respectable ranks, knows little, if anything about men, except, of course, yourself and the other imbecile.

"The young wife who will make a cuckold of you, will laugh at the scorn in which she has placed you, because, to her, every-thing will seem so unusually, so exceptionally funny.

"The prostitute will never trouble herself with all this. She will spare you the embarrassment, because she knows perfectly well that what she does is the normal thing to do.

"The respectable woman will want you to stake her lover; lend him money, and help him out of his financial worries, which are usually numerous, and then forget about it entirely.

"The prostitute will not hold you to this, because having been used to receiving money all her life, she could not bear the thought of giving any.

"Your wife, of course, will never be admitted into the up-per class, and in that way you do not have to be tortured by that disturbing practice of having to meet people and exchange visits, and get all soiled up by moving around in the best of circles and among decent folks.

"Into your home you will admit only friends like our-selves, pleasant and unprejudiced always, who will never bear you ill-feeling, surliness nor dignity in our chats together, because when in the presence of an ex-prostitute, one does not have to dress into a water-proof bathing suit the things that are said; and at the same time we will not transcend into the vulgar, because, after all is said and done, that prostitute is your wife.

"That woman will never refuse to gratify your wishes".

Tito, very modestly: "I have always supposed that no wife does".

The Man of whom nobody knows anything about: "You think so; but there are wives who have the nerve to tell their husband: 'No, dear, nothing doing tonight!'"

Nocera: "But she could never turn you down alleging that she is tired, because in that case you can very well turn around and say: 'How come, honey? Why you, of all people. Have you perhaps forgotten the happy old days when you took on about twenty males an hour?' "If, by any chance, she should want to be gratified when you are too tired to do so, you could then say: 'After so busy and laborious a career as yours, I should think you ought to have had enough of this.

"You can bestow your manly favors upon as many women as you wish, and, if she should make any complaint, shut her up by reminding her of the first male name that comes to your lips. You'll never miss the mark!

"The respectable miss will never bother to conceal her displeasure, her spleen, and will in due time train you to bear her nervous outbursts, and in yielding to you, she will show you her indifference and disgust.

"The prostitute, accustomed at all times to concede herself with a simulated smile and enjoyment, will behave with you as she would with her best customer, and give you the complete Illusion of desire and eagerness, even though her father and mother had died of yellow fever that same day.

"She will know how to keep herself beautiful, until very well on in years, because beauty being the prime requisite of her trade, she will have learned all the secrets of it.

"Perhaps someday she may do as the comedians do who have retired from the theatre when they surrender to the fobia of staging a comeback, or at least, performing during some extraordinary recital. Well, no one would be surprised then, no one will ridicule you. After all, that was once her trade.

"On the first night of matrimony you will experience a very queer emotion. You will not have the feeling that you are in bed with a spouse, but with a woman who just stopped you on the street. Doesn't that seem thrilling? You will not have to bother to break through any safety valves of virginity. Everything considered, it is a convenience not to be sneezed at! But if you were so dumb as to desire a wife who is still a virgin, believe me, my friend, you can find that much in a prostitute because only the prostitutes—and not the virgins—know, wanting to, how to give you the complete illusion of virginity".

Tito: "You are right, my friend",

Nocera: "The first thing you should do is to give up those two women. Stop seeing them. Drop them entirely."

Tito: "I will never see them again".

"Will you swear to that?"

"I will swear to that".

While they were speaking, the telephone rang:

"Someone asking for Mr. Tito Arnaudi on the phone."

Tito rose and walked to the telephone.

"Yes, my love, this is me," he said. "Over at your house, did you say? Why of course, say in a half hour, or maybe sooner than that".

"Who is that?" inquired Nocera.

"The Armenian", Tito answered, his voice sinking almost to a whisper. And he walked out.

That afternoon he arrived a little late at Kalantan's villa, having been detained before the entrance of a metropolitan depot by that certain waiter, his friend at college, who memorized all historical dates like so many telephone numbers (Peace Treaty of Campoformius: *seventeen nine seven,* etc), and had first escorted him through all Montmartre cafes when he had embarked upon the study of cocaine surroundings.

His friend seemed In great pain. He could see that an earthquake was pent up in his bosom.

"I am going back to Italy." he said with uplifted arms, in which he carried his bags, "I'm sick of Paris, I'm tired of being bossed around, tired of earning a franc or so at a time—tired, tired, I'm sick to the marrow of those whiffs of womanish air that surround and choke me. If I should stay here a while longer, I would probably throw myself into the Seine; the Seine, you know, is a River which is half filled with rinsing water which all whores, private and public, dump into it."

"I suppose you're going back to Italy to see if you can find a river that is cleaner? It shouldn't be difficult to find one, because in Italy women wash themselves less."

"I'm going to take the cowl—become a monk. There's a convent near Turin where they welcome anyone. It's a sort of mystic Foreign Legion".

Tito stared at him with genuine surprise,

"But do you know how to be a monk?"

"I guess I can fix that all right"

"Have you any faith?"

"No."

"Any vocation?"

"No."

"Well, what do you expect, then?"

"There's a small garden, the cells are well exposed, there's very little work to do, the rules are not so stiff, the diet is quite healthy; there are books to be had and one never goes out, not even after he is dead because they even have a cemetery in the house . . ."

Tito looked at him, half perplexed, half amused.

He thought he had stumbled into a lunatic, and he had always heard that lunatics must be humored. He said: "Yes, I know, you*re sore at the world because your woman has cheated you by sleeping with her husband, and left you out in the cold".

The aspiring monk lowered his eyes and threw up his arms in a hopeless gesture of discomfort. Then with a quick breath:

"Maybe, she did . . . I'll send you all the information on how to get there if you wish to call on me sometime. Goodbye,"

He was not able to say much more. His head dropped heavily forward on his breast and he rushed up the flight of steps into the station.

* * *

The velvet and pewter coffer, magnificent and complicated specimen of Caucasian craftsmanship, shrouding the past of Kalantan Ter-Gregorianz, bulged with gold coins. It resembled some fabulous treasure buried in the subsoil of ancient cities long extinct. When Kalantan said: "That coffer is full of gold coins", Tito grinned with the air of a man who had just heard a good joke, and said by way of comment:

"Little girl! There are things that happen only in Fairy Tales or in German screen versions".

It was then that Kalantan told him her story:

"My husband, as you probably know, was very wealthy. He owned rich oil wells and the most famous fisheries in all Persia".

"I know that"

"Unfortunately he was born with a fearful boredom toward life. One would say that he had been ushered into the world gifted with all the ancient Asiatic experience, diffused in his own blood. Nothing could tempt him, nothing could amuse him. Cold and indifferent toward his home and family, he would lock himself in his room where the walls were hung with placards and notices like those you see in hotels; with the price of laundry, with the cost of breakfast served downstairs or upstairs, and with reminders to the guests who departed with the evening trains to leave the room before two o'clock in the afternoon.

"His dream was to travel, but he travelled little. He was a sort of a paralytic thirsting for faraway places. His longest trips, however, were Paris-Berlin, Paris-London, and Paris-Brussels. After a month's absence, he would return home.

"He was very fond of eocottes. I think the most notorious strumpets must have passed through his hands and interpretation.

"Naturally, he would have liked to have them always around him, grouped together in a portable house, like a gipsy caravan, managed according to the precepts of a Parisian maitre d'hotel.

"Of course, he liked me too, hut only at intervals. During the first few days of our life together he loved me a great deal, and he proved it by forgiving a very serious fault I had: that of being his wedded wife,

"Eccentric as usual, in order not to feel that I was his wife, he put a price on me. Every time I received him in bed, he would toss a few gold coins into that coffer. It was a crazy thing to do. One would have considered him deranged. He said that in that way he raised me from the rank of a wife to the dignity of a courtesan. I adjusted myself to this strange formality."

"Did anybody ever try to break into that coffer?"

"I have all trustworthy servants; moreover, nobody would even suspect that there is gold money in it".

"It contains perhaps some one hundred thousand francs, I suppose?"

"Maybe a half million".

Tito approached it with a feeling of awe and studied it intently, after which he tried with all his strength to lift it; but the effort only swelled the veins of his neck and forehead. A faintness passed like a shadow over him and flitted away.

"My poor, little dear one", Kalantan sighed, drawing him closer, with a languished look, upon the couch and kissing his face, suddenly grown ashen; she began to caress his hands.

A long pause ensued. "You see, Kalantan", he gasped, "that coffer grieves me immensely—because I am immensely jealous of your past. I would like to have had you first. Each of those coins represents a quiver, a cold pleasure, a passionate fit which you have given to someone else. Think! All the spasms of many years crowded into that coffer."

"But what of it?", Kalantan exclaimed with surprise, as she showered his mischievous eyes with kisses. "You are now my only master. My other lovers, you say? I don't re-member them, because I have never before enjoyed life as I do now in your arms. After all, the past is past—it is gone, it is no longer ours!"Tito suddenly drew his hands away from Kalantan. Her words startled him.

"The past is no longer ours!"

Where did he hear that very phrase before? From the lips of another woman. It was Maud's own phrase. These two women who had come, one from the hills and dales of the River Po, and the other from the gorges of the Caucasus; these two women, though they were the products of two distinct civilizations, made use of the same words to comfort him in his grief.

Seized with an anguish quite comprehensible, his thought flashed back to his friend who sought the seclusion of a cloister, and who summed up his disgust in one single phrase: "I am sick with these whirls of womanish air choking me .

Tito was already angered against Kalantan, the moneyed Armenian, who, deep in her own heart, was delighted to be treated like a whore.

In every woman, more or less, there is some vague, latent brothel homesickness.

That day Tito could not be any too soft with the Armenian siren.

"I'll be back tomorrow", he excused himself. "But not today. Today I am sad. Let me go."

Her exhortations and pleadings were listened to with a sullen silence. In his mind there flashed but one desire.

He went to see Maud.

But if a few weeks before he could manage to forget Maud's unfaithfulness in the arms of Kalantan, or Kalantan's past while in bed with Maud, that double passion grew into frightful proportions, like two opposing and conflicting forces, both crushing him.

There wasn't a thing about Kalantan's past which he didn't know; the artificial love sales with her husband; the white orgies in the Penguin Hall; the frenzies roused by deadly excitants and by the languorousness of dope; the possessions inside the coffin, that primitive homesickness of the brothel, followed by a nostalgia veering toward chastity, which was little else but a reaction of nausea brought on by the abuse of exaggerated sensuality; a nausea of cerebral nature, which morphine had transformed into a chaste delirium.

There wasn't a thing about Maud's past and present, which Tito didn't know. He knew how and to whom she first yielded; he knew to whom she had sold herself in Italy and Paris; he had found her in bed with the negro boxer, the one with the greasy pachyderm hide; he had seen the high prefecture official leave the elevator with his little eyes purled up and filled with lewdness; he knew that the youthful surgeon had mutilated her, hastening her change of life and shortening her youth. He knew all the secret love nooks, the wine cellars, where she peddled her wares; why, every district in Paris harbored one of Maud's customers.

Maud and Kalantan were two different creatures, pertaining to two different civilizations, who agreed, however, in their lack of understanding of his anguished jealousy. Both had different accents, yet both wore the same unconscious look in their eyes when they intoned the fatal words: *"The past is no longer ours"*.

Maud and Kalantan, both different from each other, whom he loved with equal transport, because both held him chained, one with the jealousy of the present, the other with the jealousy of the past.

Maud's flesh breathed with the thyme of her green mountains.

Kalantan had in her flesh the taste of salt. They were both young; and yet both were betrayed by something pathetically, strangely old, something that was old in a different way.

Maud, greedy with carnal sensuality, sought in love the unknown form, the strange excitement, the morbid fits.

Kalantan, gorged with that same morbific extravagance, sought something wholly beyond her reach; and in Tito's love, she hoped for something that was pure and uplifting, simple and primitive.

In those two youthful women transpired two kinds of old age. One had pursued the most complicated forms of vice and sought the simple, the genuine in the sensual embrace; the other had climbed the rungs of simple love, in quest of vice.

Two opposite roads, pursued with the same breathless anxiety, an indication of two different but equally dynamic personalities.

Tito stood undecided between those two women, between those two passions. He did not know which of them he should permit to burn him. He seemed to be between two fires, distant and moving.

* * *

Just as the man who invented the rubber heel has been able to gather millions for himself; as the inventor of that flimsy metal plate which emits the disagreeable croaking sound of a hysterical bull-frog when pressed with a finger, has built for himself a very comfortable and secure station in life, so did Tito, with his journalistic enterprises win a permanent position with The Fleeting Moment. He received a generous increase in salary, but was, on the other hand, strictly forbidden to write a single word.

"If you want us to remain good friends, come and get your salary, come to see us as often as you please; play cannon over my billiard, drink at the bar, fence with my foils and swords; smoke my cigars if you wish, and you even have my permission to use my private stenographer, but don't you dare to write another line, not even if I should be the one asking you to do it, I hope I have made myself very clear!"

Tito had therefore nothing to do except to call once a month in order to sign a receipt and receive an envelope that bulged with Bank of France currency.

He spent his time taking lonely morning strolls through the eccentric quarters of Paris; he passed sometimes two or three days with Kalantan at her villa, where a room had been fitted out for the "gendeman"; he would then leave Kalantan for a whole week and trudge back to Maud; at other times he would let a few days slip by without seeing either Maud or Kalantan. And he faltered amid the shadowy, solitary haunts of Montmartre and Montparnasse, through those equivocal spots teeming with billiards and poker gamblers, master ruffians, pick-pockets; promoters of love adventures at popular prices, stool-pigeons, budding panders and slatternly whores who fed on anchovy sandwiches and *croissants* dipped in coffee.

The lame cocaine peddler had sold him six glass tubes filled with excellent Mannheim's. He roamed around Paris, hugging those six tubes in his pockets as children sleep with their toys underneath their pillows. He singled out the most solitary streets of the Villette and Belleville quarters, where the walls stood plastered with dreadful theatrical placards: "The Bastard's Daughter"; "The Secret of the Executioner"; "The Hangdog's Vengeance". He slipped through the avenue leading to the cemetery of Pere Lachaise, all spick and span, and neatly arranged like a sample; he made his way up to the slaughter-house, where he saw the restless cattle herded together in readiness for the kill.

"No one, at least, speaks to them about patriotism, as they do to men who go to war!", he thought.

A poor dog, exhausted by thirst and hunger, pranced wearily behind a light cart, which must have travelled from far, to judge by the dust it had accumulated. The driver, a peasant, could have given the dog a lift in the half-empty cart, instead of letting it suffer that way!

"But all peasants are the same" thought Tito, "They belong to an inferior breed, that's why; they are worse than savages; all their acts are prompted by the most putrid selfishness, by the most useless cruelty and by an ignorance that is most stubborn, I would be most happy if every year a hail destroyed their wheat, their corn, if their vineyards were riddled by the cryptogram pest, and a fierce cattle murrain, besides. That's what all farmers deserve."

A long line of white-clad little girls, strolling and chattering on their way to the Pare des Butes Chaumont, filled him with an almost melting emotion. He eyed them reflectively. In each of the little ones he detected something which was already definite; cute faces of future operatic soubrettes; eyes that sang gaily with the promise of future thrills; full-cheeked mamas who from one child-birth to the next, would find time to look pleasing to some reserved gentleman. All in white, all dressed the same way, almost identical in form; and yet in each dozed the future courtesan in embryo, the actress, the average woman, and the intellectual. They bear in themselves the tiny seeds from which would sprout great men or notorious criminals; they bear in themselves the typical cancer cells and the phthisis bacilli . . . . A few will become like Maud, a few others like Kalantan, to unleash despair in some little Tito Arnaudi who at that moment was perhaps picking his nose in goodness knows what part of the world!

That endless, zigzagging wandering gave Tito the blissfully apathetic aspect of a hobo. Hobo life, too, has its attractions; not to be a slave of the clock, of a goal, of an appointment; never to walk according to prescribed rules. To pass the time between a public hearing at the Assises or a lecture at some university; to sit on a park bench or at the riverfront; to be present at all auction sales; to stop and look at some heavily loaded truck, trying to steer clear of the car tracks; to inspect the morgue exhibits; to see the melancholy evening train depart; to speak to masons and bricklayers; to hear the wise cracks of hawkers; to read books over the benches of the peaceful *quais*, or maybe doze for a while over the green plush of museums; to toss morsels of bread to the clumsy and dumb bears, to those huge children, the elephants in the Jardin des Plantes.

Sometimes, he thought he saw the image of Maud projected across the sidewalks. To escape from that vision he would sneak into a cafe or a confectionery store.

"When I see an old lady crunching cookies, they seem to be wasted."

Everything irked him, in fitful spasms. But beneath all that he experienced a sort of comfort which had slowly crept into his system, without his even being aware of it. Cocaine, which

during the first stages had roused him to a pitch of sexual res-
dessness, of erode exaltation almost unquenchable (two women
were barely sufficient to gratify his desires), had now caused
a lowering of his sexual wants. He would let many days go by
without feeling the least tempted by the memory of Maud's
shapely ankles, without any desire to breathe the musk-scented
fragrance exhaling from Kalantan's tresses, And if his thoughts
ever wandered back to the beautiful Armenian siren crouched in
that voluptuous act of self-adoration over the downy softness of
the tabjia; if his memory ever wandered back to Maud, a woman
thirsting for vice and novelty, Tito considered them human beings that had long ceased to exist, while he was a survivor.

His sensuality glimmered toward feebleness and complete ex-
tinction. But now and then, a sudden pang of jealousy would burn
through him with the cooling, life giving sensation of oxygen.

* * *

He pictured Maud heaving between someone's arms, in some
far removed dwelling, goodness knows in which, of the twenty
districts, And the sudden jealousy would quickly ignite his senses
with lust.

He would then trace his way home, to look for his Maud, and
he found her (whenever he found her at all) willing at all times to
yield with all her quivering body, and her divinely moist lips.

"Cocaine!", Tito would cry in his dull bewilderment. "Cocaine! You are not Maud, you are Cocaine, the venom I crave so
much. I flee from you, swearing that I will never again see you,
but I come back, fatally I come back just the same, because I
need you like the venom that first saves and then kills me.

"I flee from you because I see in your flesh the fingerprints of
other males.

"Yes, I feel them, I see them, as one can see the soiled spots
on the petals of gardenias.

"I flee from you because you are not all mine; because it hurts me to share you with others, At times, I scorn you, I loathe you, and yet I will always come back to you, the only woman I love, the only woman I could really love."

Wearily, he pleaded.

And she, sitting upon the big bed, still undone, would listen with a quiet, almost vapory smile to the burning words with which Tito scorched her hands.

Her hands thus occupied, because Tito had brought them close to his lips, she cocked up her nose and amused herself by pawing and clutching at the turtle shell hairpins, strewn over the floor, with her feet.

Cocaine had the clutching feet typical of the ape and twenty per cent of the criminals.

* * *

Jealousy is that sentiment by which a man, having been admitted into the bedchamber of a woman once, thinks he is the only one who has the right to call there again.

No man wants to admit that this is simply overbearing absurdity.

Every woman, on the other hand, has a clear and immediate perception of this. To her, this pretense seems so awkwardly foolish that she even realizes the futility of remonstrating.

Every intelligent woman lets a man stumble over his own jealousy, because she knows by instinct that nothing she might say or do would cure him of his weakness.

Cocaine, nevertheless, said one day to Tito: "I am not wealthy; as a dancer I am worthless; I don't know how to a start a business or create an industry. It behooves me, therefore, to accept the money that is offered me and the conditions that go with it".

Before that open confession, Tito's eyes squirted and dripped like a wet umbrella.

To cheer him up, in other circumstances she would have asked him to remove his clothes and join her in bed; but since they were already in bed, she proposed, instead:

"Put your clothes on and let s go out."

A half hour later they were at the *des Invcdides* station, and rode oil for Versailles together.

Paris was beginning to weigh heavily upon Tito's heart. It seemed to him that every street there had seen her go by in a car with another man, heading goodness knows where; every restaurant had some time or other reserved a table or a private booth for her and her unknown escort! Her room at the Napoleon Hotel had received who knows how many clients, brought by herself. Even around her dressing room, at the Petit Casino, she passed semi-gratuitous love samples to everybody. For some time Tito had been anxious to give a new background to their romance; he sought 'environments which she had never visited before; he searched for new forms of pleasure, never tried before with others. From that woman he expected something which she had never yet given to anyone else, no matter how small a word, perhaps, never whispered before into the ear of another; a chemise, which he was the first to see; a restaurant which had been never visited before.

Tito discovered a small inn, frequented mostly by budding painters, students and shop girls. He took her there, to give her person a background not haunted by evocations of past phantoms.

When, however, they were about to cross the threshold, Cocaine looked around with a familiar glint in her eyes. She said quickly: "Let's not go through here, Tito. There's the kitchen, and behind that, on the street, there is a honeysuckle that big, with an odor so strong that it gives me a headache."

A shudder of jealousy mingled with disgust smote him. But

where on earth hadn't that woman been before? Where hadn't
they taken her?

When they got to Versailles, amid the gardens made bright
with Autumn shades, in that mingling splendor of sadness and joy,
sang by Musset and Verlaine, the simple, naive and childish "Cocaine", still Maud, still Magdalena, at heart, confessed to

Tito: "See? Under that lilac bush over there. That's where
they found my first white hair, two or three months ago". He
gave a swift glance and blinked.

Much to his chagrin, Tito could not attempt any new experi-
ments since that time. Once he could have gone back to Kalantan
to smother his jealousy over the soft and hospitable Asiatic takha;
but that was something he couldn't do anymore. He was through
meandering. Cocaine was now necessary to him, if he did not
want to go altogether insane without her.

"If you had a chance to earn about one thousand francs each
night", he said to her back in Paris, "a thousand francs each
night, with your dancing only, would you give up all those men
who . . ."

"Who pay me, you mean? Surely! And I won't belong to
anybody but you. All yours, of course! But do you think that possible? It's a dream! Can't you see, Tito, that I am as graceful as a
flatiron when I dance?"

Tito dropped his voice: "I've a marvelous plan. You'll see!"

* * *

Since the boss was away in Auvergne for the election campaign,
and the editor-in-chief had to undergo a small operation on his
thumb, no one was at the office to stop Tito from sneaking into
the pressroom with a thick manuscript which appeared in print,
topped by a sensational lead, in the second page of *The Fleeting
Moment.*

That night, at the Alhambra Theatre, they took in receipts to
the amount of five thousand francs, and Maud, the great Italian

beauty, dress coat dancer de luxe, was greeted on her appearance, as the one which *The Fleeting Moment,* the most influential of poor father of a family whose only daughter, after eloping with a mountebank, and giving birth to a child, chokes it to death, is imprisoned, set free, again and after six months of underworld life, returns to the parental roof. The poor father has had during all that time the opportunity to heap all his scorn and contempt upon her, to despise, hate and curse her. And when she is back, looking cowed and meek, he, having already exhausted his stock of despair and anger, can well afford to express himself softly and sweetly, with an almost subdued tone of voice.

Thus spoke, with tears streaming down his glasses, the unhappy Chief. "You have ruined my newspaper", he moaned slowly, his voice almost a whisper. "You've held me up to the ridicule of the whole Paris press."

Tito, erect before him, kept his eyes riveted on the floor and his hands crossed upon his abdomen like a seduced and pregnant maiden before her white-haired parent.

"The shock has been too strong", continued the heartbroken Chief, expressing himself in Italian to appear still more tender. "My grief is too strong to allow me to hurl my curses against anyone," He suddenly checked his passionate utterances with painful self-control. "I forgive you, therefore. But don't you come between my feet anymore, dead or alive. Give me your hand as a gentleman that you will not You can even embrace me, if you wish. I have here two orchestra tickets for the Opera Comique, I give them to you with all my heart. There is nothing else which I can do".

And he slumped into his armchair, gasping for breath, his face wearing the expression of one who had just felt the sting of a fist boring into his stomach.

When he came to his senses, Tito Arnaudi was gone. He was pounding the sidewalks, looking for a job. all Paris newspapers had described as the electrifying marvel! Terpsichore revived! According to that long write-up, Maud rose, with her legs, to the dizziest philosophical heights, to plunge the gullible awe-stricken spectators into the abyss of the absolute. The metaphysics of her dancing was the expression of the eternal and the boundless . . . .

Her dancing over, the disappointed public refrained from voicing any protest. Accustomed to the misleading bragging of publicity, everyone, as always, was satisfied to comment!

"Some nerve!"

But everybody enjoyed a good laugh.

Even the managers over at the theatre laughed; even the capital newspapers laughed; even Maud laughed. Everybody laughed.

But there was one person who could not laugh: the Chief, general manager of *The Fleeting Moment*, who had come storming back to Paris the very next day, and sent immediately for Tito who was responsible.

The latter was half dozing in the anteroom of the boss's office, when a treble ringing of a bell roused him from his reverie. One had no need to be a musician to know the wrath expressed in those three sonorous peals.

As he entered the office he saw a fierce pair of moustaches dangling over a writing desk.

The boss looked sullen and sour, his features strangely drawn, his whole body swaying. He spoke very calm and measured, though, like a man who had exhausted all his power of suffering. Think, to give you an idea, about some poor father of a family whose only daughter, after eloping with a mountebank, and giving birth to a child, chokes it to death, is imprisoned, set free, again and after six months of underworld life, returns to the parental roof. The poor father has had during all that time the opportunity to heap all his scorn and contempt upon her, to despise, hate and curse her. And when she is back, looking cowed

**The metaphysics of her dancing was
the expression of the eternal and the
boundless . . . .**

and meek, he, having already exhausted his stock of despair and anger, can well afford to express himself softly and sweetly, with an almost subdued tone of voice.

Thus spoke, with tears streaming down his glasses, the unhappy Chief. "You have ruined my newspaper", he moaned slowly, his voice almost a whisper. "You've held me up to the ridicule of the whole Paris press".

Tito, erect before him, kept his eyes riveted on the floor and his hands crossed upon his abdomen like a seduced and pregnant maiden before her white-haired parent.

"The shock has been too strong", continued the heartbroken Chief, expressing himself in Italian to appear still more tender. "My grief is too strong to allow me to hurl my curses against anyone," He suddenly checked his passionate utterances with painful self-control. "I forgive you, therefore. But don't you come between my feet anymore, dead or alive. Give me your hand as a gentleman that you will not You can even embrace me, if you wish. I have here two orchestra tickets for the Opera Comiquc, I give them to you with all my heart. There is nothing else which I can do."

And he slumped into his armchair, gasping for breath, his face wearing the expression of one who had just felt the sting of a fist boring into his stomach.

When he came to his senses, Tito Arnaudi was gone. He was pounding the sidewalks, looking for a job.

10

Tito had not laughed for a long time. His misfortune however, amused him immensely, and he looked it. He had lost his job; he lacked strength to look around for another, and the money he had was hardly enough to carry him over another week.

To save his money, he bought from an antiquarian on rue Saint Honore, two funeral urns, globular and iridescent like soap bubbles, and a gilt-silver monstrance, which had probably hailed from some small mountain shrine, now destroyed or desecrated, and over which time and incense had wrought an attractive burnished coating. The sacred host within had been replaced by one of a pharmaceutical pattern, around which, however, the silvery and gold beams shone with a brilliance truly mystic.

Back in his room at the Napoleon Hotel, he removed the host from the monstrance, which so profanated that sacred thing, and into its place inserted the portrait of Cocaine, completely naked.

He tossed the two funeral urns into a drawer from which he drew a bottle of *Avatar*, Cocaine's favorite perfume.

In its power of evocation, the scent of *Avatar* surpasses music itself.

He fastened the sprayer to the bottle and rilled the room with the intoxicating fragrance like a pagan offering worthy of the image which was encased in the monstrance. He breathed an admiring sigh.

Cocaine entered suddenly with a rustle o£ silks, while he stood still, as if lost in mute adoration of that flash of modish lines. It was a long time before she could speak; she was so moved by the rapturous scene that she tossed her parasol over the bed, and pressed her face to Tito's chest, while the quick tears that clouded her eyes pattered softly over his knitted green necktie, bespangled with blue stripes.

If you only know how fragrant are the tears that roll down the downy cheek of a woman, and how scented your necktie becomes when a woman sobs over it.

Tito's necktie was wet, but his soul was made lighter. Cocaine, too, felt her soul become light and glittering as an Andalusian mantilla. He looked at her with amazement: "I can see where your article on my dancing has yielded good results" she said,

"I know it", Tito replied, smiling acidulously.

"I have just had a long interview with a big American theatrical man. We are leaving for Buenos Aires in eight days. Will your paper let you go along with me?"

"It will", he muttered grimly.

"But will they let you stay six months?"

"Even twelve. How are the arrangements?"

"Excellent."

And she dashed into the next room and broke the good news to the maid, who answered sometimes, very arrogantly, to the name of Pierina.

* * *

When Csaky, the steward, announced that Mr. Arnaudi (he did not say the *gentleman* anymore) was asking for her, Kalantan was not surprised. She was all too familiar with the more or less prolonged periods of indefinable inner melancholy and shrinking spells; she knew how moody his nature was, and felt that it was just mere habit, if not a fatality, which led him back to her each time.

He seemed, however, strangely different: there was something forced and artificial in his tenderness; and in his love-making he lacked the usual dash and abandonment of former days. The twilight of passion was fading.

She greeted him affectionately: "Your room is still as you left it," she said, stroking his hair; "and so is my love . . . ."

That same evening, Tito felt that the beautiful Armenian siren, steeped in vice though she was, surrendered herself to him with the same naive eagerness. And the following morning, after awakening in his bed of rosewood, his eyes wandered and rested upon the familiar furniture and the velvet tapestries that hung all around, and he again saw the liveried steward, decorative and solemn-looking, who asked the "gentleman" if it was Russian tea, green tea, or Cingalese tea that he wished served.

"I want it served in Madam's boudoir. . . .

And he rose and tottered into Kalantan's room. She was still asleep, with her hands and knees huddled against her face, like magnolia petals when they sleep at night. He stared at her pale face.

Later he began dressing slowly; he knotted very carefully his green, knitted, blue striped necktie, that breathed with the fragrance of Cocaine's tears and then went to the Napoleon Hotel to gather some of his belongings.

"Come back soon", Kalantan begged.

"In a half hour", figured Tito.

A half hour later to the minute, in fact, Madam Kalantan Ter-Gregorianz's car wheeled into the garden, carrying two big yellow bags.

Tito spent many sleepless nights. Every night before retiring he took a strong dose of chloral to fight the insomnia produced by the venom of which he was a slave. But the invincible insomnia and the many ineffectual sedatives worked him into such an hallucinatory state that he spent long hours sitting up as if dreaming, in a sort of swampy inner lethargy which gave him the sensation that he was awake. To find himself in that villa as white as a charnel-house, guest and lover of a creature made up of Asiatic rhapsodies, icily greeted like an usurper by the servants; that

commingling of Oriental appearances, collected in the very heart
of Paris, which surrounded him with an environment savoring of
a Caucasian legend, and the thought of Maud, the petite Cocaine
of his dreams, only five minutes removed by car, who yet seemed
to him like a tiny human speck far, far away, shining palpably out
of the misty distance . . . all this formed in his mind like some
multicolored musical bee-hive in which the uniform humming
was now and then pierced by the ironically sentimental chirping
of a bird making love in the garden.

* * *

At the hotel they delivered to him a letter from his friend, the
monk, who remembered him every night In his prayers. He
found Cocaine occupied with trying on a *perure* of soft lingerie
in mauve crepe de chine, ornamented with fine organdy plaitings.

"You know, Tito, I'm putting on weight?" Cocaine said with
a distracted smile.

"I know it".

And how well he knew it! He had foreseen it right along. It
was the first sign of her declining youth. The cruel mutilation to
which she had submitted was now, only a year later, beginning
to prove what Virchow once said: "The woman is what she is by
reason of her generative glands."

All the feminine charm, the softness of her features, the
suppleness of her body, the silky delicacy of her hair, the fluent
opulence of her tresses, the musical richness of her voice, are all
products of that very gland. By extirpating the ovary, we will see
the harmonious lines change into obesity, the voice will become
masculine, the vivaciousness of her spirit degenerate into loss
of memory, her tenderness yield before habits of hypochondria
and irritability; her upper lips shaded with ugly hair, and her eyes
fierce and even turbulent. And after a few years we have before
us the virago in all her hybrid ugliness.

Despite all this, Tito was so deeply in love with that woman,

that he yearned for the day when she would become so unspeak-
ably ugly. "No one will want her then, anymore", he thought.
"She will then be mine, at last, wholly mine! Then I shall have
my dream come true; that of being her last love."

And when she begged him to feel with his hand that she was
really putting on weight, he gripped her with such consuming
passion against his chest that she shrieked: "Be careful; you are
ruining my organdy plaitings".

The dog began a loud bark in defense of his mistress. But
Tito, unmindful of everything else surrounding him, saw nothing but that beginning of plumpness, of that physical deformity
which he had half-hoped for and half-feared, for it marked the
critical point of her life when she would come creeping back to
him.

His eyes filled with anxiety. He looked almost grateful. It
was the first glimmer of hope that crept into that sort of amorous
redemption.

                                * * *

Csaky, steward in the Ter-Gregorianz household, regarded him
with the respectful eyes of the poisoner.

"Madam is out. But the gentleman's room is ready".

Every day, during the late afternoon, Kalantan went to a thera-
peutic institute where she submitted to illusory cures for imaginary
ailments, and returned toward sunset, with a flower fastened at her
waist; when she got home, her first thought was to surprise.

Tito in his room without ever questioning her servants, so
that the surprise would be complete.

When he was not there, she thought: "Maybe tomorrow".

And she walked back into her room, where Sonja, the
old-fashioned maid, helped her to undress.

One night Csaky said to her: "The gentleman had to leave
hurriedly for Italy".

A gleam of interest crept into her eyes.

"Did he leave any message for me?" she queried.

"No, Madame".

"Did you see him off to the train?"

"No, Madame, not to the train. Just to his hotel."

"Is his baggage in his room?"

"He left with all his baggage, Madame. But he left some clothes in the wardrobe".

"Very well. You may go, Csaky".

She laid her flower down, unbuckled her belt, removed her hat, tossed her veil upon the velvet and pewter coffer, the coffer that guarded "her past".

That coffer that collected the memory of the many fitful spasms she had offered to another man: that coffer bulging with gold coins, which her husband paid her, to give himself the illusion that she was something better than a mere wife; a courtesan.

That coffer which had caused poor Tito so much concern and anguish, that induced him to force the locks and break the hinges, to rummage through that luster of coins and empty the rich contents into two yellow bags, among his handkerchiefs and the neckties and the antelope skins and the silken pajamas. It seemed all so clear.

Kalantan, like all other women who are unable to understand what jealousy is, and above all else, the jealousy for things that are past, stood in smiling perplexity as she thought of Tito's despair when she comforted him with the words: "Little boy, the past is no longer ours!" Indeed, it is no longer ours when someone steals it from us, to cast it far beyond our reach, into two big yellow bags en route to far away South America, She sighed.

* * *

The steamer had hardly gotten under way, when Maud began flirting with a few passengers of all races and extractions. And since the sea behaved most horribly throughout the entire trip, Tito was seldom able to leave his cabin.

Someone told him the best way to overcome seasickness was to quit eating.

And Tito fasted.

Others advised him to eat.

And Tito ate.

A lady who was almost old and very religious, gave him a few drops of Saint Marie Nouvelle medicinal water.

Tito drank the water.

A *rastaquero* who was going back to his native Pampas prescribed anchovies.

Tito tried anchovies.

Another advised him to lie flat on his back.

And Tito lay flat on his back.

A third swore that one must lie on his stomach.

And Tito lay on his stomach.

But nothing that he tried did him any good. He sent for the ship's doctor.

"Doctor, what AS good for seasickness?"

"Vomiting."

That doctor was skeptic and indifferent, like all tradesmen who cater to a transient trade.

On the promenade deck the chirping Maud shone among passengers of the most eccentric nationalities. A Bolivian diplomat inquired why Tito never thought of going mad through her continuous unfaithfulness, and she replied that in matters of unfaithfulness the heart of all men is like patent leather shoes, Everything depends upon the first time you wear them. If they don't crack up on you then, they never will.

Seasickness, of course, relieved Tito of all worry, though he had an idea that the situation was not particularly fortunate.

She was even seen sneaking Into some first-class cabin, but since that was nobody's business but Tito's own, who was then more concerned with the workings of his stomach than those of the heart, it is no business of ours to waste our time upon the discussion of those innocent little happenings of transatlantic usage.

When they passed the Equator, Maud danced, and she was showered with many costly gifts and with applause.

Tito, confined to his cabin, lay on his bed on his stomach eating anchovies dipped into the anti-hysteric water of Saint Marie Nouvelle.

And the moon glittered keenly through the rifted clouds, like a match lit behind a porcelain saucer.

A Wagnerian tenor, blond as a camel, who had sung in all the famous opera houses, murmured that beside her he would have spent all his life on the ocean, because *Jamas corno en esta noche, el perfume del mar me ha parecido tan dulce.*

One day the Pampas *rastaquero,* realizing that his attentions toward poor Tito were wasted, tried to lavish his attentions on Maud.

To her that *rastaquero* appeared more worthy of consideration than that Wagnerian tenor, who had already declared that never during his whole life did he let it go through his mind to give a single cent to a woman, because women always considered it a great *honor* to grant him favor, or, as they say it in Paris, a *beguin.*

Maud, however, had long since passed the *beguins* and favor stage. The *rastaquero,* this for the benefit of those who have never seen one, was the faithful reproduction of the rustic, done over again, and euphemistically called the country gentleman. He hid the capable and well stocked pocket-book in the inside pocket of his vest, almost next to his skin, and wore drawers of cloth with strings attached at the bottom, which he tied five times around his ankles. His small, piggish eyes, diverged like road-posts indicating the opposite directions of two different towns. If he had not been so rich, he would have made a first-class watchman in some big department store, because those eyes seemed to be staring in all directions.

Since the latter's cabin was near the music salon, Maud could
go and dance exclusively for his benefit, to the rhythm of some
slow waltz, that seemed to gush from some distant isle. . . Just
to show his appreciation, the *rastaquero* allowed her to dip her
hands into the pocketbook buried. in the inside pocket of the
vest, almost rubbing against the flesh, and pick out a little souvenir of the trip for herself.

Exchanging kindness with kindness, appreciation with appreciation, Maud even allowed him to introduce his hand between
her chemise and the flesh, to help himself to a choice souvenir.

From the music salon there streamed into the cabin the notes
of a slow waltz, while the vessel turned its prow toward the south-
western route with the unchanging speed of sixteen miles per hour.

A few hours later, after the *rastaquero* had gone to bed,
alone, he found between the sheets a hairpin that breathed with
all of Maud's own fragrance, with all the exquisite scent of that
downy purple lingerie of crepe de chine ornamented with soft
organdy plaitings.

Tito knew. He sensed that Cocaine was taking several educational trips through the several cabins of the steamer. But his
jealousy was now a painless sensation. To be sure, jealousy still
fomented within, but never like those familiar outbursts back in
Paris. It was like a pulley that ran slack and failed to set the gears
of passion and pain in motion. When one suffers with some physical ailment, though it be only mere seasickness, all moral griefs
disappear instantly. I would like to create a new therapy: cure all
afflictions of the spirit through physical ailments.

Cure remorse with inoculations of influenza.

Cure jealousy with the malaria bacilli.

Cure love with germ injections.

I believe that medical science will, in the future, look into this.

The steamer put into port at Rio de Janeiro, When Tito
touched ground he wanted to continue by train to Buenos Aires.

But when he learned that Cocaine would have gone by sea instead, he again descended into the lions' den below, from which he again emerged after five more days of squeamish nausea at eighteen miles an hour.

They had arrived at Buenos Aires. We shall not attempt to describe the landing, nor the magnificence of the *Avenida de Mayo*. All those who have already been at Buenos Aires should remember it, and if there is some wretch who has not yet been there, he should feel ashamed of himself and go right now.

Nor shall we speak of Maud's tolerable success as a dancer. Her beauty was ebbing away quickly: but the electric spotlights of the great vaudeville houses, the sorcery of powders, pencils and carmine paint, still made her a desirable creature.

After dancing at Buenos Aires a few months, she went to Montevideo with Tito, Pierina and the dog.

Montevideo: three months.

Rosario: a fortnight.

Bahia Blanca: A marriage proposal from a varnish and paint manufacturer.

Fray Bantos: Vulcanic love-making by a director of a big meat extracts plant.

A year after landing on American soil Maud, dress coat dancer, signed profitably with the Casino of Mar del Plata, the most luxurious summer resort of South America.

The half-million in gold cash which Tito subtracted from the family memories of Kalantan Ter-Gregorianz, was about exhausted. Tito's health was failing. That endless roaming around from one hotel to the next, that town to town meandering, together with the realization that here and there Cocaine's lovers would spring like mushrooms along the route, had gradually weakened his nerves and impoverished his blood.

He had come to America hoping that the good theatrical contracts and the money he earned for himself by purifying Madame

Kalantan of her glamorous past, would at least insure for him the exclusiveness of Cocaine's body. But the *rastaquero* acquaintance, with that greasy face of the *Gentilhomme campagnard*, had followed them through their journey from town to town with the well provided pocketbook and the sturdy persistence of his lustful desire.

Cocaine lavished her effusions upon others either for money or gratuitously: feeling that her beauty was near its end, she bustled feverishly in her search for new pleasures without losing a single day, without renouncing a single opportunity. She even yielded to men who had later shown themselves unworthy of her prodigality.

"You give them pleasure, and they don't show you the least appreciation."

"And do you suppose that I—", she said pointedly, "aim for their respect or appreciation whenever I give myself to them? Appreciation for what? I don't give myself up for their pleasure, it is for the pleasure and for the money that I can get out of them myself. What do I care about what one says about me afterwards, if in those five minutes in which the weight of his body squirmed over mine, I felt the thrill of lust? Respect . . . appreciation. . . You poor dreamer! If you hope to chain me with arguments like these, I'll advise you to try something else, for a change."

* * *

"Your beauty is shrinking", Tito, who had vainly threat-ened her with desertion, intoned deliriously. "You are old; despite your twenty-four years you look like much more, I only love you because I am welded to your very flesh, because some elective affinity, aside from your beauty, chains me to you. You are old. Perhaps you may still be able to tempt some male who will be attracted by animal lust and be pleased to possess you sexually, but never by your charm. They seek you because you have the shape and the organs of a woman, but never because of your beauty or youth. I am the only one who can still feel your fascination, I, who will still remember your declined beauty.

"You're almost the corpse of a woman. You may yet be able to attract some short-sighted fool, because of the powder and paints; but they will then turn you down, they will scorn you like so much counterfeit money. You have before you the prospects of five or six males, at the most; a few more adventures, perhaps.

"Well, Cocaine, if you don't wish me to leave you forever, give up those few adventures still remaining. I shall be devoted to you for the rest of my life; and when no one will have any more use for you, I shall be still alongside you to love you, to whisper that to me you are still as beautiful as before, to make you feel you are still as alluring as ever.

"I pledge you my entire existence.

"But in return for this pledge I ask, in the agony of your beauty, for that loyalty which you have so far denied me.

"Think that the spectre of loneliness is now haunting you. Think of the time when you shall spend your nights all alone, icy and cold, and upon awakening, you will see your flesh turned yellow and wanted by none.

"Even then I shall love you, if you spurn today those men who are still seeking you." He stopped with a sob in his voice.

Cocaine listened to him in moody silence, and her eyes were cold and dry. She said; "The idea of giving this up now frightens me".

"But do you realize what I am offering you in return?"

"Yes, I do. But I would sooner see myself alone, forsaken, tomorrow, rather than renounce my pleasure tonight. The spectre which you say will haunt my lonely nights is to me not half as hideous as the imminent reality of renunciation itself."

He strove for composure. "You miserable wretch! But have you not taken stock of what is left of you? Can't you realize that every morning you have to pluck hair around your lips? Can't

you see how flabby the skin around your neck is and that it hangs
loose like the skin around a turkey's neck."

"I do", she sighed, "But adventure still lures me".

"Think that tomorrow you will be old."

"The same goes for you, the day after tomorrow. . ."

"With my money, I shall always be able to get myself women
who are young, beautiful and fresh."

"The same goes for me, too; with my money I can get myself
males who are sturdy and healthy".

"But that's different", Tito replied heatedly. "I've always
done the paying. It is always the man who pays, even when he is
twenty, even when it appears that the woman gives herself up to
him for love. You, instead, you, who have always sold yourself,
will yet find out what a bitter novelty it is. You will yet find out
what a dark, ugly thing it is to buy love."

"That is something I have not yet tried. It may have its bright
sides, too. We'll see. Now let me go, because it is already nine.
My dancing act at the Casino goes on at ten fifteen. Goodbye."

* * *

The performance over, the few places which still re-mained
vacant around the *roulette* tables were seized boisterously, while
the chief *croupier,* from the top of his staff, shouted: "A little
silence, if you please."

Tito circled about the tables; types of intercontinental sirens,
men of doubtful backgrounds, ladies of a certain age and an
age that was uncertain, mothers who were still amiable; naked
virgins, with some small part of their body covered, radioactive
women, with hair combed far back, leaving a forehead that was
vast and white, underlined by two wrinkled brows; verily, cruel female faces; the first who inaugurated the fad were quite charming;
but the fad has today become as commonplace as the stereotyped
police-dogs, and the snake bracelets around the wrists and ankles.

All calm, ponderous men, they were.

The smiling *ehausseur* gathered the chips from the floor and brushed the cigarette ashes off the green cloth.

Charming gamblers all, who jotted down with bureaucratic fussiness all the numbers that had been called, to check up whenever the series repeated itself. Those who believe in the repetition of chance, are like those who pretend to apply upon future lovers the experience they have acquired through association with former loves.

In gambling and in life they invariably lose out. And still Tito couldn't find an empty place.

"I wish someone here would drop dead with an apopletic stroke," he mused. "That would leave three empty places free, at least; the dead man, of course, would have to get out, and the two next to him would have to carry him out. People, as a rule, have more sympathy for the dead than for the living."

"Thirty-one, red, odd number!"

An old woman who had been trounced thoroughly and had lost everything, refused to leave her place. Hold on to the old seat, at least.

"Selfish as a tapeworm", Tito hissed loudly.

A gentleman who sat ahead of him turned abruptly.

"Arnaudi!."

He was an old boyhood acquaintance.

What a tremendous nuisance (Oh, how pleased!) are all boyhood acquaintances! Just because you have had the bad luck of meeting them when you lacked sense, you must now tolerate them for the rest of your life, no matter in what part of the world you meet them!

"I lose these thousand pesos more", said the friend, showing him two or three stacks of chips, "and then we go."

The gambling hall, with its indefinite noise, with its radiations of somber currents, reminded Tito of those sketches appearing on texts of experimental physics, representing the iron filings which are attracted by magnets according to certain lines.

In the air, upon the dazzling green carpets, he sensed those very lines of attraction, and understood why there are people who will live and die gambling.

Gambling is merely a condensation of one's existence; life is but the quarter of an hour one spends around the roulette table; the lucky ones win; to make you win, all the gentleman at your right has to do is to distract you, or the lady at your left hold you from placing your bet the way you want; have your chair near the low series when the low series come out; enough that you catch a voice floating in the air, a number breathed by some mysterious voice, and that you play the hunch, accordingly. The joy of gambling is not in the winnings but in the emotion of living intensely.

It is the folly of entrusting one's own fate to certain numbers that are like the fractions of calculus, the shreds of mathematics. To pass from earnest toil to the whims of gambling is like leaving science to try quackery instead.

Whoever in life succeeds with the quackery of a decoction or a martingale, will never go back to the sub-cutaneous injections and to the careful business enterprises.

"Do you usually win?", inquired the friend.

"I haven't played tonight; but I always manage to lose" replied Tito. "Only retired whores play to win."

The two friends parted outside. Tito walked slowly back to his hotel. It was night. Beneath palm trees and over the iron benches lining the sea promenade, sat many spooning couples, quiet as insects in love. Every now and then the lights from speeding automobiles focused upon the lovers, and outbursts of shrill laughter floated in the air as the cars swept past.

A group of lassies passed him by, escorted by dashing youths, army officers. They talked of spiritualism and theosophy, as is done in all brigades where some intellectual miss or some fashionable male idiot strut. The senoritas interpolated their Spanish chatter with a few Portuguese words. In Italy, too, they adorn their language with French words; the French with English words; in the Rome of Horatius, the intellectuals even used Greek words.

* * *

Hearing the gravel creak under his feet, the doorman in redingote opened the door for him: in the lobby, some little brat cackled and shrieked wildly as he wrestled with his phlegmatic nurse, Tito stepped into the elevator and presently three floors disappeared beneath.

Back in his room he began pacing like a cat-kin over the soft carpets.

A gnat buzzed around and flitted here and there, pausing occasionally to rest on those skinny, fleshless legs, like those of a miss ravaged by chlorosis.

It fluttered around Tito's head, and rested upon his hand.

He frowned darkly.

That insect was deadly; it was a carrier of malaria.

He squashed it with his other hand.

But then he reflected:

"How inferior man is to an insect like this? All the insect has to do to kill a man is to sting him, while man, to kill the insect, is compelled to exert himself by crushing it."

And Maud was not back yet. Tito sat on the bed. His eyes wandered over the alarm-clock: he picked it up, wound it, put it back again, A notice was posted under the bed-lamp. He read it as he nervously filed his nails: "The price of this room will be reused if one of the principal meals (lunch or dinner) is not ta\en in the hotel".

From the elevator shaft way came a noise of pulleys and counterweights in motion.

"She's here", Tito murmured to himself. The elevator instead stopped on the floor below.

He waited a while longer thinking that it had perhaps stopped off on the floor below, and that it would presently resume its upward journey to deliver him his Maud into his arms. But instead of that he heard the elevator swing softly down, displacing the volume of air in the shaft way, with the characteristic moan of a pneumatic tube in the process of deflation.

He crossed the room and threw the window open.

The uncertain glimmer of goodness knows what city fluctuated merrily, from afar like phosphoric vapors in the night, as if it were mirrored in a convex crystal; the firmament.

Tito raised his eyes to the constellations of the austral hemisphere: groups of stars, stars like dust; fragments of stars, naive combinations of primitive jewelry; he felt the blue of night rain across his burning face; he searched anxiously for the two constellations that he had heard so much about when a boy: The Southern Cross and the Hydra; but he had the impression that the sky of the other part of the world, was as arbitrarily disordered as the sky of his homeland.

The large promenade skirting the sea dazzled with the globes of arched lamps, placed at regular intervals, against the somber background of the sea; they blazed like portholes of a huge liner that steamed along with all of its lights glowing.

Now and then, the breeze wafted with the faint accords of a faraway refrain of music, coming from some villa: it was not the breeze that carried the music, it seemed, but the music which brought to him, on that sultry night, some gust of wind. Beneath the pitch blackness of huge trees, myriads of lights shone with the carbonic glitter of a jeweled clasp over quivering tresses. Tito thrust his head out of the window, as one does when traveling by railroad in August, to seek a passing comfort from the scorching heat.

He counted the floors under him. About forty meters from the sidewalk.

A motorboat whizzed over the estuary, with guitars and lie cigarettes visible in the dark. Tito raised his eyes to see if it was not Mount Vesuvius that smoked before him.

But his Cocaine was not back yet. He closed the window, switched on the fan over the night-table and began to undress slowly.

"Aren't you in bed yet?" said Maud, entering suddenly with her hat in one hand and passing her other hand across her forehead.

"Just as you see" . . . Tito answered coldly, knotting the tassels of his pajamas around his abdomen.

"What's wrong with you, anyhow?", asked Cocaine as she strove to read on his face the reason for his ill humor.

"Where have you been till now?"

"Here's where we start all over again. Where do you suppose I was?"

'That is exactly what I am asking you", 'I went for an automobile ride".

"With whom?"

"With Arguedos."

"You mean that student?"

"Yes".

"In a car, did you say? But if he had money to buy a car he would sooner invest it in a bed at the sanitarium!"

"What do you know about it?", the woman protested. It is strange, how quickly a woman's skin reacts to the scolding, which she metes out to her lover,

"Where on earth do you expect that wretch to get a car?"

Tito insisted. "Well, if it wasn't you who loaned him the money, then I suppose it was someone else who did".

"Nobody would trust him with a shoe string",

"Perhaps he rented it",

"What did he use for money?"

"Money, of course—my money. You thought nobody would give him credit, did you? Well, damn it, I did. I loaned him one thousand pesos?

"With what guaranty?"

"Friendship".

"He'll never give you that money back".

"I know it and I don't care".

He turned white, as if he were suddenly struck.

"Then . , . it's a gift . , ." he stammered.

Her voice rose in indignation, "Call it whatever you like!"

And with this, she flung open the door that communicated with her room and disappeared.

Tito, deliberately cold and hostile, edged close to the window, and in his torment pleaded for that relief which the immensity of nightdom has never yet denied to anyone who could plead with such painful eloquence.

He drank deep, with his mouth wide open, that surge of breeze and blue that was flushing his face (a phonograph played goodness knows where). He grinned bitterly and thought: "First she sold herself for money. Now she pays for the privilege."

"She will never be loyal to me I."

The nearby phonograph stopped playing.

A nightingale chirped softly in the sleepy garden below.

From another villa came the gush of a violin.

The nightingale and the violin could not see each other, but just the same, they mingled their fits of passionate weeping as they narrated their melancholy to the breeze.

It seemed as if that nightingale, that violin, were the same ones he had heard one night in Paris, in Kalantan's villa, white, as a charnel-house.

How uniform the world is! Were it not for that ocean separating us, the road between that Paris villa and this South American hotel would no doubt be peopled with nightingales and violins, everywhere!

The phonograph resumed its music. They had changed the record, which now drowned all other sounds with its own batrachian gargling.

The phonograph is the frog in that great puddle which is the city.

Much as he tried, Tito was not able to sleep that night. He heard the shrill tingling of bells; once calling for the waiter: twice for the waitress; thrice for the porter. . .

He heard stealthy footsteps moving across the ribbon-shaped carpet in the hall.

From the estuary came the shriek of a siren, marking some arrival (how sad!) or some departure (what a delusion!).

He switched on the light: just a hotel room, with the number on the door and notices posted everywhere, prices: "the management is not responsible for valuables lost or stolen, unless checked". How annoying! He turned the light oft again.

He had the illusion of falling asleep, but he couldn't. He had the impression that he was leaning with his back over a tall balustrade, which would, the next moment, break in two and plunge him, head first, into a gulf of blackness.

But as he dashed into space, he would suddenly awaken with his arms widely extended.

In the wardrobe, style Louis XV, a moth beat its monotnous call. Tito remembered that way back in his hometown they called that insect the clock of death, because they believe that the noise it makes is really the forerunner of death.

Instead, it is love. It is a love duel, it is the love call of the two sexes, as they beat their heads against the wood of their bedsteads.

"And yet men will destroy them because they are parasites", thought Tito, "Is not man perhaps the most dreadful phenomenon of animal and vegetable parasitism".

"Maud, Cocaine!"

Cocaine, frail little woman to me so tremendous and necessary; venom that is deadly and vivifying; frail woman to whom I am attached as I would be to a parasite.

His mind quickly filled with things long forgotten, distant notions, memories of his boyhood days.

Like the parasite: a tiny animal that wraps its mate with a suction cupping the size of its body.

And they stay united forever that way.

Forever, an expression that is used by every lover. And yet a dream which is only realized by those tiny insects lost in parasitology texts.

Maud and I, too, have interlocked each other with a mutual suction cupping.

Thus thought Tito in his delirium, while the worm in the wood continued to sound its love call. Tito preferred to think that it was the clock of death beating.

"Everything surrounding us is death. We live at the expense of the *humus*, which is death. Even all living ideas, modern forerunners, live through the will a *humus* with deceased ideas.

"What boredom, life! To see men. . . How beautiful life would be were it not for men. To see birds free to procreate openly; the woods invade the city; the green grass grow on cafe tables; chickens that lay eggs and hatch them upon the altars of forgotten cathedrals; mushrooms growing upon the parchment of libraries; thunderbolts falling over deserted nuptial beds. . . Man has even chained them to his will by tracing the course the bolts should follow!

"Oh, to be able at last to see horses feed on wall-flowers and run free through public parks?"

The elevator door, slamming rudely, roused him. He put his hand over his heart.

"Heart, lungs, blood. . . I am tired of knowing that my body is like a chemical laboratory, destined to renew and feed my protoplasm. I am nothing but a compound of phosphorus, nitrogen, hydrogen, oxygen arid carbonic acid, I am tired of looking myself over from top to bottom, with eyes popping out of my sockets. I am tired of love—tired of burning up my phosphorus, nitrogen, hydrogen, oxygen and carbonic compound.

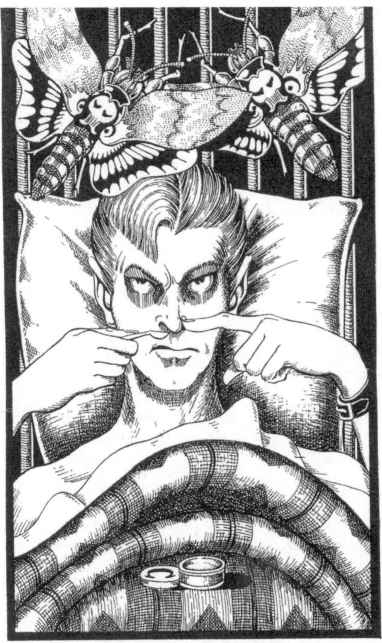

"What boredom, life!

All night long Tito raved, obsessed with nonsense of this kind.

The hours kept striking from the belfry towers, from the schools, from the stations. Then a rooster began to crow; another answered, while a third interjected.

"How they repeat themselves, the roosters; and how those clocks imitate themselves, too; like the nightingales, like the phonograph, like the fiddles!"

He squirmed and twisted around the sheets. He put his head at the foot of the bed, then lowered one leg, then the next one, to the floor. He switched on the fan and slipped into his clothes.

He rang twice. A waitress called. He rang four times: the porter appeared. At one o'clock he ordered the porter to get his trunks ready. Only his trunks. Those belonging to Madame will stay! He instructed the porter to reserve a cabin for him on the first liner leaving for Europe.

"It will be kind of hard to make any reservations today, sir", hazarded the porter timidly. "However, I will try telephoning to Buenos Aires."

"Whenever the cabins of a liner are sold out", Tito answered, "a porter of a great hotel like this should be always able to find one that is not yet taken, which is more often the best one they have aboard."

A few hours later, toward noon time, Cocaine entered his room without knocking. An Anglo-Saxon lady, recently arrived, had installed herself in the quarter left vacant by Tito and was then busy soaping the abundant fat around her plethorical snout.

When the astonished lady protested, Maud muttered a few shy apologies and rang for the waiter.

"The *caballero* has left the hotel about half an hour ago." Maud did not answer.

But like the keen psychologist that he was, the waiter added: "The boat is not leaving before sunset, and if Madame desires it

I can go and call him back. By cab, I can bring him back within the next eight hours."

"Bring me", answered Maud, "a few pieces of butter, instead".

The waiter bowed and moved to go when Maud recalled him. "And some honey, too".

PITIGRILLI
KOKAIN
Roman

11

The sea was calm. Aboard, even before the steamer got under way, he became acquainted at once with a famous Hungarian scientist, who was also a polyglot and who sputtered as he spoke, like the irked maggot and scrappy landladies, and like the grasshopper would, in self defense.

He devoted his time to important studies on the psychology of woman of the various races in relation to the weight of her organs.

German female: heart, one kilogram; brain, 825 grams; height, 1 meter, 70 centimeters. . . .

Austrian: heart, 950 grams: brain, 850; hair, 65 centimeters.

American: Just a lot of *spleen*. . . .

He also met a senorita from Granada, who stumbled into his cabin by mistake.

That mistake cost Tito two hundred *pesos,* which the enterprising and black-eyed senorita exacted in the act of delivery.

"They have nerve, those Spanish skirts", Tito said, addressing his remark to the Hungarian scientist.

"Extraordinarily so. About 2 kilos' worth", the erudite answered soberly, as though he seriously believed in what he was saying.

Like the Kings in fairy tales, the latter had two daughters who resembled each other to the dot; they were undoubtedly daughters of the same mother. One of them was chubby, rubicond, florid; the other, a trifle smaller, a trifle tinier, more refined in her appearance; they were both, however, of "the same type. They resembled each other as an orange and a tangerine would.

Tito peeled them both clean. He led the usual life aboard; speculated upon the approximate height of the boat from the waterline; strolled slowly about, questioning officers on longitude and latitude, the wireless, the compass; stared at the clouds scattered by the wind; set his watch on that of the ship's staff; taught others about seasickness remedies; basked in the sunshine stretched over a long lounging chair, and let the wind waft into his face like a caress made by the touch of shy tresses; stole into the wireless cabin and bothered the operator with a lot of stupid questions; listened to the imaginary recounting of sea rescues never staged; ordered the barman to shake some complicated cocktails. Skirting the Brazilian coast he sought the butterflies that fluttered in Kalantan's halls, the beautiful Armenian siren, in her villa at the Champs Elysees; passing the Equator he joined in the usual celebration and pocketed a cork as a souvenir; he landed for a few hours on the Senegalese coast and inspected the local brothels, with the sky as the roof.

During the first few days of the trip he bought a monkey from a Chilean merchant who exhibited on deck his loquacious merchandise of parrots, monkeys, chaf-finches and gold-finches swathed in fancy vests. At the end of the trip he gave the monkey back, as a gift, to the man from whom he bought it. The Chilean took it back as a favor. All those who buy monkeys during the first days of a trip, generally return them before landing. One thus speaks of simians that have made the trip ten times over, in this way.

They introduced him to some respectable woman, whom he entertained with that usual affable chit-chat that follows all introductions.

"But, Madam, you have such a big boy, and you are still so young!"

"Oh, I married when I was still a child", said she, very modestly. Even the respectable woman who was still so very young and yet had a boy who was so big, strayed carelessly into the common ditch of his erstwhile loves.

He ate with a healthy appetite, although the grief of having left Maud behind filled him with a vague inquietude. There are people who do not eat when they are anguished morally. Their moral pain is all in the intestines.

Tito, instead, never ate as heartily as when he suffered with the pangs of love.

He wandered very often into the engine room, and there, amid the deafening roar of the engines, he would contem-plate the firemen, stripped to their waists, bronzed, athletic-looking. Those powerfully built and sturdy males would make the mouths of virgins water with desire!

He also met a lady who, knowing him to be a newspa-per-man, and therefore something close to literature, begged him for a motto to be engraved upon the buckle of her garter.

Aboard one is not kept waiting long before he is admitted into the heart of a woman. During a trip of forty to sixty days, perhaps; but never in those lasting a mere fortnight.

The bleak Parisian days flashed to his mind; the lonely me-andering along the deserted streets, up to the slaughter-house and down again through the heart of slum-land, toward the neat and orderly Pere Lachaise cemetery, when his depressed senses envi-sioned Maud promenading stark naked in the home of someone else, without pangs of regret. And now instead he felt the rush of lustful virility searing through him. It was the excitement of the sea. The scent of the infinite is a treacherous aphrodisiac. It stimulates the sexual appetite.

One night he sat in the *fumoir* before a lady: the woman's shapely limbs were wrapt in pearl-gray silk stockings, that shone with the brilliance of fish just out of the water.

His keenly observant eyes rested upon them.

"What are you doing?", inquired the woman.

"I'm praying," Tito replied.

"1 thought you were looking at my legs", smiled the woman, looking up at him with a naughty twinkle in her eye.

'That's the way atheists pray", informed the imperturbable Tito.

That same night Tito went to pray in her cabin.

The sea was very calm.

Everyone knows that a man and a woman, not bound by matrimonial, ties, are threatened with endless annoyances if they are caught in any compromising positions aboard.

This, of course, is nothing but a clever trick which all steamship companies, generally so considerate in providing amusement and attractions for all worthy passengers, have invented. After the gipsy orchestra (the caricaturists of music), came the Holy Mass, the daily newspaper with all the latest news (those picked up before the boat left port), then the gymnasium, and now they have invented the penalty against all love smugglers, so as to make the practice more enticing for the class deluxe passengers, first-class passengers, and, of course, even those of the second-class, provided they tip well.

But nothing doing for the third-class passengers. Without the tipping, that would be immoral. Immediate arrest for all third-class offenders.

"You seem to be flirting with all the women you meet", said hi table companion one day, a rabbi from Warsaw who was on his return trip from America with a delicious soubrette, as delicate as an iris, and a lot of the money, which he had collected in the name of the Zionist cause.

"Yes", answered Tito. "For army officers a duel is considered a misdemeanor; but the offense would be still greater if they refused to fight it out. The same thing happens in matters of gallantry; if you express your wants to a woman, she feels insulted, but she would feel twice as insulted if you do not want her at all."

"You must have had quite a number of women, I say", said the rabbi from Warsaw. "I should think you know them well."

"Well, I've had my share of love affairs," Tito admitted modestly. "But to think that a man who has had a lot of women is an expert in matters of feminine psychology, is wrong; it would be like expecting a museum watchman to express himself critically over matters of art. After all, what docs one do to win a woman? Nothing, all you have to do is to let her win you. The man never does the picking. He thinks he does, but he is the one who is picked, instead. The man who pays courtship to a woman, does not conquer her, but he simply puts himself in the position of being conquered. Do you want an instance? Observe the animal species. The male is in the majority of cases more attractive than the female. What does that mean? That it is the male who is being picked. The female is not sought; in fact, it doesn't have to beautify itself, whereas the male does; look how dazzling the bird of paradise is, and how wretched the female is in comparison."

"It's true!", the rabbi admitted, stroking his moustaches that projected horizontally, as if to indicate the cardinal points. "But the really hard thing is not to win the woman, but to leave her".

"Nonsense!", Tito argued. "The man is not the one who throws the woman over, but it is he who puts himself into the condition of being thrown. If, however, there should be some exceptional cases of a man wanting to sever relationships, there is always some infallible way in which he can withdraw from the picture gracefully; and that is, to say to her point-blank, in a threatening voice: "I know everything!".

"Know what 'everything'?" the rabbi marveled.

"Even the most guiltless among women, believe me, has had sometime or other, during her past, I don't care how far back, something which might be that 'everything' about which you ask."

Two English misses, sitting opposite them, listened quietly, with noses shaped like clarinet mouthpieces and the wild staring eyes of heifers at the passage of an express train.

The rabbi from Warsaw was a charming person. He tittered
at the caricature Tito made of the Bible during one of his periods
of cocaine frenzy, and, in return, confidentially explained to him
that the money collected in America would go toward the re-
building of the Israel kingdom in Palestine, that the Jews who are
at present dispersed around the world may have a home to go to.

"Will you, too, go to live in Palestine?". Tito asked.

"No, not I", the rabbi answered. "I'm all right where I am in
Warsaw."

"But how about the persecutions, the pogroms. . . . "

"Tommyrotl", laughed the rabbi "These are only rumors
which we, Polish Jews, circulate. We make everybody believe
that the Jews of Poland are living a dreadful life, so as to make
the rest of the Jews stay out."

During the twenty-two day trip, Tito had paid court to five
different women, his senses excited by the sun and by the scent
of the unruffled sea. He appeased his senses, and by appeasing
them he killed the memory of Maud, who drifted farther away
with every revolution of the ship's propeller. Love (an erotic
attraction) decreases, like the force of gravity does, in proportion
with the square of distance.

When they neared shore, Tito regretted leaving the Dutch
miss of the perfect curves, round and sweet like her Daddy's
marmalades; the respectable lady who had a boy who was already so big, because she had married when she was still a child;
the professor's two daughters so like and unlike each other, as
would be a tangerine and an orange; the lady of the dazzling legs
who wanted a motto engraved upon her garter; that dry Hebrew
joker, the rabbi from Warsaw, with his girl friend who was as
delicate as iris, but dumb as elder-tree blossoms. . .

He regretted having to part from all those women whom he
would never see again. And yet he experienced no regret for Cocaine, the Cocaine of his thought, whom he never wanted to see

again in his life; Cocaine, who at that moment squirmed in the
arms of that multi-millionaire *rasquatero* who must have oozed
castor oil if you squeezed his snout, and over the keel-shaped
chest of that Arguedos student, who bid vainly for a semi-gratuitous bed in a sanitarium.

* * *

When he boarded a train for Turin he remembered very little of
the trip, except for a few cigarettes given him by some generous
fellow-passenger and a little tropical tan over his skin.

And his thoughts darted back to Cocaine, the petite Cocaine,
whom he had left on the other side of the Atlantic: his Cocaine
who exhaled a fragrance which he had never been able to detect
on the flesh of other women; his Cocaine, upon whose flesh all
fragrances reacted prodigiously as in no other feminine skin;
Cocaine, Maud, from whom one flees and to whom one returns,
venon-woman, whom one hates and loves, because she is exaltation and ruin at the same time, grief and ebriety, the most delicious of all known deaths and a life most terrible.

In Turin, cradle of Italian independence and custodian of
the Holy Shroud, he saw many familiar faces, the usual things.
Hundreds of martins continued till dusk, ruffling their wings and
weaving the paths of their flight into a disordered skein, as they
skimmed over the towers of *Palazzo Madama.* He saw those
same people mounting in a trolley, at the usual starting point, to
get off at the usual stops, at the usual hours. He met also a few
friends, a few women who, as he happened to think, had once
belonged to him. We sometimes meet a woman whom we have
once loved for an hour or for a month, and of whom we have
almost forgotten. But it doesn't always happen that way. That act
seems to have such little importance. Nothing is left in us of her
flesh, of her fire, of her breath. Nothing!

And yet, if we hear that the woman we love today, belonged
for only five minutes to someone else, we feel, even though

many years have since elapsed, an unbearable grief. The act she
has performed with others seems to us like some unforgettable
contamination: we feel as if her very blood has been polluted,
that her flesh has been ill-used, defiled beyond repair by that very
act, by that same act, which we hardly remember ever having
performed with that very woman we meet on the sidewalk.

Jealousy is a fever originating in some stupid, groundless
exaltation of our thoughtless brain. Jealousy is a phenomenon of
auto-suggestion.

Your woman has gone to bed with Ipsilon, let us say. You
hate Ipsilon, and you hate her; before your eyes you have always
the vision of your woman and Ipsilon interlocked in that act
which dismays you so.

And yet, you, too have once cheated on your woman and did in
bed with Madame S. exactly what Ipsilon did with your woman.

Well, what is there left in your flesh, in your soul, of that
woman? Nothing, Nothing more than Ipsilon's kisses over the
flesh of your woman.

An auto-suggestive phenomenon, therefore. Do you want a
proof? If you do not see that individual, you imagine him to be
hideous, repugnant, loathsome, and you feel you would even kill
him if you met him.

But, on the other hand, if you should chance to see a picture
of this man, you would begin to understand that you can look at
him without feeling the least disturbed.

And if he should ever be introduced to you in person, you
would, mind you, greet him with a broad smile on your lips; you
would look straight into his eye, without faltering, and if you
happen to have reached that degree of perfection which I have at-
tained, you would most likely tap him cordially upon his stomach
and say: "Good for you!"

Through reasonings through education you will be able, in
a not too distant future, to make men realize how groundless

jealousy really is. The day will come when our beloved children (the cuckolds of another day), will be trained for the cuckold role they will play and will no longer regard the fact as humiliating, because during that time we shall have made some injections of common sense into them, some anti-cuckold vaccinations, so to speak.

Tito's jealousy had grown stronger now that there were no males around, stronger than it was twenty days before when he met them at every step and caught them sniffing in the air, to catch the last invisible sparks released by Maud's body.

* * *

He tried many women. They were beautiful, they were young, they were experienced. But they were not Cocaine!

He poured Cocaine's perfume over them, the delicious Avatar, over their flesh, but the odor which they emanated was not like that of Cocaine.

He roamed around Turin's most eccentric quarters, as he used to do way back in Paris in the bleak old days, gone by. But as he walked he felt the burden of his body weighing on his legs. It was the first sign of old age. It is the time In life when a man begins donning somber brown cloches.

Tucked away in some forgotten corner of his travel bag he found that familiar knitted green necktie, with broad blue stripes, and he wore it one morning as he set out to call upon his friend the monk, in that convent which was like a sort of Foreign Legion to the victims of sentimental failures, A ray of sunshine beaming over his necktie enlivened the spent Avatar aroma. If you only know how perfumed are the tears that roll down the fresh cheeks of a woman, and how gloriously scented a cravat becomes when a woman sobs over it!

In the convent's garden some swallows fluttered, skimming the earth and then taking to the sky, as if to wipe their beaks against the clouds.

A poor monk tossed small bits of bread to the sparrows, humble like himself. His friend, the monk, moved forward with the sleeves of his cowl extended and greeted him a brother in Christ, Then he said, "Yes, I am happy".

And he advised him to take the cowl.

"But that's not an easy thing to do . . ."

"Very easy, my friend! Are you a Mason?"

"No."

"Well, it's like being initiated in a Masonic Lodge."

He told him how the Good Shepherd rejoiced in finding his lost sheep.

"I don't blame him" said Tito, "because if he hadn't found it, he would have one less to milk and shear."

Together they visited his cell, the library, the laboratory of an old monk who delighted in the study of coleoptera and butterflies.

He drew him into the church.

"I'm sorry", said the little monk to Tito," that I cannot offer you any vermouth, as I used to in Paris. But if a Mass will do . . ."

"That's fine", Tito accepted, "the Mass will do."

"Do you want plain or High Mass?."

"Which is quickest?"

"Both last the same time".

"Will you sing it for me?"

"Naturally."

"Then go ahead and sing it".

And he attended the service.

"Do you want the Benediction?"

"No, thanks. I'm all right the way I am".

They visited the dining hall.

"How's the food?"

"The food here is table *d'hote*. Only sick people here eat *a la carte*."

The little monk explained to him that we all must love Christ because He had sacrificed himself for the good of humanity. And Tito replied that the rats and the rabbits that we sacrificed experimentally upon the physiological laboratories, for the sake of humanity, are then like so many Jesus Christs.

Horrified, the little monk entreated him not to curse, and he very patiently explained that a rat saves nobody, while Jesus Christ has redeemed mankind.

"Then a fireman who gives his life to save a man is more admirable than Christ, for there is greater merit to die while saving a man, than saving billions and billions of them".

The monk did not seem convinced (perhaps he was convinced from before), and couldn't find anything better to say but insisted that Tito take the minor religious orders. And he waxed so persuasive that the latter would not dare to call him crazy when leaving, but promised: "I'll think it over."

He answered, in other words, like a woman, who, in wanting to leave a store without buying a thing, would say:

"I will call later, with my husband."

* * *

For two or three nights he went to a cafe on Po street, familiar to his student life, and there he again saw the dialectical poet, a great consumer of unsweetened coffee, and the old painter who reproduced on canvas landscapes from Mars and fantastic flowers of Saturn, because he did not know how to paint the flora and the landscapes of his own homeland. Every one an artist, these boys! People are loaded with diplomas. When someone has been able to put a little mud together and shape it into a nose, he is forthwith consecrated an artist; all another one needs do is to have four books and a microscope in order to become a scientist. But unfortunately, with that same fickleness with which glory is built, it is also destroyed.

They told him that Pietro Nocera, his colleague in Paris journalism, was also in town. In fact, the two met a few days later.

"Yes," said Nocera, "I heard all about that half million haul
of yours. It didn't surprise me a bit! There is nothing astonishing
about a man who steals. And since man is a potential thief, according to circumstances, I don't differentiate much between the
man who has stolen and the one who has yet to steal."

"That was just a chance I had", Tito explained. "I have always been honest in the past. I guess you understand that."

"Of course, I do". He smiled faintly, tolerantly. "My friend
Mark Ramperti says that honesty is very often shrewdness in
disguise. What are you doing now?"

"I live in a furnished room: I still have a little money on the
side. When that is gone I will either commit suicide or I will take
shelter in a convent."

"Feeling the call of Faith?"

"No. Religion reminds me of those great firms, staked by the
government, for the exploitation of mines one has never seen. All
other religions wage a little war upon it, but not any too openly,
of course, so as not to attract the people's attention to the fact
that they, too, are founded upon mines which never existed. But
since the Almighty is the honorary president, everybody takes
them seriously. Perhaps, I, too, will someday take one of them
very seriously, especially when you figure that I have nothing to
lose in the bankrupt speculation. And what have you been doing
in Paris since we left each other? And why did you come back to
Italy?"

"I fell in love with a woman who was a trifle vulgar, but
whom I liked just the same through some little faults she had; but
they kept growing, and some of them I did not like very much;
I tried to induce her to reason, tried to polish her up a bit, with
a few restoring orthopedic lectures, but they didn't work; say,
if you expect to refine a woman with honeyed words it's like

dousing a chestnut with sugar and expecting it to yield candied chestnuts.

"I reacted to that by falling in love with a highbrow woman (blue blood guaranteed under chemical test): of very ancient aristocracy; and she was even beautiful But I learned that in every woman, be she superior or inferior, there are three ingredients: nobility, prostitute and servant. The proportion is the only thing that varies, but the substance remains the same. In the superior woman you will find ninety-three parts of nobility, but as to the other seven parts. . . .

"Unfortunately, they do not know how to conceal those seven parts. You hear them talk with the air of great minds; every thought uttered sounds as vast and as pure and as sublime as the rainbow itself; they become fussy and prudish before the little miseries of life. When they step out with a man, all public conveyances seem all too vulgar for their downy softness; but when alone, they ride very cheaply in trolley cars, and like it. If you escort them into a tearoom, the tip you leave the waiter, even though it may exceed the cost of the beverage, will seem all too niggardly before their generous eyes. But if they should stroll into that same tearoom unescorted, they would leave a tip which you would most likely feel ashamed to give to an organ-grinder.

"If you should lose your pocketbook, they titter; and act in an insulting manner if you show that you are worried about it; but when it is they who save to buy a shoe string, they will bargain stubbornly, heckle heatedly to save a few cents, as quibbling diplomats would."

"That's right", interrupted Tito. "These, of course, are things, which I can teach you. But these are all very charming faults to have, when you find them in a superior woman, because they are the corresponding pits to their dizzy intellectual minds. I beg of you to conclude."

"And so I left that woman in Paris, and came back to Turin. I am now in the real estate business. Want to buy a patch of pasture ground?"

"A patch in the graveyard, perhaps. But we can talk about that later. Got a woman lover here?"

"Yes", answered Nocera. "Just the average sort of a woman, she dresses very simply and acts likewise; but under that modest appearance she has many hidden treasures of delicate ingenuity, and beneath the sober dress she wears lingerie of the finest fabric."

Tito saw in a flash the lingerie of mauve crepe de chine, ornamented with fine organdy plaiting.

"Just like the homes of Mohammedans", continued Tito, "that are very plain, square, and calcimined with lime on the outside; while they are rich with fine mosaic workmanship, gardens, spouting fountains on the inside."

"Aren't you going back to Paris?"

"No, Tito, I am not, but I gather that neither will you. You, me, your friend the waiter, who is now the monk, your Maud, your . . . what's her name? . . . Calomelan . . . ."

"Kalantan", Tito corrected him.

"We are wallowing together, led on by a common fate; we are like dying dogs that go into hiding under the beds, under the tables; we are like wildcats, tired of roaming, they go back home to die. We are all members of some tragic, somber society in process of dissolution; daunted at last! You, me, your waiter friend who, for one reason or another, have left Paris, the great thoroughfares, the great appearances, the stupefying intoxications, because we feel the end of our desires approaching: not to have any more desires, to cease being curious, is to die. Your Armenian siren, if I remember well what you told me about her many times, completed her cycle of vice quite rapidly, to take refuge in love which was pure, a chaste frenzy as you used to express it

Your Maud, instead, pursued the simple and unadorned stairway
of clean love, but parted midway in quest of vice, which lured
her on with a prospect more seducing, and even had her organs
mutilated that she might enjoy to the fullest her sexual tourna-
ments. Our lives are but a cascade of ideas; your waiter friend,
who was an atheist, has suddenly turned mystic."

"Don't you believe it! He wears a cowl, all right; but in himself he despises it!"

"Better still! Because of his need to shriek from the crush and
thunder of his spiritual unrest, he chooses the monastic seclusion without having any faith, which is like becoming somberly
resigned before some undeserved punishment. Our life today is
but a rush of uninterrupted passions; for a long time you have
wavered undecided between two women, and because of your in-
tensity of sentiment you have loved them both at the same time.

"You say that Maud has grown old; so even she has joined
the rest of us in our mad race to the end.

"We all kill ourselves, in many different ways, in a paroxysm
of silent agony, and we die chained to our frailty, even though our
heart keeps beating. Do you remember what that good devil, that
charming editor-in-chief, that alcoholic who, rather than because
of any innate desire, got drunk because of system, method and
conviction. What? Don't you remember what he said at the Cafe
Richelieu the day we introduced you to Madame Kalantan?

He said: "Women are a lot of wandering magnetic bodies,
with fools rushing after them, speaking of glory and ideals. To
avoid seeing this ugly thing before my eyes, I, a drunkard by
conviction—drink, drink, and kill myself I'm sure, we all kill
ourselves. All of us, men of our times. And the spreading cocaine
venom is but a symbol of the death to which we all succumb.
Cocaine is not merely the hydrochlorate of cocaine; it is also
the fierce and subtle and sweet death—truly, a thing of black
shadows, like some nameless cataclysm, which we inflict upon

ourselves voluntarily, with different voices and different words, while waiting for the consummation of our fate."

They continued to walk until they came abreast of a dwelling.

"Well, here's where I live, on the second floor. Come up when you feel like it . . . . Goodbye."

Tito, alone, started walking home. In a trunk he found the funeral urns and the monstrance. The urns were round and iridescent like soap bubbles, and in the monstrance, the picture of Maud, stark naked, still stood out bright and radiant.

He removed it and put it into his pocket, to have it always on him. And he went out again.

* * *

He came back a few minutes or a few hours later, moved by a determination which was firm and resolute; to become a monk, to join his friend in the convent where all the spiritual failures gathered.

"I will dedicate my time to the study of butterflies, just like that old monk did; an insect is far more elegant than the most elegant of women; there is greater dazzle in a butterfly's wing than in the shops of Parisian jewelers; during ambassadorial receptions.

I have noticed a lot of discordance; but never upon the wings of insects!

"I will take care of the orchard: I will witness the miracle of the sprouting seed, that peeps out with its verdured smile over the earth.

"It is as marvelous as the sweet mystery of love, and it unfolds without cowardliness.

"I am going to raise a beautiful beard.

"A huge beard that's full of impressive graveness.

"A flowing beard that will be the headquarters of all my butterflies and all my coleoptera. I will never again use cocaine, not even when I have a tooth to pull.

"Tomorrow at this time I will knock at their door. Day after tomorrow I will be wearing sandals; not everything at once, of course; but I will wear something, anyway. Probably it will be the cordon around the loins. The first thing they give soldiers is a spoon and a porringer.

"And in eight days I will feel as if I've been a monk all my life".

Someone knocked: "Can I come in?"

It was the landlady with a radiogram. The tense look relaxed.

"I am wiring you from aboard the 'S.S. Caronia'. Amon my way to Genoa but will stop eight days at Dakarto dance at Governor's palace beg you meet me Dakar. I love you.

Cocaine".

Tito took a sheet of paper and wrote:

"Maud Fabrege, danseuse, S.S, Caronia; via Buenos-Aires-Genoa: Am leaving for Dakar with first steamer desire you infinitely.

Tito".

And he dashed to the telegraph office.

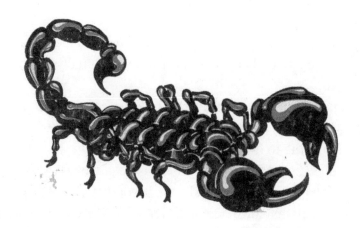

12

"You can still see Genoa", said a table companion of his as he handed him the twelve-power prismatic binocular. "In thirty minutes well be on the high seas. Where are you bound for?"

"I am going to Dakar. And you?"

"I'm going to Theresina."

"Who's Theresina?"

"It's a Brazilian town. I'm the owner of a big plant where I make food extracts of my own invention."

"What are they good for?"

"It's a novelty which I shall launch throughout the whole world in six months from today. A most amazing thing. You know that we have flower extracts from which we prepare toilet water: rosewater, vervain, carnation; and we also have fruit extracts, like citron, raspberry, tangerine, from which we manufacture syrups. But fruits and flowers have nothing to do with my case; mine are all chemical syntheses, extracted from tar. Well, I've invented special essences which, poured over bread and flour, would give these ingredients the taste of certain familiar foods; the illusion is complete: Thus you will have breaded-veal-cutlet extract served with young potatoes; roast-beef, rare or well done, as you like it, served with truffles; roast chicken, served with asparagus tips, A few drops of my extracts and pronto—dinner is ready!"

The sea was not as unruffled as during the last trip. "If you'll pardon me, I am going to retire to my cabin", stammered Tito, turning suddenly pale as he brought his hand over the haunch bone, like the dying Meleagrus, The sea was beginning to work on him.

"Aren't you interested in what I am telling you?", the Theresina chemist resented it.

"After eating, it sort of nauseates me to hear food mentioned."

And without going further into the subject, he vanished into his cabin, and did not come out again until eight days later, to land upon the aromatic Senegalese coast.

* * *

Dakar.

Along the wharf, amid the throng of negro longshoremen, flaunted Arab barracans and the light uniforms of European army officers, over whose beaming faces the cork helmet shed a black shadow, making them look like dominoes.

Cocaine? Not here. Her white line would have been readily recognized, resplendent under the dazzling parasol disc.

After all landing formalities had been cleared, he took the road that lay straight ahead of him: a Berber settlement to the left, and a European one to the right; in the background a white minaret sprung up out of an oasis into the vermilion sky.

Senegalese soldiery, khaki-clad Europeans, Arabian bazaars, non-commissioned officers, loaded with galloons; negroes of indefinite age squatted peacefully over leaf mattings before their *tukuls* and puffed imperturbably at their *narghile*.

Two negroes accosted Tito and, speaking in broken French offered to shine his shoes and shave him for a few cents, Tito rejected the offer. After a few steps he saw a decently attired man who suffered, upon a chair, the simultaneous vexations of a bootblack and a barber.

Tito finally found the only presentable looking hotel. The polyglot doorman informed him that Miss Maud Fabrege honored the hotel with her presence and, in fact, occupied suite 9-17.

Tito figured: nine and seventeen, equals twenty-six; divided by two, it makes thirteen. That means good luck.

* * *

"My love, you come at a very bad moment, In about an hour I have to be at the officers' mess to attend a reception given in my honor: and I am unable to make the paint stick to my lips. It's so terribly hot in this country! Pierina, in that flat trunk you will find a finer pair of stockings for me; can't you see how heavy these are? Look! They are all right for ice-skating. Well, it doesn't matter, give me what you have, but hurry."

She looked at Tito, while Pierina knelt before her to put her stockings on'

"I see you're looking quite well. You haven't kissed me, yet, I am going to give you lots of kisses when I come back; but not now; I am not able to make my lip-rouge sack: think I got uglier?"

"On the contrary."

"Oh, I know, you will not tell me, but I know it just the same. And yet, look, there's a wire over on that table."

Tito picked up the telegram,."Read it aloud."

Tito read:

"Barbamus Falabios Tagiko Ramungo Bombay 200,000 Viagaros Wolff."

Then he asked:

"Is this Esperanto?"

"No. Evidently you are not familiar with the code of telegraphic abbreviations; it's a vocabulary they use in com-mer-ce: the senderhhhhhhh of this wire is a wealthy rug merchant from Bombay, and his name is Wolff. And that *Barbamus Falabios*, and so on and so forth, means that if I go right away to him, he will pay me for my *Ramungo,* that is my precious and delicate merchandise, two thousand francs, beside all of the round trip expenses."

"And what did you answer?"

"That the *Ramungo* is retiring from business. Poor devil, that's going to make him suffer a lot, because he loves me, but I have gotten to a point where I can stand neither him nor any other man any longer: the only one I still love a little is you; I love you like a brother, like a son, and I send to the devil all the *Barbamus Falabios* in the world, I have renounced him, who would have been quite willing to go and live with me in Italy, He said to me:

"From Bombay we shall visit Persia, Arabia, Assyria, the Northern coast of Africa, and then we can settle down in Italy; it is the journey pursued by the swallows on their return trip home'. Because he is even a poet, my merchant is. It's now four o'clock, I'll be back at the hotel at six-thirty, and we will dine together. After that I am going to dance at the French Consulate. You'll go along with me. So, I'll see you later. Goodbye, in the meantime."

Tito followed her with his eyes as, with a hip movement altogether too soft, she crossed the sun-baked streets, that burned with dust.

"Pierina", said Tito, "do you think that through a strong recommendation on your part, they could be prevailed upon to get a bath prepared for me?"

"I was just corning to get your orders", answered a waiter, wih an appearance almost Parisian. "But you will have to wait a little while, sir."

"For the water to get hot?"

"No, to let it cool of! a bit, sir."

When the cake of ice had melted, Tito stretched himself in the bathtub, and remained there for an hour.

Then, slowly, slowly, slowly, he began dressing, while now and then he paused to sip a green, iced beverage.

Maud Fabrege, dancer, came back loaded with heat and roses.

* * *

The concert hall at the Governor's palace had the blue sky for a ceiling, rich with stars, as if they had been raked from all over the firmament and had been collected in the space of that small rectangle overhead.

When, almost unnoticed, Tito arrived, the guests had already taken their places; European army officers so blackened by the sun that they would have passed for so many natives, except for the gold-gallooned khaki uniform that distinguished them; the town's notables, solemnly shrouded in dazzling white barracans: some wore silken turbans over their heads, strapped leggings; the Innocuous poniard thrust into the white sash. The bare arms of the ladies, a few of them were draped, dangled upon the luxurious, rustling silk. From all those men and women there breathed forth, rose and rushed heavenward heavily laden whiffs of air; as if the earth wanted to give back to the sky the thermic energy it had borrowed. A small orchestra, composed of negro cello players, led by a conductor who was almost white, clad in a tuxedo almost stylish, stirred beneath a stage surrounded by palms and fiabells.

The Governor's servants, scampering here and there, served rapidly melting ice-cream on tinkling trays.

The tropical heat and the local coloring are much more charmingly represented in the imitations of Paris which they put on in the underground night *tabarins.*

Tito glanced at the program: and since an English juggler, an Egyptian hypnotist and a German singer preceded Maud, he went out into the street.

In the dark, the small market-square fermented with rotten vegetables and fruits. In a cafe where he ordered some iced tea, he found a newspaper from Marseilles.

Beside him sat a Senegalese sergeant, full of medals and golden hieroglyphics; he was waiting for the absinthe to sip through. A French soldier, of the nonchalant boulevardier youth type, entered with an elastic swagger and sat down.

The Senegalese sergeant rises and starts admonishing him; "Why didn't you salute me?"

And the Parisian soldier, flashing a contemptuous look in the direction of the gallooned negro:

"Don't you bother me, you old fogey!"

"Here, here." the Senegalese protested, pointing to the stripes over the sleeve.

"That? That is all junk," answered the gallant Parisian.

And he proceeded to order a mug of beer. The non-commissioned officer of the many stripes and the many medals was so taken aback that he did not know what to answer, so he walked back to his table where the filtered absinthe awaited him.

He drank it with tropical sternness.

Tito walked out into the street. From a sort of a hut came the sound of guitars and castanets, and the voice of a Spanish entertainer, singing:

"Donde vas con manton de Manila?

Donde vas con vastido chines?"

A sort of a *regisseuyr* invited him with smearing politeness to enter the *Variete*.

The performance had just started.

A boy sold him some oranges.

Everything in Africa tastes as if it were cooked, burnt; the flowers smell like hot house samples; the flesh of women tastes as if it were cooked, boiled; and when you bite into a fruit, you feel in your mouth the warm, sweetish savor of pastry.

He traced the road back, re-entered the concert hall of the Governor's palace.

The German singer, blonde like an egg-punch, sang, to the score of the Merry Widow, the melancholy verses of Alfred de Musset:

". . . Quand je mourrai,

plantez un saule au clmetiere".

The audience, composed of intellectual native ladies, applauded with a good deal of sweating and enthusiasm'.Maud's
turn was next.

Tito had never before seen her looking more beautiful. She
squirmed in a new dance, accorded to the tap of the wooden
heels over the musical stage; her whole body seemed disjoint-
ed, and the soft, rounded, almost boneless arms, rose to the sky,
toward that rectangle of African sky where all the stars in the
world seemed to have gathered to watch her dance. Oh, those
arms of Maud, so miraculously bare, how they rose, how they
stretched and extended toward the stars! All of her a soft thing,
elastic, which curved to the right and to the left, to slump forward, with the flexibility of a lily stem the flower of which has
become so heavy that it droops to the earth, dazed and felled by
its own fragrance. Around her breast and her arms and ankles roll
the moisture-like dewdrops, and from her flowing tresses fall the
roses and the hairpins alike; she smiles, showing all of her dazzling white teeth, and her two great, big eyes, the astonished eyes
of the bird of prey. The paint on her lips drips with sweat; they
looked like drops of blood.

And the dancer continued to toss and roll, and she weaved
like a lily-stem shaken by a storm.

The serpentine contortions alternated with the lazy amorous
pliability of the feline: an evil glance flashed sud-denly in her
eyes, and vanished before a smile full of soft sweetness. Flashes
of lust, whim, cruelty and murder, shone alternately in her eyes.

Tito remembered having seen a dance like that before, during
a white orgy in a distant Parisian night, in Kalantan's villa, at the
Champs Elysees. How everything repeats itself, how everything
comes back!

Cocaine dropped on her knees and curved backward, arch-like.
Tito saw nothing but purple nails over hundreds of agitated black
hands.

* * *

A long line of ancient-looking cars stood in the street. The scorching heat had vanished: a dewy breeze blew in from the sea.

Tito put his arm around Cocaine's waist, and they walked toward a white patch, a mosque, set like a jewel in a green oasis, where began two long roads that would stretch far into the desert,

With the lightheartedness of two children, who take their first stroll the night they have confessed their love to each other, they walked amid night and solitude. But the fatality of agony hovered over them.

"I left Buenos Aires to go back to Italy, and I have danced tonight for the last time. I am no longer beautiful: I have put aside a little money; I will retire to my home, on that fourth floor apartment facing the courtyard where the odors of rich cooking have filled me with the frantic desire for comfortable living. Remember? Perhaps I will still find some man to whom I may not look so bad. Perhaps I will die in loneliness, In life, I find myself facing a dilemma: who knows how far into Africa the two roads before us stretch; whichever of the two I take, I believe that it would lead me to being burned to death, near or far."

Thus spoke the woman, dejectedly, Tito, however, never believed in the dejection of men and women. Deep at heart we are all optimists. There are people who seek a "clean love" on the fourth page of a newspaper. But as time wears on, there develops in ourselves a faculty of compensation, similar to that which in blind people develops the sense of feeling and hearing. As we grow old we experience within us an adaptation that satisfies us . . . the actors who consider themselves through at the sight of the first gray hair, will consider themselves still young when their beards are snow white. The women who at thirty become sincerely resigned to remaining spinsters, at thirty-five will once more hope they will still find a mate for themselves in time. When the first wrinkles appear, they say: "I'm ugly: no man wants to look at me!" But ten years later they are positive that they can still awaken a burning desire.

It is impossible to be a woman's last love, because, no matter how old she is or what her age is, no matter how unsightly, she still hopes to be able to find another male after you are gone.

Cocaine continued: "I begged you to meet me at Dakar, so we can be together during the last lap of our trip back home. The letter you wrote me about the sad and lonely life you led in Turin, has filled me with grief. You spoke of dying. I, too, would be willing to die."

Cocaine uttered these words in a quiet, humble tone of voice, while one of her soft arms dangled listlessly in Tito's burning hand. They walked at random, under the starry canopy overhead; all deserted immensities fill one with dismay and are more difficult to walk through than the most complicated labyrinths.

A military patrol, coming out of the dark, stopped before them. "Watch out", said the corporal in fairly good French, "in a little while the great Western Africa express is due to pass by, and you are too close to the tracks. It is a train that plays tricks, for it overtakes you, without your hearing it, since in this solitude there are no walls to collect and transmit the noise that it makes,"

"Thank you, Corporal", said Tito.

"Don't mention it, my lad Good night to Madame."

And the patrol vanished.

That night Cocaine seemed more beautiful than ever to Tito, desirable as never before. That renewed beauty of hers, filled him with added grief, rather than joy. He felt that in order to be her last lover he would have to wait a long time yet before the dissolution would complete its work, Cocaine regarded herself as ugly: Cocaine felt herself growing old; but not too old yet not to please anymore. Therefore the joy of being her last was again denied to Tito.

Her last!

Tomorrow, in the house of the Custom House Chief, there would be another reception for her; for Thursday night she had been invited to the English Consulate; for Saturday, she was expected at the villa of a wealthy native merchant. Tomorrow or the day after tomorrow, Maud would have roused a few passions In that settlement of Europeans nauseated by the savage scented flesh of ne-gresses. Tito was sure that the resolutions of renunciation she expressed a moment before would vanish at the first smile of some European gallant.

That was what Tito felt. But Cocaine, whose will was sick and nerves tired, was like a lifeless thing, easily influenced by a will a trifle stronger than her own.

"Did you say you would be willing to die?" murmured Tito.

"Did you say that you feel all was over for you, that there is nothing else to look forward to, anymore? I, too, am a walking corpse, I, too, have no other road ahead of me but the one leading to death.

"If I should propose that we die together tonight, would you accept?"

Cocaine hesitated a moment. A star shot across the horizon. Suddenly, as if she had been touched by someone, the woman turned. Tito's eyes shone as when he was drunk with the white drug which the crippled merchant at the Montmartre cafes sold him.

"Would you be willing to die?"

"Yes".

"With me?"

"Yes".

"Even now?"

"Even now".

"Well, I propose to you the most beautiful of deaths: that which gives you the most maddening of thrills. In a little while, over these very tracks, the great Western Africa express will roar past us. It is a train that has been running for days and days, and will run many days more before it reaches its destination. Blindly it goes forward, without ever knowing where it is going, without ever knowing what it crushes beneath its wheels; the engine-driver dozes over the brakes, and they go on and on along the straight rails, day and night . . . ."

"Would you want that train to pass over your body?"

"Yes".

"But can't you see, Tito, that you are talking like a person who is out of his mind, that you are using words that one reads only in books? You are only upset, excited."

"Not excitement, exaltation, I am exalted Exaltation and ebriety are but a hand which Fate holds out to us to thrust us forward when our will power is not enough, to assist us when our will fails us. This African night, your voice, all this exalts me; and even your dejection toward life encourages me to put an end to all this. Think how thrilling it is to stretch ourselves across these endless tracks, with our cheeks resting over the cold steel, feel for the last time our bodies throbbing with fear, adhering together. Every light in the distance, every noise we hear, will thrill us with madness lasting an eternity. And at last, when we will hear the roar of the steel rails, when we will see the train moving like a shadow out of the shadows, getting closer and closer, we will shriek like two cowed dogs. But that black thing will already be on top of us, crushing, grinding us to pieces, mixing our flesh and blood together, forever.

"Think that neither you nor I have anything to expect from life. We are tired, our spirit is broken. We are like dead. Come near me, and let me kiss you for the last time, Cocaine".

The sky was like a perfect niche: one could see the perfectly rounded frame encircling it as when one is aboard a steamer on the high seas. Cocaine was pale: her brow was moist with sweat, and her eyes were dilated frightfully as if she saw death's face over her.

But it was only Tito's face, close to hers. He kissed her on her mouth, throat, and eyes. Under her back, the rail track stretched like a blade, into infinity.

"Cocaine!", he moaned, without ceasing to kiss her cheeks, without ceasing to bite her lips, "Cocaine, this is our last. Tell me again that you love me."

"I love you!", sighed the woman, with agony in her voice.

"I want you!", Tito hissed in a death rattle, as he choked her with the pressure of his mouth on her throat and clasped her in a grip of death, as if to kill her, "I want you! I want to die when I possess you for the last time. I want to be your last lover."

Cocaine was still lying in the same position. There was nothing immoral about that lifeless form, a beautiful white statue, her pouting red lips relaxed into serene content, in that boundless darkness, under the purity of stars, under the blue canopy of the infinite.

But her lover, her last one, focused his eyes southward and saw an ominous shadow approaching like a black hearse moving in the dark over the shining rails. He gasped.

He hurriedly picked her up and deposited her over a patch of grass a little distance from the tracks.

The Great Western Africa Express loomed distant. In another moment it approached with the force of a tornado, passed and vanished into the desolate expanse.

Cocaine opened her eyes and saw that gleaming wreath of lights run through the dark of night and vanish from view, leaving behind the glittering steel rails, extending like drawn daggers, piercing the infinite.

The train swept over its own sparks, grinding them.

Without saying another word, Tito helped her to her feet and they resumed their trek through the unfrequented path back to the hotel. His face appeared calm and untroubled. The struggle with fierce desire was over.

They kissed each other again at the threshold of her room.

* * *

On the afternoon of the following day, while Maud was sipping melting banana ice-cream at a reception in her honor, Tito secretly embarked on a steamer en route for Genoa.

When the moment of departure arrived, and the propellers began to hum their melancholy and gay farewell aria, Tito, thrusting a hand into a pocket of his traveling suit, found a visiting card.

"Who is this? Where have I met him before?"

Then he remembered. . . .

He was that European who, shortly after his landing, had praised the excellence of Berber women and promised him he would keep a few at his disposal, the oldest among them not over sixteen.

Tito read the card over again, and smiled.

He thought:

"If I had listened to him in the first place, my suicide resolutions would have disappeared right then.

"My jealousy, even this last time, was caused by the languishing and long collected desire."

And he remembered that the previous night, when he returned back to the hotel with Cocaine, he felt his sense vibrate in a sudden lull. He had thought that tomorrow perhaps she would have yielded before others, and he did not feel hurt.

Dakar was already far away, Tito, erect and motionless, reminisced about the times when he used to dash to Kal antan and vent upon her flesh the jealousy which Maud caused him. Since that time he felt that jealousy is but a physical, glandular phenomenon.

And yet, at times, too many times, to be sure, he had forgotten about that.

His senses were now appeased, because the night before, under the wafting breeze and under death's very breath, he had spent, over the endless rails, all his jealousy. His desire was now dead. His passion stilled.

A pause of self-reproach suddenly followed that thought,"But now? Now that the steamer was moving further away, now that the passing of time and the exciting fragrance of the sea would stimulate him once more, his jealousy would again ravage him; now, that he had seen her reborn to new beauty, now that he had seen her dance so wonderfully, now that the joy of life throbbed everywhere around, now that Cocaine attracted him as never before, how, oh, how, could he live without her?" Skeptical thoughts whirled through his mind. Fear and jealousy returned. Again it would sweep hot as flame over him.

And now that he had tried to die with her, how could he gather courage to face death alone?

He gazed with wondering eyes and a beating heart in the direction of Dakar. It was gone.

Something like a throb, a painful shiver, ran through him like a stab.

The ship was now rolling across the choppy sea and the glittering firmament above it, turned upside down, with the perfectly round frame encircling it, just as he had seen it the night before, resupinated, majestically beautiful, over Cocaine's brow, then whiter than a ghost, in their last embrace in the desert.

And to the sea he murmured one sweet name; the expression of his indefinable brooding: "Cocaine!"

13

Just as Tito had foreseen, only a few days after leaving her, he was assailed by Cocaine's memory. Every now and then he stopped in the street, and stealthily, to avoid anyone's seeing him, he drew Cocaine's picture out of his pocket and cast furtive glances at the naked form.

"Back in Turin again?" asked Nocera.

"Just as you see."

"But what brought you here this time?"

"I came to die."

"Couldn't you have died where you were?"

"I tried, but I couldn't."

"Right you are; it's too hot in Senegal, It takes less effort to live there."

Nocera amused himself on this score because he never took Tito's idea of suicide any too seriously. Already he had bragged too much about it. One who is resolved to die, keeps quiet, so as not to put his fellow-man in the position of having to thwart his act or warn him from carrying out his purpose. One seriously bent upon committing suicide does it, without informing anybody beforehand.

One day Tito said: "I tried everything in life: love, gambling, dope, hypnotism, work, idleness, robbery; I have seen women of all races and men of all colors. But one thing I haven't yet tried: death. I want to taste it."

Sensing that those words expressed the love of idle talk more than a resolute and irrevocable determination, Pietro Nocera replied: "Stop playing the tragedian, Tito! Quit talking about dying. Life is, after all, a farce."

"I know, Nocera, But since it fails to amuse me, I want to leave before the performance is ended."

"Your funeral shroud seems to be slabbered with literary drivel", observed Nocera, "You are not going to kill yourself. You talk too much about it; in your very words you seem to be looking for a loophole you could hold fast to, to prove to yourself that you are wrong. What you say to me has but one purpose—to provoke objections on my part to which you could gleefully say: 'What you say is right, you have convinced me, and I am not going to kill myself anymore." But instead of that, my answer to you is this, dear Tito: 'Of course, go ahead kill yourself; it's all right with me."

"Bravo, Nocera! That's the way I like to hear you talk. All I wanted of you was a word of encouragement, and my purpose is set. The only thing that perplexes me is the kind of death I should choose. Snuff myself out with gas? That's too slow. It isn't polite to keep death dancing at attendance, when we ourselves have sent for it; it isn't ethical to have it come through the service door; it should rather burst through the main entrance, suddenly, The ideal thing would be to die on the ocean. It's the most beautiful death, that one. To be in a first-class salon, on a fantastic night, during one of those celebrations aboard, all athrob with music, with blue distances and speed. To be amid the many millionaire ladies in *decollete,* clad only in ribbons and diamonds: beautiful ladies, radiant with beauty, who have bedecked themselves with costly jewels and un-burdened themselves of years, to worthily greet the occasion. Men in dinner coats discussing business between continents. Toasts, champagne, an orchestra playing ragtime, a dancer rotating her international form upon a stage surrounded by palms and wreathed with lamps. Cosmopolitan bustle: Chinese, negroes, mulattoes, merchants, matinee idols, *viveurs*, diplomats, cocottes who change continents to raise their tariff. All of them people who have been called together aboard that steamer by their common lot, by fate, by fatality, with different pretexts, but with an identical purpose: death.

"Suddenly the hubbub ceases. There is a crash; thousands of lives shouting; a few gun shots, and the water begins to slip in, surround everybody; it submerges, drowns all, snuffs out the shrieks, stifles all voices, makes all tables float and all carpets swell, snuffs out the lights. And rapidly we sink, we are buried beneath a dim veil, under a *charmeuse* of blue water, while our ears still ring with ragtime tempo which acts as a delicious funeral march. I believe I could die almost without struggling, and while others would toss and writhe frantically over the billows, I would still feel myself able, perfectly at ease.

"But what can you do, my dear Nocera? I don't choose this kind of death, for I suffer with seasickness, I must therefore give up the idea of dying this way; but believe me it would be most elegant to be buried in mid-ocean, without the humiliation of being tucked away in a hearse, and the burial in the ground, in that filthy thing, which is the earth!

"It will be you, Nocera, who will have charge of my body. I want to be cremated."

"What nonsense!"

"I know it is. Jean Moreas once said: "I want to be cremated because I know it is silly.""

"As far as I am concerned", commented Nocera, "I won't care whether they toss me into a swamp or bury me in Westminster Abbey."

"I, instead", replied Tito, "would enjoy thumbing my nose at those eight legions of underground worms which had already figured upon feasting on my hide. To be devoured that way after death is repugnant, It would be different if you were alive. Take the oyster, for instance, which is eaten alive—what a noble animal! Then it is agreed that you will take charge of my cremation: it's an interesting thing to watch; have you seen it? The body looks as if it is still alive, it rises, it twists, it kneels, folds over, the arms contract, and it takes on postures that are grotesquely obscene."

"It isn't true."

"When you'll see them cremate me you'll be convinced that I was right. But let's not wander from the subject. Tell me of a good way to die."

"Throw yourself from a ten-story window."

"I might land on someone else's window."

"How about throwing yourself under a train?"

"I tried it once. I don't like it. And then, with all those trains running behind schedule . . ."

Pietro Nocera lost his patience. "Frankly, I don't know what to advise you. When one is so hard to please as you are, one does not seek any advice, nor kill oneself. One just lives, that's all."

* * *

Tito then began thinking it out for himself, and after mature reflection, concluded: "If I should swallow strong poison, or sink five bullets into myself, then I am sure I will die. Rather than to have that happen, I would rather like to find some way where.I would have a chance; to be more exact, I would like some sort of violence done to myself, which fate, if fate exists, would allow, and if it is opposed to my dying, then it should save me. If I should eat a few sublimate tablets, I am sure to die, and fate cannot stop me from dying then; it can't be otherwise. If I throw myself off a steeple, I would most assuredly crack my skull on the sidewalk and my lot, my fate, or God Almighty, for that matter, cannot hold me suspended in mid-air . . .

"I want to give fate a chance to save me, if fate has ordained that I should be saved."

He thought all this over on his way to the hospital. He read a few notices, entered through a door, turned to a watchman, breathed the mingled scent of disinfectants and cleanliness, climbed a few steps, and slipped through a corridor.

The doctor whom he had sought greeted him with a manly handshake, and a laboratory smack, which enhanced the charming scholar's smiling, feminine grace.

Together they had gone through the University College; they had worked upon the same anatomical marble slabs, they had walked many times together through the same street, on their way from one clinic to the next. There had even been a time when Tito vaguely loved the signorina; she, too, had loved him at a different period; but it was a light case of love, more of the joking than the sentimental and soulful kind. Circumstances had never been favorable for a reciprocal confession of their love for each other. When Tito left college, he promised they would meet again. From Paris he sent her a postal card with a view of the Eiffel Tower, and she exchanged the greeting with a view of the Carignano Palace, and also with the question: "How are things with you?"", a question which Tito never answered.

"Yes, Arnaudi, we could have shaped our lives along an altogether different course. I remember that one winter morning we walked together to the clinic. You said to me then, with a shyness which had me quite moved, a few polite words. It was cold: the trees along the lane were bare and branched out like the bronchi of many anatomical specimens. Suddenly you went into a tobacconist's shop, 'When he comes out", I promised myself, I will tell him that I love him. But you came out looking very mad and cursing against the State, or tobacco, or the tobacconist, I don't remember which, and the subject shifted, and the clinic was close by. We walked in and not another word was said about that which was uppermost in my mind."

"I would have been most happy!", confessed Tito sadly, "if you had spoken then. Our whole existence may sometime depend upon taking one trolley car instead of another, upon entering a cigar store, or leaving the house a minute sooner or a moment later".

Tito added that all those who have been compelled to change trade or cease their educational pursuits, regret bitterly that they had cast aside the books and the tools: it is like first love: it can never be forgotten, for it seems the only one that is really worthwhile. He confessed to her how his life had been embittered by the nostalgia of the microscopic call, which he had cast aside, the auscultations, the tubes, the analyses, the reactions. And he besought that they visit together the laboratories, the operating room, the surgical instruments.

"Very happy to do so. Let's start from the wards."

They trudged out of the laboratory, crossed a long white vestibule, with huge frosted windows, Taciturn nuns, A smell of cooking and disinfectants. They walked through the long double line of white cots, all built alike, and marked by notices. They drew near to the most interesting cases, the most strange forms of disease. How many different diseases in all those beds so like one another; how many different fates In those wards, all so symmetrical and uniform! The signorina led Tito here and there, stopping before the most interesting patients, and explaining to him the new diagnostic methods used and the new cures.

In the surgery ward, filled with the pungent odor of chloroform, a sister tried to comfort a delirious patient: "Think, my good man", the nun said, "that you already have a leg in heaven and that you will soon join it there."

They slipped into another hall. Other cots, other wards. Silent nuns walking quietly about, white smocks everywhere, tall frosted-glass windows from which poured a gray light.

In the mortuary chapel, upon a cot, lay the body of an army colonel, with his sword and all his medals. Over a pillow, near his head, lay his military cap.

"That cap over the bed brings hard luck." Tito warned smilingly.

"But what else could happen to him if he is already dead?"

"He might rise from the dead again".

He entered the auditorium. Tito remembered having sat upon those very circular seats a few years before.

"We used to sit right here", said the woman doctor. "Remember? I sat here, and you sat at my right."

They climbed to the next floor, visited other halls, set some of the apparatus in motion, and then re-entered the laboratory.

The adjoining room sheltered show cases filled with many small tubes, standing in serried rank, and sealed with cotton tops which looked like hairdressings of the eighteenth century pattern.

"Are these bacilli cultures?"

"They are", answered the signorina. "Diphtheria, pneumonia, malaria, typhus . . ." and she pointed meanwhile with her finger to the various tubes, each carrying a tag. While she explained to him about the coloring of bacilli for microscopic purposes, a man with big feet shooting out from underneath his smock, passed by.

"Doctor," called the young woman as she moved away from Tito, who now stood alone before the bacteria tubes. "They telephoned from the Anatomy Institute; they are asking for the body of a woman, preferably young."

"I have nothing to give them for the moment", answered the doctor after brief thought, "but I hope that by tonight at the very latest, we can have one delivered."

Taking advantage of the woman's temporary absence, Tito snatched, without being seen, one of the tubes, and thrust it quickly into the pocket of his coat.

He lingered a while longer, listening distractedly and impatiently to the explanations of his charming guide.

When he finally was able to get out, he hurried home, caressing the bacilli tube with one of his hands from the outside of the pocket.

"Typhus! Typhus! Typhus bacilli, that's what they are. I am going to drink them—swallow them. I am going to face death. The kind of death I have been waiting for; if fate wants to save

me, it will put me in the hands of a good doctor who will cure
me."

He shook the mucilaginous fluid, poured the contents into a
glass, and drank it in one gulp. It tasted kind of saltish and acidu-
lous.

"Bacilli cultures are not such a bad drink."

And he drank a tumbler of *chartreuse* for a chaser. He drew
Cocaine's naked picture out of his pocket, gazed at it and put it
away again, He next sat before his desk and wrote: "I kill myself
because I am weary of life. Every intelligent human being who is
twenty-eight should do the same.

I don't want any clergymen at my burial. But since priests
are of no use to the dead but might be of some use to the living,
if there should be any priests I would also want a rabbi and a
Valdeian pastor. I have a great admiration for priests of every
religion, because they are either in good faith, in which case I
consider them worthy of admiration; or they are not sincere, in
which case they are to be admired like all clever mystifiers.

"I want to be laid at rest in my coffin in green pajamas with
my hands in my pockets.

"I demand to be cremated.

"You will fill the two round and iridescent funeral urns with
my ashes; one will go to Pietro Nocera as a memento; the other
will go to Maud Fabrege.

"I am also leaving all my books and clothes to Pietro Nocera.
To my friend, the monk, goes my gilt silver monstrance; to Maud
Fabrege, (Magdalena Panardi) my few jewels.

"All my money will go to the S.P.CA."

He signed, dated it, then sealed it in a large envelope. On it
he wrote: "My will, to be opened shortly after I am dead."

And to dispel the melancholy that was gripping him, he left
the room and crossed the street warily, careful not to be run over
and perhaps die under a truck.

He sniffed a few pinchfuls of the pale drug and went to a movie. But he didn't see a thing.

"When I used to tell my mother that I had a toothache, she had the tooth extracted for me; when I complained about a boil I had, she squashed it for me; when! confessed to her about my love for a woman, she called me an idiot. Shortly after I was born, my father sent for a clergyman, and since my father had sent for that priest and not for another, I was brought up to honor and love one God instead of one of his competitors; when 1 changed my religion they called me a renegade because I refused to deal with the priest who dealt with my father. When I was a boy they taught me good manners; to be well-mannered means to deceive people willfully, to feign to ignore a thing which someone would hate to have us know; to have to smile to people, right into whose eye we would enjoy spitting; to say 'thank you', when we would much rather say 'bust'. A few years later I rebelled against that sort of good mannerism, and have flaunted since that time the joy of speaking just what I thought. Later on, however, I began to understand that sincerity led me into trouble. And so I turned to lying again. I would have been better off if I had followed the original course from the start. At first they told me that the *POX populi,* public opinion, is always truthful; in many cases which have occurred around me, I have been able to learn and discover that public opinion was very often wrong: but I then deepened my inquiries, and finally had to admit that public opinion was right. When everybody says that Tom is a thief and May a prostitute, you refuse to believe that it is so; for a year or maybe two you would swear as to their innocence; but on the third year of your acquaintanceship, you begin to find out that there is a good deal of crookedness about Tom and a good deal of prostitution about May, In this case, one would be better off believing the *vox populi* rumors from the very beginning, instead of wasting all that time investigating. When I was twenty they taught me to swear allegiance to the King, a man who plays the King because his father played it before he did, and the grandfather before both, I swore because they compelled me to swear. If I hadn't been forced to obey, I would never have sworn allegiance. After that they sent me to kill people I never knew existed, but who dressed more or less like myself.

"One day they said to me: 'See that man there? He is your enemy. Shoot him down. I shoot, but miss him. He shoots back at me. He plugs, and wounds me, I don't know why they told me that it was a glorious wound."

Meanwhile the picture reeled before him; intermissions succeeding each performance, new faces and spectators kept changing, and Tito remained nailed to his seat, day-dreaming. He had sniffed all the cocaine that was in the box. An usher walked up to him and told him that he had already sat through three performances, and politely invited him to get out.

On the street he continued to ruminate upon the most impossible and distant things; he felt that he was already twenty-eight, the tragic age of all male lovers; one lacks the vigor of the youthful lover, and one has not yet the money of the older lover. He thought that woman would be willing to make any sacrifice when she loved a man, but when she doesn't love you anymore, she is liable to do you untold harm, just to satisfy her beastly anger; she is apt to invent slanders, conjure plots, become an accomplice to things detrimental to you. He laughed at ideals scornfully; In the most noble of human aspirations there is always present the metallic reflex of money. He felt old emotions surging back to him; there is no love without jealousy; only the ruffians and women sustain the contrary. He thought up new forms of suicide: to throw himself headlong from the second balcony of a theatre into the audience below. The women who would submit to anybody, the day they cease loving the man who loved them, will refuse him gratification; the day they yield before you, they want to impress you with the loftiness of their body, but when you reprimand them for having yielded to someone else, they will answer that their contact with that man was an accident of little or no importance.

He meandered through cafes frequented by tradesmen.

"I have never been able to understand how I could ever manage to live by trading, that is sell for a hundred what costs me only ten: whenever I sold anything, I gave for ten what cost me one hundred and fifty."

He decided that if he should be born over again, he would become a vagabond or a beggar. . . . Money is useful because you can spend it. If you must work, you would lack time to spend all the money you earn. One must be either born rich or else steal.

"What is difficult about killing a man? In five minutes you have time to premeditate, execute, regret and forget all about it. What's painful about an operation (on somebody else) that lasts only thirty seconds, compared to the happiness of a lifetime?"

Every now and then it dawned upon him that death was approaching. The bacilli had already gone mercifully to work on him. He felt he was fading out of life tired and bored, as if rising from the bed of a courtesan, and it pleased him to have always been bored in life. What a happy lot those have who are easily bored by life; they will leave it without regret.

And since woman was the torment of all his life, his dis-jointed thought returned to her invariably.

"One wonders", he thought, "which might be the psychological, physiological, pathological and degenerative reasons by which the woman you love cheats you. But most of the time, a woman will yield before you because she has a pair of new garters which she wants to have admired."

He recalled, but without pangs of regret, a few scenes of his life as a lover. Cocaine, his Cocaine, now so far away, gave him the exaltation of an hour; after having possessed her, he felt a frenzy of creation, an enthusiasm toward life: but an hour later a sense of prostration, the *taedium vitae*, jealousy, the fear of losing her, the incurable despondency succeeded the previous emotions. That woman and that white powder had planted into his blood those same venom-phenomenae which would hasten him toward his end. If he hadn't met that woman, he would perhaps be a physician by now, peering through the microscope, without detecting a thing, or, perhaps seeing everything; the blind eyes of poets like Homer and Milton can see far better than the instruments of precision blinded by presumptuousness.

He fancied he could see the image of Cocaine, grown old, uglier, but cleverly painted, "My unhappiness is all due to a small tube of lip rouge, a blue pencil for the eyebrows, and a box of powder."

He felt a vague regret for not having accepted the advice of his friend, the monk.

Asceticism, whether the individual lacks sexual desire, like the eunuch, or has ceased desiring like Saint Francis of Assisi, is an indication of scarce vitality, I could be a mystic by now. Mysticism is nothing but virility in liquidation; semen gone wasted.

"But why do I puzzle my brain with these things? I must have a little fever, I guess", he muttered to himself feeling his pulse, as he bent his steps homeward. He pulled a drawer of his desk open and found a thermometer; he placed it under his armpit.

He put the thermometer down, removed one shoe, then the other one, then his clothes, and slipped into bed.

The ailment manifested itself with symptoms of angina; fever, and a general weakness.". . . . But, why angina?" he marveled, "Typhus bacteria is what I swallowed. Must be some anomalous case of typhus? I guess."

He recapitulated the death program: "I want to give fate the fullest liberty of either killing or saving me; I will behave like any other patient would: I will first call a doctor, to whom I will explain my symptoms and then follow the cure he will prescribe for me. If it is so ordained that I live, fate will make me live; it will be life and I will not object to whatever arrangements fate will make for me toward that end. If fate wants me to die, I will not resist death, and in that case I would behave like any other patient would in my place. I will not tell how I have caused myself this ailment. If fate wants the doctor to know how this happened, he will find it out by himself.

He dozed a few hours, but his sleep was disturbed by feverish tossing and groaning. When he awoke he saw Pietro Nocera, the landlady and Maud at his bedside.

Maud, who had arrived a few hours before from Senegal, had sought him out immediately.

He frowned a little; at the sight of that woman a vague desire to live suddenly smote him. Remembering that in case of typhus one puts ice bags over the stomach, he asked for one, while waiting for the doctor to come.

"Can I make him an egg-punch, Signor Nocera?"

"Yes", approved Nocera.

"No", resisted the patient. In a case of typhus the most rigid diet was in order. Absolute fasting and ice bags over the stomach. Ice bags over the stomach and absolute fasting!

"The doctor is here", Maud announced, opening the door. Entered the famous Professor Libani, a young and very modern scientist, with fair hair, gold spectacles, and a great deal of dangling jewelry over his stomach and fingers.

He sat; his clinical eyes widened over the patient; he felt his pulse, pulled down the bedsheets, raised his shirt, touched, felt, listened and looked: then he sat once again as he jotted down in so many humble words science's profound response.

The instant the scientist opened his mouth, Tito thought he saw one word come out of his mouth: "typhus."

Instead of that, the eminent scholar spoke briskly: "You drink too much goat's milk."

"No, sir, I do not."

"Yes, you drink goat's milk."

"But that's impossible, doctor."

"What do you know about it? You drink whatever the milkman gives you."

"The milkman gives me nothing because I loathe milk, that disgusting glandular secretion. I drank some when I was a child, till I was ten months old, because I had no other choice except drinking what they gave me. But when I became of reason. . ."

"Never mind", the scientist cut him short, "You have. . ."

And Tito expected any moment to hear the dire pro-nouncement: typhus!

"You have a *septicemia du coli*, that is, an infection of the blood . . ."

"Is it serious?", inquired Maud, who had turned suddenly pale.

"No", spoke the doctor encouragingly. "Here is the cure to follow: first of all we must do away with the ice bags over the stomach: then we will make a few high pressure enemas to clear up the intestines."

"Enemas with what?", interposed the landlady.

"Several liters of physiological serum, that is water and salt, in plain words. When the temperature decreases, or lessens, he can be allowed to eat whatever he likes."

Tito's eyes opened wide in astonishment.He shook his head dolefully.

"Can this be possible?", he thought. "Typhus produces ulcers in the intestines. Not to irritate, not to tear those ulcers, is what fasting is prescribed for. This man, instead, authorizes me to eat, and orders high pressure clysters, which will swell my belly like a balloon. But that is all right. I must not interfere with fate's scheme of things; for it was fate that placed me in the hands of a doctor who mistakes a disease, prescribes a cure contrary to that which would save me. I will eat, take enemas, and then burst".

However, he hazarded timidly: "Pardon me, doctor, but couldn't it be typhus instead?"

His face grew hard. "I exclude it most emphatically. Let's understand each other thoroughly. All the general symptoms of typhus are missing; headache, torpor, diffused aching of the bones; the spleen is hardly palpable, there is no roseola on the stomach, the pulse is too frequently composed for the present temperature. You know that in typhus the pulse is inversely proportioned to the temperature; whereas you have a high fever and a high pulse. But if you want any further proof, we can perform the serum diagnosis. Later in the day I will bring my instruments along."

Tito made no reply. The doctor rinsed his hands, dried them gravely, and strolled out of the room, very much hurt.

In the anteroom Nocera," Maud and the landlady spoke to him in a low tone of voice; they then returned to the patient to ask what it was that he wanted first: eat or. . . .

"It's all the same to me", Tito replied somberly; knowing the real nature of his ailment, he sensed that either thing would have been fatal to him.

'Then well first start with the hydraulic operation", said Nocera, "while the lady here will prepare a juicy steak that big. . ." He looked at him curiously. "All right!" came the patient's stoical reply, And he lay on his stomach, his lips pursed grimly, to receive that two liter deluge that crashed noisily into his flimsy viscera. The coquetish looking rubber tube hanging from a wall, called to his mind the *narghili* which he had seen smoked by wealthy negroes at Dakar, as they sat over their mats, before the entrance to their tents.

"Now turn over and sit", decided Nocera; "now you must eat!" Very patiently, the doomed man did as he was told; he sat up and

took the steak with both hands, like Socrates when he took the
hemlock from the hands of the servant of the Eleven, When he
had it all stored away in his stomach, he stretched himself out
on one side and with shut eyes, followed its journey through his
body; "now it slits through the gullet, then crosses the cardea re-
gion; know enters the stomach, where it is feasted by the gastric
juices; it is a trifle ill-treated by the peristaltic movements, it next
passes through the pylorus, then journeys through the duodenal
tube and moves on into the stomach where it spins round and
round the ileum. If mine is an ileotyphus case, goodness knows
how many bacilli it will find there! Oh, here we are at last, before
the ascending colon; "the colon: the colon with its vermiform appendix attached; watch out for this dangerous railroad crossing,
there is danger of appendix ahead; but let's keep moving; next
it crosses the transversal colon, and after that it slides down the
descending colon, I remember seeing a theatre at Buenos Aires
with the name Colon."

"Calm yourself, calm yourself, dear," Maud begged sooth-in-
gly, worried by his agitation.

The slight fever filled his brain with the same ravings to
which he succumbed that first time at the hotel on the Place Vendome, when he had become inebriated with cocaine. Even now
he thought: "No, God is no such great humorist. He is a small3
miserable humorist. He has the mentality o£ the land-surveyor.
To snuff the life out of multitudes, he resorts to wars and epidem-
ics. He doesn't know what refined injustice is like. The only odd
thing I ever saw him perform is the work of pickpocket thieves
in churches, where one is picked while praying; outside of that
He has never been able to invent anything that was really spec-
tacular. If I were in his place the first thing I would do would be
the immediate staying of the forces of gravity. A man would try
throwing a cigar butt away but the stump would stay in his hand,

He would try to come down a flight of stairs and would be forced to kneel, with his head upside down, and walk down on his hands, exerting himself more in climbing down than in climbing up. Or I would accelerate the centrifugal force of the earth. Instead of one revolution every twenty-four hours, I would make it spin around in one hour. Then everything would be projected helter-skelter, flung through immense distances, in catastrophic ruin. Japanese pagodas launched upon the glaciers of Mont Blanche, mohammedan minarets would go dipping like biscuits into the crater of the Vesuvius, Cheep's Pyramid would go hurling into the Place de la Concorde. No, God is not such a good artist. To kill men he hires cut-throats so small one does not even know whether they are vegetables or animals. How small-minded that Almighty God! And what lack of dignity!"

"Calm yourself! Calm yourself, my love!" entreated Maud, tenderly. "He has fever. Doctor, suppose we perform a morphine injection?"

"That won't be necessary. We shall perform the serum diagnosis, instead. With this method," the scientist explained briefly as he tied two bandages on Tito's arm to swell the veins, "we will prove beyond doubt that it is not typhus, I, for one, am already convinced that it is not; there is no swelling of the spleen, and there is no roseola. . . ."

And Tito, who, despite his mounting fever, still preserved a little of his mental lucidity, and was still able to grasp a few words, upon hearing roseola mentioned, said: "There may be no roseola, but the germs are there. Goodness knows how many billions of them I have swallowed."

When his vein was sufficiently swollen, the surgeon plunged the needle of the Pravaz syringe into it and drew some blood, which he then poured into a sterilized tube, ready for the testing. And he took it away.

He came back the next day (Tito had slept very well), stating that the serum had been negative for the various forms of typhus, paratyphus A and paratyphus B.

Tito believed he was still under the hallucinatory influence of cocaine; he knew that he was infected with a disease which could only be cured by leaving his system in absolute quiet and rest, but, although they kept torturing him and forced him to eat, he did not die. In fact, he was feeling much better. They were doing exactly the opposite of that which science prescribes in cases of typhus, and still he did not get any worse.

"The diazoreaction test is also negative," the doctor announced triumphantly, when he called for the fourth time, "We had, on the other hand, excluded the possibility of typhus since the very beginning. I am pleased to observe that the patient has improved considerably."

"Yes" said Maud. "He is restless in the morning and at night only. His afternoons are quiet."

"One would think", interposed Tito, smiling feebly, "that the microbes are taking their afternoon nap."

"His fever, however, continues."

"It will pass", promised the doctor, as he slipped on his overcoat. After he was gone, Nocera said to Maud —"I fail to see any improvement. It looks the same to me, just the same as on the first day".

"Suppose we consult another doctor".

"Rather. . . ."

Tito did not interfere. If they had proposed to call an electrician or talked him into drinking a potion of hot vitriol^ he would have agreed.

Came the new doctor. He was the old type of diagnostician, the serious doctor. He stood before the bed, with arms folded over the stomach, as if he were leaning upon a window-sill. He felt his pulse, took a look at his tongue, the watch, the thermometer, and made all other routine motions.

"Who is your doctor?"

Nocera mentioned a name. The great doctor deftly Indulged in a caustic opinion, and made a grimace.

"What did he have to say?"

"That he has infection of the blood, *Septicemia du Coli*".

"Nonsense!", laughed the serious doctor. "The gentleman is infected with . . ."

Tito saw one brief word forming upon the lips of the serious doctor: typhus.

Instead he said:

"The patient has Malta fever."

"What did you say?"

"Malta fever."

"Is it very serious?"

"No. Serumtherapy does miraculous wrok in this case. It is cured with Wright's serum. But we must act quickly. Let us begin by suspending the cure followed so far. I am going out, in the meantime, to get the serum, and shall return as quickly as I can. In an hour, I suppose."

This serious doctor read medical reviews and was very fond of the latest methods. Six months before, one of his patients had died of Malta fever, and since that time he saw nothing but Malta fever in every patient he visited.

"It's easy", he explained to Tito, "I am going to inject a few billions of attenuated bacilli into your blood, See this tube? There are three billion of them right there".

The patient behaved like a martyr. He let them inject the bacteria into his blood; without twitching a single muscle of his face, nor of that part where they stabbed him with the needle.

He said simply:

"Doctor, you have now injected Malta fever germs into me?"

"I have."

"Let us now suppose that I did not have that disease before; it will mean now that you have injected it into me".

"Of course".

"So, should your diagnosis have been wrong, and I were infected, let us say, with typhus, now that you have injected your Malta fever into me, I will have two diseases, instead of one".

"Naturally, But you have no typhus."

"I know, doctor, I know", the patient added earnestly, "I was only supposing. A queer case, that's all."

Tito knew that instead of one, he now suffered from two ailments, typhus and Malta fever, "One of them is sure to kill me", he thought.

The fever, which had lessened, now rose a little, Tito complained of pains in all parts of his body.

"Nothing to worry about", said the serious doctor, "When we are in the presence of Malta fever, Wright's serum gives precisely those very reactions. The pains you feel are only the natural reaction, and proves in the light of science that my diagnosis was correct. I have every reason therefore to reach auspicious conclusions."

Maud and Nocera were not so sure about anything; neither the first nor the second cure convinced them.

"If it is possible that the first doctor was wrong, why couldn't the second one have been."

"The first one discovers one thing; he performs the reactions; the reactions prove that he is right.

"The second one finds that something else is wrong; he performs his reactions, and they prove that he, too, is right. . . . I would advise calling a third doctor, I would call in the most famous physician in town, without any delay."

Before evening, the most renowned professor strolled into Tito's room; he was the infallible one, the specialist, the medical luminary, the marvel of science.

In a very dignified manner he shook hands with the other two doctors who attended upon the patient and said, "The patient has typhus I Why, even a dentist would see that!"

"Impossible!", exclaimed the first doctor.

"Have you performed Vidal's serum diagnosis?"

"I have".

"How many times?"

"Once."

"Not enough", pronounced the luminary. "Do it once more".

Tito had at last found the doctor sent by fate to save him. They took more blood from his veins. This time the serum diagnosis was positive.

"So, it is typhus, after 311?" asked Tito.

"Typhus," the three doctors chorused.

Tito thought: "up to now they could not cure me because they did not know the nature of my ailment. Now that they know it, they will no doubt prescribe the right cure, and I will be well again."

"No more food!", ruled the medical luminary, as he paced about the room with long, swinging strides, his forehead puckered in thought.

And Tito thought: "I knew quite well that with typhus one doesn't eat."

"To reduce his fever you will dip him into an iced bath. Is that clear?"

"Yes sir", answered Maud, Nocera and the landlady.

"After the bath you will put him into bed again. We shall be back tomorrow". And they walked out.

The patient felt that he was coming back to life. Nothing strange that a certain cure should prove intellective when one mistakes one disease for another; but when the diagnosis is correct. . . . In this case the diagnosis was most precise: he knew he had drunk from a culture tube upon which the word "typhus" was written.

And yet he could not understand how those steaks he ate and how that "deluge" of two liters daily, as Maud called it, did not dispatch him rapidly.

In the hands of those three doctors he felt as if he were being tossed by his feet by three acrobats suspended from the ceiling of a circus, spinning dizzily around on his flight from one of them to the other, and being caught when he was just about to plunge downwards.

His two friends broke his reverie by dipping him gently into the iced bath.

"Awful!", chattered Tito, writhing and gnashing his teeth as if they were two fling-stones, grinding at each other.

"Be patient, dear!"

"Be patient, my love!"

"One more minute!" pleaded the landlady, holding a watch in her hand.

"It will kill the fever," said Nocera.

"It will cure you, dear,",Maud moaned, in a persuasive voice.

"This is the end," groaned the victim.

They dried him summarily and then, half-led, half-dragged him to bed. His face was livid, and his flesh purple, as if he had just been fished out of the water.

"You will get warm again, love!"

But instead of warming him up, the bed was icier than the iced bath, and he felt a painful stab in his right side. And he coughed. He coughed again. Then he spat blood.

The first doctor, who had come shortly after they had taken him out of the bath, said that the stab was merely a pain between the ribs.

The famous physician, the scientific luminary, reassured everyone: "It's nothing to worry about. That is only a bone abscess caused by typhus. Why, an army doctor would understand that.'

Tito knew that in that bath he had caught a galloping pneumonia.

Maud rushed out to call the doctors, who had made themselves scarce at the first blood sputums, back again.

And Tito saw a priest, black and solemn, who whispered to him in a voice beyond a human one.

"Who was it that sent for you?" inquired the patient.

"Nobody did", lied the landlady.

"Priests as a rule have an uncanny way of sniffing where there is somebody dying", said Tito in a weak thread of a voice, "They are like those flies that lay their eggs in the nostrils of the dying. But since he is here, let him stay."

The clergyman showed him a crucifix, and assisted him in repeating a prayer after him.

"Look here, Father", groaned Tito, "in that drawer there is a box; in the box is a photograph. Bring it to me."

The priest brought the box. Tito took out the photograph of Maud, stark naked.

The priest became horrified. "You'll destroy that, I hope", admonished the clergyman, with flashing eyes.

"No. I want to take one last look at it," sighed Tito with serene eyes.

"But in these supreme moments God is right near the deathbed!," thundered the minister.

"And now, you will confess", ordered the priest, snatching the obscene effigy from his hands and thrusting it between the pages of his breviary.

"Confess? Is this magnesian lemonade really necessary for my soul?"

"You blasphemous wretch—stop cursing!"

"Then get out, you idiot!"

The priest left. When he was mid-way down the stairs he opened his breviary and blushed.

Nocera brought in Tito's aunt, a carrion he seldom saw. In every family there is a carrion of an aunt. In mine, also.

She was happy to know that Tito was dying; and yet she shed burning tears.

"If you weep," said Tito, "it means that 1 am getting well again; because if I were really to die you would burst out laughing with joy."

A man brought three oxygen bags.

"Three, But why three?", inquired the carrion aunt, one of those carrion aunts whom one finds in every family, even in mine. "Why did you buy three? And if you use only two, what then? Will the druggist take back the unused one?"

"Yes,"

"Will he refund you the money?"

"Look here, Nocera", shouted Tito with the last breath remaining in his throat. "Throw that carrion aunt out, or else I'll wreak vengeance upon her; I am going to be spiteful and won't die."

Came the marvel of science, "How is everything going?" asked the illustrious doctor as he felt Tito's pulse.

Tito grinned sadly. "Yes, we're going".

His head rolled over languidly. He was dead.

Nocera, Maud, the landlady knelt in prayer around the bedside, their foreheads bent over the quilts, like in those prints showing Anita Garibaldi or Camillo Benso Count of Cavour in their death-beds, surrounded by mourners.

So this is how, having swallowed typhus bacilli and having been cured for septicemia first, and Malta fever afterward, one can be cured. But if one tries to cure typhus the right way, one can die of galloping pneumonia.

14

Only Maud was present, her eyes reddened by tears, when Pietro Nocera proceeded to open the Will.

Tito had expressed himself very clearly: "I kill myself", he had written," and he had killed himself because of her.

It was the first time that Maud felt smitten by remorse.

"If I had only been loyal to him, or had at least given the appearance of being loyal, perhaps at this moment . . ."

"But, don't you worry, Signorina". Nocera spoke encouragingly; "Remorse is the most useless of all things. You should go home and sleep, rather, I will arrange for the funeral."

Maud kissed Tito upon his brow for the last time, put a little red paint over her lips and went home, to that very room, where she had spent her girlhood days, toward the courtyard, where the kitchens on the floors below sent up an aroma of expert cooking.

Her father greeted her, and with all the respect due her grief, timidly inquired if, perchance, the deceased had not left a spring topcoat which might fit him.

* * *

To the deceased one's home came the medical examiner, who left a short while after, then a priest who stayed about thirty minutes.

"My poor friend was an atheist", objected Nocera to the priest.

"It doesn't matter if the deceased was not a believer", explained the clergyman. "So long as the living ones believe."

"But frankly, Father. . . ."

"Perhaps you don't, but. . . . ."

"Briefly, how much will it cost?"

"Each clergyman will cost you twenty-five lires."

"How many clergymen do you think we will need to make a good showing?"

"At least eight."

"That would be two hundred lires."

"Then the nuns, of course."

"How much for the nuns?"

"Two lires each, if they use old candles; three lires with new ones."

"How many nuns do we need?"

"About one hundred."

"That makes two hundred lires."

"But that's without the new candles."

"Since they have to be lit, I don't think it should make much difference if they have been burnt before. . . ."

"Then we must add fifty lires for the rugs at the doorway".

"Necessary?"

"Absolutely". Then the Mass and the Benediction."

"Let's make it a flat rate. The very minimum."

"Mass, Benediction, rugs, one hundred lires. Priests and nuns, to be reckoned separately."

"Agreed."

"Will you advance me a part of that sum for the initial expenses?"

"Will two hundred lires do?"

"Yes."

"Will you take charge of everything?"

"Everything! Then all is set for tomorrow evening at four?"

"At four, Reverend? But how can they celebrate Mass at four in the afternoon if the Holy Host must be taken after fasting?"

"We have an all-day faster."

Next came the agent from the undertaker to make arrangements for the hearse and the caparisoning. Nocera telephoned to the cremation company, and received their representative, to whom he introduced the band master.

"I'm first clarion with the prized 'Music at the Head' band, and I can settle for a very reasonable price with you. We have a selection of funeral marches by Gounod, Donizetti, Wagner, Petrella, Grieg and Chopin. We also have a weatherbeaten flag, where you cannot see what is written: it looks like the flag of some welfare home, which the deceased has benefited. Every musician wears a cap, and, with a slight compensation, also a sword."

"How much for the sword?"

"Two hundred lires."

"Agreed, Tomorrow, then."

"Have you selected the pieces?"

'What pieces?"

"The pieces of music."

"I leave that to you. Be sure that you select the best in stock".

They brought in the coffin. Nocera took out the silken green pajamas and called someone to help him dress the deceased. Then they tucked him into the box.

"Shall we close now?"

"We can close right now, if there's nothing else going in".

* * *

The hearse was held in readiness before the doorway. The sextons lowered the casket and slipped it through with precision and elegance, and the procession got under way. The balconies were thronged with the curious and in the doorways along the route chit-chatted the town's chatterboxes.

A sexton with his moustache trimmed like an American, led the cortege.

Next came the band, composed of: An octave-flute, eight flutes, two cornets, two trombones, a triangle battery, two bombard ins and a bass.

Then followed the nuns all dressed in green They tossed like salad on parade.

Then came the clergymen, singing psalms. Eight in number. But one hobbled. The hearse, very much revered and loaded with chrysan-themum wreaths, fluent and soft like ostrich feathers. Sumptuously caparisoned horses.

Maud, with her black flowing veils.

Nocera.

Maud's father, wearing an overcoat of the deceased that fitted him to perfection.

Many women. Many men. All people whom Nocera had never seen before. Some old towns woman made the sign of the cross as the cortege passed by her.

A boy mounted on a bicycle, sped along the band, with one hip on the saddle and both his legs to one side, and pedaling with one foot.

"She's the deceased one's sister", said one of the mourners, pointing to Maud.

"The wife."

"The lover."

 "Not bad looking".

"She's got a swell. . . ."

"And some swell. . . ."

"And how."

"Is she old?"

"Don't think so. About thirty-five."

"Maybe more."

"What is she doing?"

"She's a. . .

"That's been her business for a long time."

"What did he have to say about it?"

"He closed an eye. Feigned not to see."

"And opened the purse, instead."

"But he did it in a sportsmanlike manner."

"So everybody could see."

"He was even in jail."

"Passing bad checks, I suppose?"

"What did he die of?"

"Consumption."

"Syphilis."

"Really?"

"American, I suppose?"

The band, the nuns, the clergy, the hearse, the cortege came to a stop. The sexton removed the coffin, brought it into the church; then he took it out again and slipped it into the hearse.

Again on the march. The band struck up a melancholy dirge. Slowly, slowly. Very slowly.

All funerals should be done with motor speed: the deceased should ride in a car and all the mourners in motor-cycles. The nuns in motorcycles, the musicians in motor-cycles, the relatives, bereaved by the untimely loss, also.in motorcycles.

Nocera turned around. The crowd had thinned down considerably, but there were still a great many present.

Any poor devil who never had a loan of two hundred lires or a word of comfort in a lifetime from anyone, is escorted to his grave by a phalanx of kind souls, The humble country school teacher receives the funeral eulogy from the school board official; the barrister receives the extreme salutation from the President of the Bar Association; the town's quack doctor is mourned like a veritable loss to science. The derelict who was seen reading a newspaper alone, on a park bench, will be accompanied to his resting abode by a hundred kindred souls, gathered in "sad and orderly" procession.

The living man represents something that is ambiguous and circumspective; he is always apt to do somebody harm, betray, change opinions, rewrite his will. The dead one instead is something more definite.

The hearse is always followed by the closest enemies of the deceased: the husband, by the wife's lover; the man who has been killed in a duel, by the man who killed him; the debtor by his creditors.

And the passers-by doffed their hats.

And the procession wiggled on.

"I feel sorry for her."

"She'll get over it."

"Not right away, though."

"She'll be all right when she digs up another one."

"She may have one already."

"Maybe more than one."

"Men will hitch on to anything."

'Especially women of her type."

"With that face painted like a clown's."

"And the false teeth."

"And the periwig."

"What work does she do?"

"She works for men."

The cemetery was near. The crematory oven reared its white stack into the air.

The hearse pulled up and passed through the stiff gates, along the graveled path, in die direction of the oven.

Halt!

Out with the coffin! Silence. A speech by a gentleman nobody had seen before.

Anyone else who wished to talk?

Nobody.

Two sextons took the coffin, entered into a white chamber, placed it over a cart and slid it away.

The man in charge at the crematory warned that only the closest friends of the deceased were permitted to view the ceremony. Maud remained in the chapel to pray, while Nocera watched in silence before the iron studded spy hole, through which he would see the body of his friend devoured by the flames.

"It will take about an hour", said the man in charge.

Nocera handed him twenty lires.

The operation over, they drew the cart against the door, and with a silver trowel gathered the ashes.

Nocera had taken the two round and iridescent urns with him: he had them both filled. A few fragments of bones were locked in a regulation urn of red clay and immured in a wall lined with small tomb-stones.

He pocketed the urns, and offered his arm to Maud. Everybody was gone. Every murmur hushed.

"Where are we going now?" asked Nocera, helping her into a taxi which had stopped before the graveyard.

"I should go to the dressmaker for my mourning clothes".

"You should look well in black". I hope so. But not that dull black. I look well in black satin. I will order them made with satin, so they will not look like mourning."

The driver sped toward the city, without haying been given any direction.

"I'm not hungry", said Nocera.

"I couldn't touch any food," said Maud,

Nocera sighed. Maud sighed.

Sighs!

"And still we cannot go on fasting like this for a month. Let's go to a restaurant."

"But I can't eat a thing."

"Neither can I,"

"Just a little broth. An egg."

Nocera gave the name of a restaurant to the driver, and Maud suddenly realized that a little weeping would be the proper thing to do.

She shed a few tears, while the taciturn Nocera reminisced over the Dante-like spectacle of the corpse in the oven.

And so they arrived at the restaurant without knowing it. All the waiters in the place rushed forward to offer them chairs and help them remove their clothes. Maud was not hungry. The food wouldn't go down. Nocera had the same difficulty. However, they ate.

He paid one hundred and eighty lires. That wasn't so expensive because of the liquors served, to help digest the lobster and the seasoned partridges, stuffed with truffles.

What a sad journey, the way back home. "Suppose we go to a theatre?"

"That would be a sinful thing to do."

"Oh, I don't mean we should go there to amuse ourselves. Just so we forget our grief for a while."

"What are they giving tonight?"

"*The Pills of Hercules.*"

"Risque?"

"Rather."

The play over, Nocera accompanied her to the carriage, and saw her home. He opened the door for her and let her choose one of the two urns.

"It's all the same, either one will do", she said, picking one up at random. Never before was inheritance divided with greater harmony.

Nocera pocketed the urn remaining in his hand, and walked back to the carriage.

How barren that home appeared to the poor woman, now that she had grown so accustomed to the fashionable hotels of the metropolis, and to the rich villas of modern Croesus!

She had been back in Turin since a week before, after having danced her last under Senegalese skies, when a bit of African fever had sipped into her blood. She had returned to Turin to retire from life, to lock herself up in that humble room of her childhood days.

She found some old postal cards, empty candy boxes, books, with pages torn and faded, notebooks, grown yellow with ink, bits of chemise-tattered ribbons. She found many bygone memories come to life again: the exact spot where Tito had given her his first kisses, the very door against which, one hot afternoon in August, she had yielded for the first time to a man.

It seemed almost sweet, pathetically sweet, to be able to hide forever in that humble room and die amid her souvenirs. She locked herself up with the remorse of not having been loyal to poor Tito, and not having given him at least the illusion that she was loyal. A penitent woman, she now offered him her infinite devotion, the eternal exclusiveness! Tito would from now on be her *last love*, just as he had always wanted to be.

She threw her chinchilla across the bed; in an angle of the room she fitted out a soft bed for her little live dog that resembled the stuffed dog to perfection, and was grieved by the departure of Pierina, the encyclopedic maid, who had been given an unlimited furlough.

The room was clogged with trunks plastered on all sides with the names of different steamers and different hotels. Her furs and coats exhaled the scent of *Avatar.*

Over a little table that she used as a writing desk, near the window, she put Tito's picture and the funeral urn was placed over a pointed lace; the round and iridescent urn, filled with gray dust.

That gray dust was all that was left of Tito, A leg, perhaps? The head or an arm, maybe? The hips, or maybe the neck. Who knew what parts had been her share in that division of spoils? And now, how everything had lost its original form in that yellowish-gray dust that looked like powder!

"Amid all these souvenirs", she thought, "I can prepare myself to die."

* * *

**. . . . a crystal globe, pearly
and iredescent . . . .**

Nocera paid the doctor, the druggist, the undertaker, and called at the parish-church. "How much is it?"

The bill was waiting for him. He disbursed the money without asking for any reduction, although, among the eight priests (at twenty-five lires each), there was one who hobbled.

He paid all others who had assisted in the burial service.

Goodness only knows, why so many people should mobilize when someone dies!

There will come a day when corpses will be flung into swamps like dead cats.

He executed all of the deceased one's last wishes, sent a few acknowledgments and thanks to those who expressed their sorrows, gathered the few things remaining around the room. Under the bed he found a pair of shoes.

Ah, the shoes of the dead, what a sorrowful sight they are! Those two black things that still have the shape of some-thing that is no more!

* * *

When in Paris, Pietro Nocera had never had an oppor-tunity to approach Maud. If he had seen her then amid those electrifying Parisians, she would have revealed herself to him in all the poverty of the Provincial Italian.

The moment he saw her in Turin, he felt captured by her fascination of the great traveller, exquisitely Parisian. Her devotion to her deceased lover, moved him; and from commotion to concupiscence there is but the same distance that separates those two words in the dictionary.

One morning, three days after the funeral, Magdalena was having her breakfast on the balcony, facing the courtyard, when they brought her a letter. She read it once, and wrote in pencil, over the first sheet that came to her hand. "Dear Nocera. You don't love me. You think you do.

Please do not write anymore to me as you wrote today, I will never be yours nor anyone else's—never! Tito must be my last lover."

The next day they delivered another letter from Nocera to her. He told her of his great desire to kiss her magnificent body.

She paraded in front of the mirror, which reflected her whole person, then answered: "Dear Nocera. My body is wasted. I cannot love anymore, and do not wish anybody to love me. My last lover will be poor Tito, to whom I shall be loyal throughout eternity".

The next day she waited for another letter, which never came. She waited two days, three days, which she passed in a state of inquietude and suspense.

"Why didn't Nocera write anymore?"

"Here's a letter for you, Magdalena."

It was one last passionate letter from Nocera who pleaded that she go to his home, in a street almost poetic of a quarter that was almost peaceful. He told her he loved her, he longed for her, he needed her, her flesh, her fragrance.

Magdalena remained a few moments absorbed in deep thought, then took paper and envelope, and wrote, very calmly and with a springtime smile: "Will be over at four. Kiss me."

She searched for blotting paper. There was none. She looked high and low, unsuccessfully. Not even a little sand. But beneath her eyes shone, over that pointed lace, a crystal globe, pearly and iridescent, filled with a yellowish-gray dust, just like powder.

Magdalena picked it up with nimble fingers, and poured the contents over the moist ink, and ran the dust over the writing; then, bending the sheet of paper, she spilled the ashes back into the urn, She sealed the message in an envelope, which she had delivered by messenger, and remained deeply absorbed in thought, briefly, like a musical pause.

She moistened her lovely lips, then dried them by rubbing them against each other, and then, very slowly, skillfully, she passed the carmine red over them.

She singled out the smallest among a bunch of keys, the one that opened the flat, cabin trunk.

Her soul felt light and luminous like an Andalusian mantilla.

She hummed a song through her tightly drawn lips, and kneeling before several pairs of stockings, she carefully selected the sheerest ones, the ones that made the flesh look naked.

THE END

**New Vessel reprint
of the Hamlyn 1982
UK translation.**

PITIGRILLI
& THE FASCISTS

An anti-Semitic Jew, Dino Segre (1893-1975), who wrote as Pitigrilli, was an illegitimate child whose father did not marry his mother until young Dino was eight years old. His father, also named Dino Segre, was Jewish; his mother was Catholic, and arranged for young Dino to be baptized. In the short run, this did him some good; in the long run, not so much. Pitigrilli founded the literary magazine *Le Grandi Firme* ("The Big Names," a bit like *People* and other celebrity magazines today), publishing it in Turin from 1924 to 1938, when it was banned by the Race Laws of Mussolini's Fascist government. This, despite the fact that Mussolini was a fan of Pitigrilli's writing—he once defended Pitigrilli, whose *Cocaine* was placed on the Catholic Church's Banned Books List, by saying, "Pitigrilli is not an immoral writer—he photographs the times. If our society is corrupt, it is not his fault."

In fact, Pitigrilli did more for the Fascists than depict the times: he actively helped create them. He spent years as an informant for OVRA, the Fascist equivalent of the Nazi Gestapo (the initials stand for "Organizzazione per la Vigilanza e la Repressione dell'Antifascismo," which translates as "Organization for Vigilance and Repression of Anti-Fascism"). Mussolini's OVRA had some 5,000 agents, who infiltrated most elements of everyday Italian life.

Pitigrilli fit right in. It all started in March 1934, when Pitigrilli's first cousin, Sion Segre, was caught trying to smuggle into Italy, from Switzerland, newspapers and leaflets of an organization called "Giustizia e Libertà" ("Justice and Liberty"). This group was at the time the main leftist but non-Communist anti-Fascist organization; its leaders were living in exile in Paris.

Fascist police, after arresting Sion Segre, picked up 14 others suspected of ties to "Giustizia e Libertà." Nine of them were from Jewish families—which led some Italian newspapers to talk about a Jewish anti-Fascist conspiracy.

In his autobiography, published after World War II, Pitigrilli said directly that he hated his first cousin and the Jewish portion of his family. His father's relatives never really accepted Pitigrilli's mother as a daughter-in-law and did not treat Pitigrilli himself as a true grandson, possibly because of his illegitimacy or his mixed Jewish-Catholic background.

In his book *The Chastity Belt*, Pitigrilli wrote that "revenge is a great safety valve for our pain," and his motivation for his work with OVRA may have had just that simple and strong a basis. Some of those on whom he informed were intellectuals and writers who would later become important in Italy's anti-Fascist cultural elite. Among them were publisher Giulio Einaudi, painter and writer Carlo Levi, Adriano and Paola Olivetti, and Leone Ginzburg and his future wife, Natalia. Pitigrilli's best year as a spy was 1935: his secret reports led to the arrests of some 50 suspected anti-Fascists, many of whom were sent to prison for several years. Among those arrested were the editorial staff members of the magazine *Culture*, which was known for its independence; the entire magazine was suppressed in 1936.

The successes of 1935 constituted such a coup that Pitigrilli feared his success might reduce his usefulness in the future. He went so far as to suggest to the Fascist police that he himself be arrested to head off suspicion and maintain his value as an informant, but the police did not do this.

Within a year, Mussolini's regime stopped reprinting most of Pitigrilli's books, which had until then been quite popular. Then, in 1939, Pitigrilli, who tried without success to be recognized as an Aryan both before and during the war, received a note saying, "We thank you for all you've done up until now for us, but given the present situation we are compelled to renounce your further collaboration." The situation that resulted in the final rupture between Pitigrilli and OVRA had to do with a file including Pitigrilli's name being found by French police in the flat of Vincenzo Bellavia, the OVRA director in Paris.

From then on, Pitigrilli's onetime handlers referred to him as "the well-known Jewish writer Dino Segre, alias Pitigrilli." By mid-1940, police in Turin included Pitigrilli on a list of "dangerous Jews" to be interned in the south of Italy, in Apulia, although when he was actually held for a time, it was in the town of Uscio.

In 1941, when Pitigrilli was living in Rome and writing movie dialogue anonymously because, classified as a Jew, he could not do so openly, he again offered his services to OVRA, saying his status as a persecuted Jew would provide him with cover. But he was not rehired.

After Mussolini's regime fell in 1943 and the Nazis occupied Italy, Pitigrilli fled to Switzerland, where he lived until 1947. By this time he had married a Catholic woman, his former attorney, and had a son with her—his first wife, however, had been Jewish, which was certainly another strike against him during the rise of Fascism and in the war years.

Yet although the Fascists had deemed him a Jew and refused to keep working with him, Pitigrilli's years as an informant for OVRA came back to haunt him in the postwar world, and he was at risk of prosecution as a war criminal. For that reason, in 1948 he emigrated to Argentina, as had many Fascists and Nazis, most famously Adolf Eichmann. Pitigrilli remained in Argentina for a decade, but eventually returned to Europe, dividing his time between Paris and his home in Turin, where he died the day before his 82nd birthday.

Pitigrilli's involvement with Fascism was certainly not born of belief in it as a political system; he was too cynical for that. In *The Chastity Belt*, published the same year as *Cocaine*, he had written, "Fatherland is a word that serves to send sheep to slaughter in order to serve the interests of the shepherds who stay safely at home." It is virtually certain that his anti-Semitism, propelled by anger at a well-to-do father who shared his exact name but whose family never accepted the illegitimate son, explains some of his work for and with OVRA. But there is likely more to it than that: Pitigrilli may have seen his work as an informant as a form of self-preservation.

Here is a possible motivating factor. In 1928, some people who wanted to take over *Le Grandi Firme* got one of Pitigrilli's former lovers, an ambitious writer named Amalia Guglieminetti, to agree to provide them with some incriminating personal letters that insulted Mussolini and Fascism itself. Guglieminetti was by this time the mistress of a powerful Fascist official named Pietro Brandimarte. But the letters were forgeries—such obvious ones that, at trial, Pitigrilli exposed them and Guglieminetti admitted the fraud on the witness stand. Nevertheless, the episode surely made Pitigrilli feel vulnerable as Fascism took deeper hold in Italy. In 1931, Pitigrilli actually sent Mussolini a book bearing the dedication, "To Benito Mussolini, the man above all adjectives." The adjective that Pitigrilli could not escape, "Jewish," likely combined with the adjective "fearful" to turn the acerbic writer, for a time, into a servile but willing participant in some of Italy's darkest modern times.

—Mark J. Estren, PhD
Fort Myers, Florida
January, 2016

Ronin Books for Independent Minds

COCAINE FIENDS AND REEFER MADNESS ....Stark $19.95
History of drugs in the movies.

THE HEALING MAGIC OF CANNABIS .... Potter/Joy $14.95
Healing power of psychoactivity, tinctures, food, list of med conditions.

PSYCHEDELICS ENCYCLOPEDIA ....Stafford $38.95
LSD, peyote, marijuana and hashish, mushrooms, MDA, DMT, yage, iboga, etc

LEGAL HIGHS .... Gottlieb $12.95
An encyclopedia of relatively unknown legal psychoactive herbs & chemicals.

PLEASURES OF COCAINE .... Gottlieb $16.95
Everything you need to know to save your life!

ACID TRIPS & CHEMISTRY ....Cloud $16.95
History, blotter, ergot rye, chemistry, bad trips.

MARIJUANA BOTANY ....Clarke $34.95
Sexing, cultivation, THC production and peak potency, continued production.

MARIJUANA CHEMISTRY ....Starks $24.95
Species, seeds, grafting, and cloning, growing techniques and essential oils.

DIVINE MUSHROOMS ....Allen $19.95
Abundance of beautiful photos, mindblowing descriptions of hallucinations

SEXY, SACRED 'SHROOMS ....Allen $19.95
Amazing sensuality. 'Shrooms turn on the heat.

COOKING WITH CANNABIS .... Gottlieb $12.95
Soup to nuts—tasty recipes for every occasion.

MARIJUANA RECIPIES & REMEDIES..Staywell $14.95
Mj foods, tinchures, polstices and more

MARIJUANA FOOD HANDBOOK ....DRAKE $14.95
Make potent extracts to use in cooking almost any food

CANNABIS ALCHEMY..Gold $16.95
Cult classic. How to make hashish

PSYCHEDELIC CHEMISTRY ....Starks $24.95
THC, analogs. Biggest, best, most complete

LITTLE BOOK OF ACID...Cloud $12.95
Natural sources of acid-like chemical, acid experience

A HISTORY OF UNDERGROUND COMICS.....................................Estren $34.95
Most lavish collection ever; tells history of undergorund comix

Check out books at our site, roninpub.com with lots of info, use
ISBN to order Ronin books from your local bookstroe to save
ship fee or from amazon at a discount.

Ronin Publishing, Inc.
POB 3436, Oakland, CA 94609 • Ph: 800/858-2665 • Fax: 510/420-3672
Catalog online www.roninpub.com
• Over 18 years old only • Prices subject to change w/o notice

Printed in the USA
CPSIA information can be obtained
at www.ICGtesting.com
JSHW022217140824
68134JS00018B/1111

9 781579 512187